Maureen Duffy

is a much respected po
several novels, includir
cosm, Love Child, Cap
novel *Gor Saga* was recenuy
as *First Born*. She has also published a co....
amount of non-fiction, including *The Erotic World of*
Faery and an influential biography of Aphra Behn. She
is past president of the Writers' Guild and is currently
chairman of the British Copyright Council and the
Authors' Licensing and Collecting Society. She lives
in London.

MAUREEN DUFFY

Illuminations

A FABLE

Flamingo
An Imprint of HarperCollins*Publishers*

Flamingo
An Imprint of HarperCollins*Publishers*
77–85 Fulham Palace Road,
Hammersmith, London W6 8JB

Published by Flamingo 1992
9 8 7 6 5 4 3 2 1

First published in Great Britain by
Sinclair-Stevenson Limited 1991

Copyright © Maureen Duffy 1991

The Author asserts the moral right to
be identified as the author of this work

ISBN 0 00 654473 8

Set in Galliard

Printed in Great Britain by
HarperCollinsManufacturing Glasgow

'A writer cannot avoid politics and the situation of his country is always reflected in his work, directly or indirectly. A writer can never rid himself of the period he is living in, on the contrary his senses are particularly adapted to make him feel it. Literature is a means of human self-awareness and it reflects the spirit of time, of place, of history, of civilisation.'

Vaclav Havel. Prague October 1990

'Fortis est ut mors dilectio.'

Berthgyth after the Song of Songs

THE FOX begins it. Hetty doesn't know this as she opens the back door on a late summer morning luminous as pre-lapsarian Eden where each leaf on the holly tree is a polished heliograph. Afterwards, looking back, she'll remember that this is the brush mark in the margin saying, 'Start here', but now it's only a fox beached with its nose against the bootscraper grid as if it had run for dear life to her door to die, couldn't run away any more because the nylon noose has cut deep into its throat and half severed its neck. For a moment she's afraid as if it's a portent, the day overcast, and perhaps someone's left it there. Meaning what? And though she doesn't believe she thinks of witchcraft and the trappings of malice.

Then she sees that the rusty coat is sewn with seed pearls of dew and the smart black lips are drawn back in a desperate snarl of horror and pain. If she had known could she have saved it? She bends down to look closer and sees that any intervention she might have made would have been too late. It's a young fox. She can't tell what sex, and now she'll have to bury it before the sun brings out the flies. But not until she's given herself some breakfast strength while the problem adjusts in her mind to the practical where and how and whether she should remove the snare, and before the desperation of that last run into the dark is shrivelled by the sunlight.

She shuts the door on the morning and the heavy lump of death on her back doorstep and turns to put on the kettle and assemble cereal and milk and orange juice on the pine table where she can sit and munch, looking out at the front hedge of blackthorn where sparrows have begun the daily round of indignant chirp and flaunt. Predatory Reynard has got his come-uppance sneaking down to drowsing henfolk. The snare was meant for rabbit or hare. He'd had the strength to tear it free but not without garrotting it tighter. She shouldn't feel sorry for him but she does, for a burn of vivid life extinguished as he snuffed out others. Nature red in tooth and claw as the wild-life programmes on telly always show it, picking on those creatures who kill and are killed with all the distortion of drama. She will lift the carcass up on the spade to carry it, she plots, her hand shying away in imagination from contagion with the dead.

The sun has moved round to fall through the French doors in a glistening puddle on the table as she smears marmalade on toast and licks her fingers of sweet and sour stickiness. She drinks her bitter coffee slowly, reading the cereal packet with complete concentration. It offers a body of dazzling svelteness and vitality, a holiday for two in Bermuda if she can consume, alone and unaided, twenty packets of chaff by the closing date and come up with a formula encapsulating life and a morning bowl of forage. Maybe she should have a holiday but where and who with? Isn't life one long holiday now? 'Stop shilly-shallying,' Hetty says aloud as she often does. 'Go and bury it. Nothing can go on while it's lying out there.'

She dives her feet down into the rubbery dampness of her Wellingtons, takes the spade from where it leans upright against the corner by the bathroom door and opens again into the garden. The morning has fallen quiet as if waiting to assist at a ceremony. She bends and gets the spade under the furry body. The dew has dried leaving the coat staring and harsh. She wants to take off the snare as some kind of evidence. Surely they must be illegal. But perhaps that's only gintraps. She'll have to bury the fox in its noose like the human sacrifices found in peat bog or barrow with a meal of gruel in their crops, her breakfast muesli that this morning seems to be sticking half-way down.

Hetty climbs the brick path up from the cottage, with the spade and its balanced body held awkwardly but somehow ceremonially in front of her. The nemesia and snapdragons flanking the path make a deep banner of colour down to the small terrace. A whiff of goat comes over next door's wall. At the top of the path she turns left over the thin green pile of grass, proceeding towards the chestnut tree in its heavy summer dress, embossed with small green maces of conker husks, to where the ground is soft with mushroomy leaf mould from a century of autumn droppings and the spade will go in deep and easy.

Hetty rakes the dark crumble with its litter of broken chocolate shells over the foxy grin and burnished fur and stands for a moment drained and still. 'You didn't even know the animal. Suppose it had been a cat or a dog you'd lived with.' But her stillness is for death itself, the extinction of warmth and breath and beating blood. Above her the chestnut bows and sighs the layers of its shaggy cumulus of greenery. Suddenly she thinks she hears the distant call of the telephone or is it just the blackbird that's learnt to imitate it and sent her blundering across the grass and down the path as it does now, conjuring it not to stop just as she reaches the door. 'Keep ringing you bastard! Keep ringing!'

'Where were you? I was just about to give up.' The voice is shaking and irritable. For a moment Hetty can't answer, out of breath, and stunned by the once so familiar voice she has heard now for two years only in her dreams.

'I was burying a fox.'

'What curious imperatives you have out there.'

He had never liked the cottage, the idea of it, even before his one encounter with its physical manifestation. 'Why were you burying it?'

'It had died on my doorstep.'

'Anyway how are you?'

'Fine, and you?'

'Com'ci, com'ça. You know what it's like here.'

She does remember of course. After a dozen years of it how could she forget. She waits for him to elaborate. 'We've got a mid-term crisis. With the students all away you'd think there'd be some peace. Anyway when this thing blew up Bob wondered if you might help us out and I said, just the person, and volunteered to ring. I hope you don't mind?'

His words are opaque, without real substance, calcified translucencies like the cockle shells he had heaped in her lap on a rare day at the seaside, a child's gifts to please or appease the mother he had roamed from along the tide line. Then she'd been charmed by him or by them: false mother of pearl; bits of bottle glass polished to gem stones that faded as the salt water dried, agate and emerald, chilly to the touch; curiosities of cuttle-fish bone and honeycombed whelk-egg cases; trash of the ceaseless fetch and carry of the waves. Yet she could catch some of his passion as he showered her with them where she leaned against a blackened breakwater. The sea had hollowed out a little pool at the foot of each upright post where see-through shrimps scissored their tails across into the safety of water and a small green crab sank itself into the crack under the plank wall, beside a colony of closed blue-black mussels waiting out the ebb. Left alone to troll the shore she would have gathered treasures in her own right. Now she peered into the pool with its parallel life and waited to be brought them.

The smell and cascading light of that day almost overwhelm her as she stands at the kitchen table with the receiver like a plastic seashell at her ear. 'Are you still there?' His voice buzzes her.

'Yes, sorry. What were you saying? A conference?'

'In Germany. One of these EEC things. Charlie Caswell was going but his kid's had meningitis and he can't really leave Christine to get on with it all.'

'Which one?'

'There's only one Christine.'

'Which child?'

'The youngest.'

'Gerald?'

'I expect so. Can you go?'

'When is it?'

'Three weeks tomorrow.'

'What would I have to do?'

'Give a paper. The conference is called *Towards an Idea of Europe: Origins and Expectations*.'

'Hardly my kind of thing.'

'It's got to be everyone's these days.'

'But I'm out of all that.' She means the jealousies, the lobbying for promotion, the dismal publication of footnotes and studies.

'I bet you miss it. Anyway we're so short-staffed nowadays no-one would have let you go. You just got out in time.'

His rewriting of history makes her smile. It must if she's to keep back the surge of indignation, recrimination that threatens her calm, her control of the conversation.

'All expenses paid and fee. Not much of course.'

'What would I talk about?'

'Charlemagne?'

'Not my period.' Nothing was any more. They had ceased with her job at fifty, had drizzled unspectacularly for half a year and then stopped. Once she had thought she detected the traditional hot flush, and that had been that. 'You'll have to give me a day to think about it. Ring me tomorrow morning.'

'Why don't you ring me when you've decided.'

'No. You might not be there. You ring me. Where is it by the way; Germany's quite a big place.'

'Oh Hamburg or Frankfurt. I can't quite remember. I'll let you know tomorrow.'

When she has put the receiver back on its cradle Hetty realises that she's trembling, dry-mouthed, her head not quite in touch with the tingling body. 'It's the shock. That's all. Hardly surprising really.' Automatically she switches on the kettle for more coffee, something to do, to hold on to. *Towards an Idea of Europe: Origins and Expectations*. It was as nebulous as an idea of heaven, happiness, love even. What could she say, shut out in rancorous insularity? With her mug of instant coffee in her hand she opens the door and steps into the garden again. From the distance, beyond the cornfield that stretches further every year as the farmer effaces bush and verge and barrow, the motorway slurs. In the field itself the throbbing stamp of a combine has silenced the birds.

He thinks she will go, and suddenly Hetty thinks so too if she can dredge a subject out of her past, the history she's no longer allowed to teach and has hardly thought about since she moved to the cottage with its unending chain of practicalities to fetter the pain that had clawed and savaged her. Now she's uncertain, diffident of her ability. 'I ought to be able to think of something.'

Europe: Europa, a woman enamoured of a bull, seduced not raped though that, she thinks, is the title of Titian's picture. Riding away with her fingers twined in its curly forelock, passively side-saddle. There had been England's long love affair with Europe: Renaissance, Baroque, Classicism; the paintings, bronzes, marbles, music brought back as emblems of civilisation and pleasure until the long night of the French Revolution had shown us the dark and bloody underside and we had recoiled on ourselves in shock, to native Gothick and mock Tudor, to chinoiserie and the decorative tat of the Empire while waves of tribulation battered the continent spawning monsters until now we're exhausted. 'I could make something out of all that but it's very negative and backward looking, very British in fact. It's what they'd expect to hear from us but perhaps it's just a projection of my own state, a political version of the Romantic fallacy.'

Hetty's pleased with this, with the unaccustomed activity of flexing her mind. It elates rather than depresses her and she feels as if she's stumbled on or fought her way through to something very important, a vision conjured by the pure energy of mind that must therefore be true and told to someone, to the conference: that gathering of unknowns who will nod and agree. Except that it doesn't quite fit the theme.

'Well, it does in a way. Every positive contains its negative and vice versa. If I talk about the dissolution of an idea then that's a step to its recreation.' She will go. She will get on an aeroplane and fly away to Germany where she's never been. Jack's voice on the telephone has set her free. She will leave the orange and scarlet flames of the nemesia to burn themselves out in the garden, and the farmer to set fire to his field with all the small life in it that rains down in ash on her terrace and her clean washing, and if the dead come to her door they will have to lie unburied. 'Let the dead bury the dead,' she remembers, and then thinks that Mr Powers who comes a half day a week to help with the garden could be asked to see after such things. She's forgotten to ask how long she's needed for but in the nature of these affairs it'll only be a few days. Hetty turns away from the reproachful eye of the garden.

An hour later she's on her way to the city, driving the same motorway, abandoning the forty-year-old upright bicycle she uses for shopping in the village. Gouts of smoke cloud her windscreen from the fiery stubble with the blurred black forms of beaters vanishing and reappearing amongst them like some ancient mural of hell. Hetty hears the air plangent with small unshed cries. The road falters on the outskirts and becomes entangled in narrow streets hazy with car fumes. As she inches sweatily in the rank exhaust of a rusted pick-up she remembers how even this small market town, citified only by its cathedral, stinks. She winds her way to the market square, beats someone to a parking place, buys her pay-and-display ticket and leaves the car to blister in the sun while she slides into the cool quiet of the public library.

Of course she could have gone to the college library and worked there among their books which Bob had said, at the leaving party she was almost too ill to attend, would always be available to her. And of course she had never been back, afraid of embarrassed encounters in corridors and between bookstacks, afraid of challenge from a new member of staff who didn't know who she was, afraid of a still heavily menstruating heart that left her weary, edgy, yearning. Anyway brought up on the public library she feels at home here. She likes the mix of ages and sexes, the feeling that everyone is after information or recreation and not there as part of a job or a course: the eruption of a group of hushed six-year-olds beside the unkempt old man who came in to read the newspapers.

Hetty climbs the stairs, past the donated prints and engravings showing the history of the town, and the cases of miscellaneous relics. She hesitates guiltily where a local artist is sitting at a trestle table with photocopied catalogues of the flower paintings that paper the corridor on either side behind her, and then goes firmly on through the heavy moulded mahogany of the reference library door, finds herself a seat which she marks with the *Guardian* and heads for the old catalogue still kept in small binders which allows browsing unlike the microfilm reader which will tell you only if you already know what you want. Hetty fingers her way through the Grand Tour and the French Revolution and then takes her note of the titles she wants to the staid young woman behind the information desk, reflecting as she does so on the continuing aura of virginity even married librarians give off, both male and female.

Back at her desk she unfolds her newspaper but refolds it hastily on the blurred disintegration of a jet liner with its chronicle of torn metal and seared lungs. Maybe she won't go after all. She isn't committed to it yet. Out of a dead childhood she hears the elderly woman who had adopted her intoning the folk belief that lightning never strikes twice in the same place. No planes will drop out of the air for a couple of weeks. Those deaths have made her flight safer by the laws of chance, the randomness that allows those coincidences life is shot through with.

Chance had taken her into the supermarket that afternoon and set a train of events going that had led her to here and now. Chance had decreed that rounding a gondola stocked high with all the fruits of the earth (not just commonplace globes of apple and pear or hospital visitor's grape and orange offerings but hairy, ugly exotics, paw-paw and cactus, kumquat, mango, kiwi and passion fruit, expensive delicacies raped from tree or shrub whose leaf and shape she couldn't even envisage) she should see at the far end, wearily pushing a burdened trolley with one small child clinging to its polished silver frame and another perched on top of it like a marriage mascot, Jack's wife Mary, she had met once at a college social, and had ducked back out of sight behind the mineral springs of Derbyshire and Vergeze.

'Do we really need it all?' she had once asked Jack, and he had answered:

'Trade makes the world go round. It's been going on ever since men had anything to swap with each other.'

'And women.'

'Women too. And then sometimes the men swopped the women.'

'And the women swopped the men.'

'Ah the myth of the ancient matriarchy.'

Mary had dark curly hair, a little dishevelled and a face that had the smooth pallor of an opal. She was younger, much younger than Hetty had remembered or allowed for and her youth and those two small children were an acid bath to Hetty's illusions. She felt herself stripped, flayed. She abandoned her attempt at shopping and drove back to her flat near the station, shaken and sick.

'I saw Mary in Allways.'

He sighed. 'I expect she had the kids with her. She looks such a mess when she's shopping as if it's the end of the world. She can't really cope.'

Why then, Hetty wondered but not aloud, had he let her have, given her in fact, two more children, when the first two were at last away at school and she could have had time to herself? 'She doesn't want it,' he would have said. 'Mary's the earth-mother type.'

To Hetty she had looked more like a lost child herself, a true sister of the young unmarried mothers who pushed and dragged their children wearily between the market stalls hunting for bargains to eke out their social security money, a substratum of semi-rural urban poor, girls in strained, stained T-shirts and mini skirts, with thin, scuffed plastic shoes.

Hetty hadn't known about the family until she was briefly pregnant herself. Jack had been alone at first, in cheerless digs. She'd invited him round for supper and so it began. He'd mentioned Mary but not specifically as his wife. Later he had said, 'But I assumed you knew. That's why I've been looking for a place. We met as students. Married too young. It doesn't really work but I can't hurt her.'

Later again Hetty had realised how she'd led herself on, unwinding a long thread of delusion as she went further into the labyrinth, a skein she would gather up again painfully re-winding on the way back. But that wasn't to come for years. In the beginning she was lost, dazed, as bewitched as if the fairy king himself had carried her off to another land where time and the whole semblance of the external world were warped by the flow of energised particles that seemed to have replaced her previously commonplace human blood.

'You look a bit pale,' Jack had said. 'You alright?'

'Something happened last night.' Hetty laughed a little trying to skate as lightly as she could on the dangerous surface that suddenly had cracks flowing in all directions from under her feet. 'I think I must have been pregnant without knowing.'

'Christ! I thought you were on the pill.'

'I am. But they go wrong sometimes.' The doctor had recommended a low dose because of her age.

'Anyway, it's alright now?'

She had felt a pain and been pleased because she was a bit late getting the curse. She hadn't been really worried. There was just an undertone of question but her periods had never been very regular. She had got up and gone along to the bathroom, had strained a little and felt a rush, a gush, and sat for a moment. The tissue when she wiped herself was brightly bloody, a giant red peony flowering on the white paper, and the pan seemed to be full of cochineal-coloured water with a little dark clotted nucleus to it. She heard her mother say, snatching away the boiled egg Hetty had just taken the top off, 'Don't eat that. The cock's been at it.' And she had glimpsed a black heart to the yolk with filaments of red she knew were blood.

She sat for a while on the edge of the bath with a towel under her. She knew she must flush the mess away but she felt stunned, her numb brain unable to direct her hand to pull down the chrome lever and put an end to it all, her first and almost certainly last chance of the child she'd never really thought about before. Still she sat on, feeling slightly sick, until quite suddenly the first shockwave receded and she was able to bend over, deliberately not looking down and pull the handle. Only after the flush was finished and the filling cistern dwindled to a trickle could she make herself look. The water was quite clear. Hetty felt that any trace of what had happened would have made her lose her fragile control. Holding the towel between her legs she went back to her bedroom, got another towel to put under her from the pine chest of drawers and lay down on the bed with a pillow under her feet.

Although she had never thought in terms of marriage and children she felt drained, diminished and somehow unable as yet to plug herself with a tampon, as if she were being let blood, sacrificial blood that needed to flow. She felt herself drifting off to sleep to jolt awake scared that she was bleeding to death and then fall away again unable to bring herself to do anything about it. In the morning she found that she had soaked through both towels but the flow was less and she felt her practicality restored. She threw the towels away in a plastic bin liner, ate some toast though she couldn't face the egg that usually went with it, padded herself with a swag of cotton wool and went to work by car.

'Yes. I think I'm alright now.' She wanted to ask if he would have liked her to have his child, even though as she had driven through the clotted streets towards the college she had taken herself through the whole impossible script of might-have-been.

'I don't think I could cope with any more at the moment,' Jack had said. 'Mary rang last night. She's sick of being stuck up there with the kids. She thinks I'm not trying. She's right of course.' He had turned on Hetty the full frontal intensity of his gaze which usually made her head sing like any teenager in a women's magazine romance but this morning she felt dull, an ache dragging in her gut that seemed to be reaching up to squeeze at something she imprecisely thought of as her heart.

She should have stopped then, refused to go on with it but after she was over the shock, pleasure returned, sweet and sour at first but still greater than the pain, and sinking only slowly as dead weight followed dead weight of experience and insight, filling up the other pan until the two were held in a dull equilibrium. The sight of Mary and her children in the supermarket hadn't quite tipped the balance. That had come from seeing Jack across the junior common room at a freshers' tea flirting indiscriminately with a group of girls and boys from the new International Baccalaureate course whose golden skins oozed richness. When she had charged him with it jokingly he had given his guilty boyish smile and said: 'They're all so attractive the young these days, don't you think?' Hetty had finally realised that if he did ever leave Mary it wouldn't be for her. That's when she became ill.

It was easy enough to put it down to the menopause. Hetty grasped gratefully at the accepted excuse that allowed her to take days off, she who'd hardly missed a seminar in twenty years, to have headaches and weeping fits, to be late with marking while she sat listlessly in the senior common room staring out at the students laughing past the window, always on their way to possibility as it seemed to her. Bob gave her a lighter timetable, urged a holiday and when the proposals for early retirement came with the next round of government cuts, suggested she should put her name forward.

The shock of that interview made Hetty realise how far she had slipped. She had bought a derelict cottage half an hour's drive from the town in the hope that Jack would come there and they could be more relaxed away from the possibility of his being seen calling or the demanding voice of the telephone. He had driven out one Saturday afternoon at her insistence, sniffed at the damp brick floor, been squeamish about the plastic Elsan and the goaty smell from the neighbouring garden, and when she had taken him up to the low-eaved but double bedroom with the cello-shaped brick chimney breast, had looked at his watch and taken her, there was no other word for it, from behind with hard painful thrusts that made her cry out but not with pleasure. Hetty had been aware of his anger cantilevered above her back where once they had lain face to face while he traced the contours of her body. He had never come there again.

Twice more, while she still had her flat, he had made a furtive dash in and out, duty visits that left her feeling as if she had picked up a stranger and paid him for sex. When she left, retired, she had withdrawn her bruised eyes and antennae into the shell of the cottage, glad of its small overgrown windows, and the high bank and dense bushes that shut it in on three sides as if she had crept underground to hibernate after the leaving party.

The obscure books she's ordered have to be fetched from the bookstack in the basement and are a long time coming. Deprived of the newspaper by the picture of the plane crash, she's forced to find something else to read and runs her eye along the nearest shelves which turn out to be rather boring bibliography until her search picks out a title and she takes down the illustrated catalogue of the cathedral library in a faded-ink binding with the thin shiny pages and hatched line drawings of the early nineteen hundreds, compiled by Canon Samuel Wren, gaitered in shiny black. The book falls open at a grey photograph of the cathedral's chained library, heavy books manacled to upright lecterns and massive oak tables in case they should run away. Hetty feels an upsurge of her oldest passion that had been reduced to a flicker, had even she'd thought, guttered out in those last two years before she had left St Julian's as the policy had been increasingly not to teach history but to teach the teaching of history to students who knew none, had no well of knowledge in themselves to fill children's cups from as Hetty remembered her own teachers doing.

'The swollen sheep look up and are not fed,' she'd interjected one day into a staff conference.

'Aren't you lucky you'll soon be out of it all,' Bob had silenced her with, smiling.

Canon Samuel Wren scurried about the cathedral library in wire-rimmed spectacles, compiling his catalogue: the only record he would leave to posterity. Hetty turns the pages, surprised that a provincial cathedral should have such a collection of not only printed books but also hand-written manuscripts. She had supposed all such rarities would be in some public or academic institution.

'No. 77,' she reads, '*Evangelia quatuor*. Vellum; 12½ by 9 inches, 86ff. Fine hand XI and XII century. Grotesques in red outline drawn in lower margins. No. 80. 1. *Pauli diaconi de gestis Longobardum*. 2. *Eginhardi vita Caroli Magni*. 3. *Monarchi Sangallensis [Balbuli Notker?] liber de gestis Caroli Magni*.'

Jack had suggested she should talk about Charlemagne. Hetty reads on. '*Epistolae Bonifacis*.' Canon Samuel Wren had commented: 'Very much discoloured by damp. A XII century copy see Introduction.' Dutifully Hetty turns back, skipping her expert eye until she has what she thinks is the right bit. Canon Wren twitters dustily across the years.

'The twelfth century saw a revival of interest, and many manuscripts were copied afresh to coincide with the Norman rebuilding of what had been the abbey church. At the same time the copyist was not above turning author or forger and several MSS from this period must be viewed as highly suspect although it is not always possible to deduce the forger's motives. Charters of course were often forged and it is easy to suggest a practical reason for this but it is hard to see what could be the significance of the long letter which forms part of MS 80 which purports to be from an English nun Tetta, circa 790, in Germany. (For further comment on this see my article in *Transactions of the Dorset Archaeological Society*, Vol IX 2nd Series.)'

Hetty is out of her depth, out of her time, which has always been that modern age of the Enlightenment that was supposed to have begun around seventeen hundred. Before that, as history stretched back, it grew increasingly shadowy, murky even seen through the deepening refractions and layers of time. Those years after the collapse of the Roman Empire used to be called the Dark Ages in the old school history books though now she's noticed they're given the less evocative title of Early Mediaeval. She must see if she can find the article, perhaps even visit the cathedral library. Meanwhile her own books have arrived but after her glimpse of that other, through the eyes of Canon Wren, they seem lacklustre, the sons of the English aristocracy on their package tour of the sights of Europe, unusually charmless forerunners of badly behaved football fans with their contempt for foreign inn-keepers, their hostlers and their daughters. How can she make a lecture out of these complaints of bedbugs and broken carriage wheels?

Tetta could almost be a version of her own name. What could an English woman be doing in Germany at the end of the eighth century? It sounded like a forgery. Could English women even write as early as that? She finds it hard to concentrate on her chosen theme but she bends her mind to it. Unless she can convince herself that she has something to say before Jack telephones again she will have to turn the trip down and now she longs to go. It was just coincidence that she had come upon an English nun with a name like hers who could have been writing home from Germany, and Hetty of course is too much a child of her generation to believe in signs and portents. Nevertheless she feels a frisson of excitement as if an important event has overtaken her. For the first time for months her mind is engaging with something that's neither the practicalities of everyday nor the treadmill of loss and grief.

Transactions of the Dorset Archaeological Society turn out to be on the local history shelves. 'If this is indeed a twelfth-century forgery,' Canon Wren had written, 'then what we have here is the first epistolary fiction by an English hand though of course in Latin. One may imagine the bored scribe, tired of copying the life of Charlemagne, turning his hand to a little light invention. The style is based on that of St Aldhelm, florid and, alas, too easily imitated. It is indeed close to that of the so-called Nun of Heidenheim, author of *The Hodoeporicon of St Willibald*, who may or may not be his sister St Warburga, whose name has quite mistakenly been appropriated for the carnival festivities of Walpurgisnacht.'

The stage is filling with a ghostly cast of robed figures, dead for a thousand years whose existence Hetty has never suspected. Even as she dredges back to her student days, when they were meant to know the whole of human history, she can't recall these names and shapes. Perhaps because they had reminded her of her childhood, of the parlour with its heavy curtains, embroidered chairbacks and sonorous clock where no-one ever laughed or sang, of chapel three times on Sunday, she had grasped at reason, the explicable, and her mind had refused them entry. Across the page from the Canon's article is an illustration in black and white, an impenetrable tracery of line and convolution and hatching, as ornate as an oriental carpet or the computer-graphic delineation of the order at the heart of chaos which Hetty had watched unravel one night on television, going out after the programme to look afresh at the cloud race in the moonlit sky and the dance of dark leaves and boughs in the night wind.

She had had her first affair at university, eager for liberation from the gloomy parlour yet terrified of pregnancy. She and Derek had gone to the Proms together, downed the halves of bitter their grants could afford, gone for walks in the Great Park at Windsor on weekend courses at Cumberland Lodge, and finally lain down fumblingly together to get it over with, lose their virginities in each other before he went off to do his National Service, carrying buckets of shingle up a beach on the Isle of Wight while Hetty stayed on to write her thesis on the Enthusiasts for her MA. Their letters had become spasmodic, full of apology for not writing, until with mingled relief and apprehension she had read that he was engaged. Now she could barely remember what he had looked like and that, said to be the greatest moment of her life, had reduced to a memory chiefly of pain and messiness.

Still she was grateful to Derek. It had been a relief when Jack had first made love to her not to be a virgin, to know what to expect. She had enjoyed their lovemaking and in the beginning he had been a good lover, making her, with his tenderness, able to ignore the eight-year difference in their ages that seemed so immense when she was alone. Only later he had become peremptory, impatient, but by then Hetty was too enmeshed to try to play games that the women's magazines she sometimes saw at the dentist recommended, to try and turn him back to how it had been.

Staring blankly down at the pages she suddenly feels a longing, a lust she hasn't felt for months. This won't do in the public library. How did Dark Age nuns cope with such feelings? Prayer and cold water or the dubious efficacy of flagellation. What did they do when they got the curse? Canon Wren wouldn't have an answer to that problem, the cyclical concern of feminine life. She's glad that's over at least.

'For the benefit of members I have ventured a translation of this previously unpublished curiosity which the editor has kindly allowed me to publish in full in spite of its length. In some places the meaning is rather obscure and the author's or authoress's syntax not of the purest but I have preferred to give a consistent reading which I trust will render some of the flavour of the original.'

My dearest father after the flesh and the spirit, Baltheard, Tetta lowest servant of those who bear the sweet yoke of Christ and your daughter greets you. I long to clasp my arms around your neck and press my lips to yours. Know that although I may not see you with the eyes of the body you are always present to my love. Whatsoever our circumstances on this earth we can never be separated from each other's loving care even though cruel waters lie between us.

There is a messenger going for England from the court and I will entrust this to the hands of Aelfwin your servant, who is to travel with him since I promised to let you know of my safe arrival. I shall never forget the sight of you on the shore at Hamwick as we left the port. You had chosen me a good ship and a skilful captain, admonishing him to take care of me among his wild galley slaves so I had no real fear, only the creaking of the oars and the groaning of the timbers as we braved the mountainous seas beyond the harbour mouth seemed loud to me. Then the sailors shouted and set the sails full and we were soon out of sight of land and you, with a following wind from the west that made us fly over the water like a bird. The night before I had felt a great cloud of sadness come over me at the sweet voices of the sisters singing the *Officium Peregrinorum* to send me on my journey to foreign lands as I lay before the altar on the cold stone but now I was strengthened by the thought of the call that has come to me and by your trust.

A fellow traveller seeing me standing alone looking back addressed some words to me and when he saw I did not understand his speech spoke to me again, this time in Latin with the pronunciation of Brother Dungal, which let me know he was a Scot from Ireland. He asked me where I was going. I answered that I was going to the Abbey at Erfurt. He laughed and said that I would be safe there now but not to go further north or the Saxons would eat such a succulent dish. Then I remembered our kinsman Boniface's advice to the Lady Abbess Eadberg about women, even nuns, travelling abroad and their temptations, and that there was no town in Gaul, Lombardy or Frankland where there was not a courtesan or harlot of English birth as he wrote to Archbishop Cuthbert. And I saw how easily temptation comes in a few words, especially to those who have lived innocent of the world and that my pride in understanding Latin speech had earned my first fall from which I prayed God to lift me up and so moved away from the stranger, glad of your servant Aelfwin with me for my greater protection.

Of the fleet of boats that had set out together we were the swiftest and the first. The oars were unnecessary, wind and tide carried us so fast towards the coast of Frankland. At first we were protected from the open sea by the Isle of Wight but when that was past there was nothing but open water and our boat very small in that immensity of sea so that I could no longer make out the coast of England and I wondered how men could navigate when there was nothing behind or before but water and sky above. The spray dashed against the boat and there was no way to keep our clothing dry. Some of the travellers began to feel sick and lay down upon the deck but I found it better to stand looking out. After a few hours there was a cry that someone had seen a ship and at once we were all afraid that it might be one of the pirates from the North. The captain ordered the crew to take up their oars and every man to have a weapon, knife or staff ready, while he buckled on a sword. The other ship was very faint against the grey sky to the North when the waves lifted us and I thought that perhaps they too were as frightened as we and ready to defend themselves. However they came no nearer and then they were gone and the sailors put aside their oars.

It was now the hour of noon by the sun high up overhead and your servant took bread and meat and a flask of wine from his bag begging me to eat and drink and saying that he had promised you to look after me and that if the sea sickness had not taken hold of me I should sustain myself with food. Then I broke some bread into wine in a little cup and so made a sop which refreshed me and made me sleepy so that I lay down with a wallet under my head and drew my cloak and cowl around me while the faithful man kept watch. I tell you this so that you too may reward him when he returns to you with this letter.

When I awoke my mouth was very dry so I drank a little water mixed with wine. I describe you these small acts that you who have never been to sea or left our native land may travel with me in your thoughts. Then it seemed to me from the position of the sun that it was the hour for Compline and I repeated the office silently to put myself in mind of God and commend you to Him, for it also seemed to me already that to travel is to occupy the mind with strange sights and little by little to push our accustomed thoughts away until God is forgotten, unless a fear of death or destruction arises and then we quickly recall Him and call upon His aid. Now I told Aelfwin to sleep while I watched lest someone should try to steal our goods while he slept. He protested that his lord had told him to watch always but I answered that night would soon come and then he must watch through the darkness and he would do that better if he was refreshed now, and he was persuaded.

No sooner had he lain down than the strange Scot approached me again and asked me in the name of our Saviour for a cup of wine which made it impossible for me to say no although I had heard him make the same request to several others in the boat and he had not been refused. He drank the wine and asked me where I came from. I told him that because of my vows I was not accustomed to hold conversation with men, at which he replied that he was a bishop and therefore there could be no harm in it. It was clear to me that he was one of those wandering bishops according to the Hibernian custom without a diocese, of whom it has been written that they toil not neither do they spin but lead lives of idleness and lasciviousness to the great scandal of the Church. However I told him that in our monastery of Wimborne when the bishop comes even the lady abbess speaks to him through a window and therefore he must excuse me. Then he left me alone again.

It is plain to me that it will be necessary to speak to men from time to time and indeed I had already made up my mind to thank the captain myself but I perceive a difference between needful speech and the loose indulgence of the tongue. And what is true of the tongue is also true of the eye and ear. It is necessary for the eyes to be open to see one's path but not for them to rest lustfully on objects or persons. The ear should be open to God's words and music but closed to idle chatter. All these things which I have often impressed upon novices, I find I now have to teach myself anew because I have gone out into the world.

Soon after, twilight began to fall and the captain ordered lamps to be lit. The night was mercifully clear and we sailed on under the moon and stars in a bright radiance that was reflected from the water's surface so that we seemed to move across the face of another moon which had fallen to earth. I pointed out and named the constellations to Aelfwin, believing that this was permitted for his education and as a manifestation of the power and beauty of God though I was careful to tell him that the names of the stars were those of the pagans before our Saviour's birth and their stories were not to be believed but rather as we might tell stories of our own heroes, of Cerdic from whom our family and all the kings of Wessex are descended. Then he said that in Mercia where he was born the kings are descended from Wotan who was held a god among our forefathers and our cousins, the German Saxons whither I intend to go, God willing, to look for your sister, and this I could give no explanation for. For if he was a god then how could he beget human children from whom other children are begotten? Our Saviour although perfect human did not beget children on a human woman, although the Arians and other heretics may claim so, for if he did where are they now? Therefore I think this Wotan was a hero like Cerdic whom men foolishly set up for a god. All these too were thoughts that had not come to me before and I prayed silently that I was not being led into error and pride.

The breeze had dropped with the coming of night and the captain ordered the sailors to row. I asked Aelfwin why we could not lie still and wait for a wind with the morning but he pointed out that if we were not in motion forward we might drift back and lose what we had gained and that a boat that is lying still is more easily surprised and taken. The sound of the oars was very rhythmical and I found myself growing drowsy. I prayed to God to protect me and laid my head down again with great confidence.

When I woke again there was a bar of grey between the water and dark sky. The moon and stars were gone and it was as if a curtain was being drawn up to let in the dawn. The wind had come back and the sailors were drooping asleep at their oars having rowed all night. Now the sea grew rough. White caps appeared on the waves and the ship was pitched from end to end and side to side. It was very cold and the spray flew over the side of the boat. I saw some, who had given no thought to them the night before, hastily beginning their prayers for deliverance but I found myself quite calm and with a steadfast conviction that God would not let us perish.

Observing this I suppose, the Hibernian was bold enough to approach me again with my third trial. 'I see,' he said, 'that you alone are not afraid.' I answered: 'We are in the hands of God.'

'True,' he said, 'but we are also in the hands of the winds and sea, and of the captain and the sailors and those who built this boat.'

'Then,' I said, 'where there are so many elements which are unknown, and which we cannot affect except by prayer, our course is simple.'

'You are a philosopher. However I think we can trust in the boat. It is large and strongly built. In my country men put to sea in small round boats of skin in which they travel to the Holy Island and go where men have never gone before, except in their minds, as far as the Land of Promise as the Blessed Brendan did.'

I was silent then for both these things I knew from Brother Dungal but I did not wish to display my knowledge and give occasion for further talk. I thought that my rule must be to answer questions briefly for courtesy but to ask none and in any case I doubted whether his knowledge was much greater than my own. 'I have made this journey many times,' he went on, 'and sometimes we are driven back to England and must begin again.'

I saw that all this was an attempt to provoke me into further speech. Our ship was being driven forward by a great wind that bellied out the sail as if it must split and the ropes and timbers groaned under the strain. At one moment as we were lifted up I thought I saw a low line of shade brushed in between the sea and sky on our right hand but I could not be sure and then it was gone again.

Now Aelfwin brought me a little bread and wine which he offered me as well as to the stranger and I was able to sit apart while I ate and drank and hear what they were saying. First Aelfwin asked where he was from and he named the great house of Clonmacnoise, and then where he was going and he said that he was going first to the court of the King of the Franks, to stay for some time among the Scots there because the King liked men of learning about him and always welcomed them. This meant that our way might lie together which I found disturbing and I was sorry that I must present myself at the palace before I could travel on further.

Our ship continued to fly forward under the clouds which seemed to bend low towards us. The captain approached and accepted some wine. 'I am afraid,' he said, 'that with the strength of the wind we shall be unable to make our landfall and turn towards the mouth of the Seine. Indeed we must run before it and try to land higher up the coast at Quentawick, unless God will hear your prayers lady and cause the wind to drop. I do not want to spend another night at sea for fear of being driven ashore in the dark.' Shortly after this the wind indeed began to moderate and the ship was able to turn south by means of great tacks to right and left. After several hours I saw again a dark blue ahead of us which Aelfwin told me was the land of the Franks. The wind ceased altogether as we drew closer and the sailors were forced to take to the oars again but more cheerfully this time, seeing an end to their labours and gradually it became clear that we were entering the mouth of a great river with watchtowers on either bank. Aelfwin told me that the Romans had built them in the time of their Empire and that the King of the Franks keeps them repaired against the Northmen.

'The prayers of virgins are incense in the nostrils of God,' the stranger said as we passed into calm water. 'Nevertheless I should have been glad to see the harbour of Quentawick with all its busy life of merchants and sailors, and the English house there at Saint Josse is a comfortable enough lodging.' I realised that he was playing with me, or upon me, again.

The boat drew towards a wooden landing stage. Aelfwin called up our servants and we prepared to disembark. The stranger wished me a good night's rest. 'We shall meet again,' he said, 'either in this world or the next.'

The captain came to wish us goodbye. 'I shall always believe that your prayers tamed the wind and brought us in safely,' he said when I praised his skill and thanked him. My limbs seemed very weak after the journey and it was with difficulty that Aelfwin helped me ashore and even then the ground appeared to sway under my feet as if we were still on board. However our tents were soon set up, a fire was lit and a little fish was cooked for my supper. While it was cooking I fell on my knees in my tent and gave thanks for our arrival. My bones ached with weariness and my head too but I went out after supper to stand at the flap of the tent. A little night wind soughed and all around under the stars were other stars, the fires of the pilgrims and travellers camped along the shore and from one, where I thought the galley slaves must lie, came singing in a language I did not know. The great river shone against the darker land. I looked to where it flowed to meet the sea and knew that you would be watching beyond its black waters, anxious for my safety, my dearest father.

Hetty lifts her head and looks about her. She has been transported from the library and its other fidgeting readers, and the hushed business of the librarians. She is standing on the right shore of a river bank with the wind in her face bringing the smell of the sea and of reeds and mud mixed with the barbecue of charcoal and roast flesh. She is caught, entranced and she can only bend her head again, turn the page and read on. Words, letters, symbols, small scratchings on a page, have warped her time by a thousand years, even through the filter of Canon Wren.

In the morning I was covered in weals from the midges that abound in that marshy place where the river bends many times on its way to the sea so that although we were still weary from tossing on the water I determined to move on towards Rouen before any of my party could fall sick of the marsh fever. Also I prepared an infusion of thyme, feverfew and fennel and made all my servants drink it. First I drank myself and then Aelfwin, although he made a great face, and then the others, and thanks be to God none of us has so far taken ill. It is thirty miles to Rouen, a journey of three days, where there is a great market with goods and people from many lands, and also thieves and harlots. Therefore I decided to camp outside the town while Aelfwin went in to see if it was clear of plague, for we had heard some rumours on the boat, and to buy more food.

From Rouen we travelled for four more days beside the river to the great shrine of St Denis and then to the abbey of the King's sister, the Lady Gisela for whom I had letters and gifts from our abbey of Wimborne. She received me very kindly. When I came into her presence I prostrated myself and she raised me up and kissed my face saying that we were sisters not only in our profession but also because of the love she has for our race through Master Alcuin who comes often to see her, and with whom she discusses many matters of scripture and doctrine so that she may the better teach her people. She spoke too of her love for Mother Lioba and therefore of her desire to help any of her family. She said that to be a ruler of an abbey was not easy and that she had had to learn many things and would always be ready with her advice and experience when I should encounter difficulties as I surely would, even though I was going to the rule of a much smaller house than hers, for Chelles is a royal estate where she often entertains the King on his journeys about the country. Then she laughed and said she always remembered with pleasure a story Lioba used to tell of my namesake Tetta who was abbess at Wimborne in the time of Boniface's first coming to Frankland, and how one night the keys of the chapel were lost after it was locked and when a general appeal to Heaven was ordered by Tetta for their return they were found in the mouth of a little dead fox lying outside the chapel doors by the watchman in the morning.

I said that I should try not to bring disgrace on my name and to follow the many examples of holy women who had gone before and left the accounts of their lives in the mouths of those who had known them. Then I presented her with that copy of the Epistle of St Peter which I had made myself and which I showed to you on our last day together. I reminded her of the copy in letters of gold of this same book that the holy Father Boniface had asked the Lady Eadberg to make for him, sending her the gold for it from Frankland that the words of St Peter might shine in the eyes and illumine the hearts of the heathen Saxons and said that I would have written hers in the same way but that there was no gold in English land but, for our sins, only blood and destruction as the world draws towards its end in these last days. Nevertheless I had embellished it as best I could, and she was kind enough to praise the penmanship and the painting of the capitals. She asked me why I was accompanied only by male attendants, apart from one servant girl, and I said that I had thought that if I had taken sisters or novices with me that this would have caused jealousies and she said that mine was a wise head for all my young years. And I remembered how Ethelhild begged to be allowed to come with me and I would not hear her because God had stopped my ears.

When we had rested at Chelles where the words of the venerable Gisela and the calm voices of the sisters were a refreshment for my spirit as well as for my body, although they sang the office in a way new to me, we set out again for the north-east towards the city of Rheims where the Franks first received the word of God when their King Clovis was baptised there and which is one of the twenty-one metropolitan cities of Frankland. After six more weary days of wandering we came to its walls which are entirely surrounded by vineyards whose fruit hung in ripe purple drops below the leaves so heavy that I understood more clearly the words of the psalmist: 'and every man shall sit each under his vine'.

It is a city splendid with high thick walls, a great arch, many churches and buildings in stone, that seems the work of giants rather than of the Romans who built it. We arrived in time for the feast of their saint, Remi, he who baptised King Clovis, and all the public squares were hung with coloured cloths, and the churches with white hangings and smelling of incense and sweet-scented candles which made a perfumed paradise. Then I understood, my father, how we live in Britain on an island at the edge of the world where there is storm and darkness in the long months of winter when the sun withdraws into Africa and our hands are too cold to write.

Here in the basilica where I had gone to pray at the shrine of St Remi, which the King has ordered restored to its former state and the walls are bright with painting and the floor with tiles, I thought I saw the Hibernian but I drew my cowl over my face to avoid speech and hurried away. Beyond the city to the north lies the forest of the Ardennes, a dangerous place where there are wild men and beasts who fall upon travellers when they are camped at night and so it is best to travel on, however tired, to a safe house of which there are several maintained by order of the King.

We passed the first day of our journey in safety but towards noon on the second day we came out into a clearing in the dense trees where there was a cross set up in stone. Against it stood the Hibernian surrounded by four or five brutish men with knives and staves whom he was keeping off with his own staff. When they saw us they turned upon us snarling like beasts. We were more than they in number (but two of us were women plus the boy Hereric); of grown men we had only Aelfwin and two porters we had hired in Rheims who were as likely to join with the brigands to rob us. Suddenly the Hibernian called out something in what I took to be the Frankish tongue and they fell silent. Then he said: 'Tell them to depart in your best Latin.'

I lifted up my hand, feeling a power that overcame my fear and said: 'Go. It is finished.' They began to mutter and back away so I said again: 'Go.' They turned and ran and we could hear them crashing through the trees in the direction of Rheims which was a great relief for if they had gone the other way they might have recovered their courage and lain in wait ahead of us. Then the Hibernian requested permission to join our party for safety and I could not refuse.

'Are you not curious?' he asked, 'to know what I said to them?' I bent my head in assent. 'I told them that I had seen you calm the wind and waves and that you would destroy them as you had the storm.'

Once again I determined not to answer him or to speak at all on what had happened for I could see that I was being tempted by the sin of pride and that in some way the Hibernian has been sent to test me to see if I am fit for the work I have to do. When we stopped to eat therefore, I sat apart with my servant and the boy, and took care to bless our food and drink before we began on it. Some time after when we were again upon our way he came up to walk beside my horse. 'Have you noticed,' he said, 'that few birds sing in this forest? In my country where the ground is open many larks start up from the grass singing their way up into the sky, towards heaven, in praise of the sunlight and their freedom.'

'A bird will also sing in a cage,' I said, thinking of the linnet that I allowed the novices to keep when I was their mistress.

'But always with a kind of franticness as if their little hearts were bursting. Do you not sometimes pine for the freedom of the lark climbing the air in your cage of poverty, chastity and obedience?'

I answered that I did not feel them as bonds since I had freely given my vows; that I was fed and clothed and housed and therefore not poor, that we are all obedient to fate and made free by obedience to God and our Rule since by them we overcome fate, and that chastity gives us true freedom for as St Jerome says: 'When a woman wishes to serve Christ more than the world she will be called a man and no longer subject to men'. After this he dropped back to walk with the porters. Nevertheless I noticed that what he said was true and that in the dense forest we were travelling through where the trees pressed in on both sides of the path there was a broodingness, broken only sometimes by a rustle and the cracking of branches as if some large wolf or bear was walking unseen beside us.

It seemed as if we must wander through this wilderness forever but after many days of travelling in wind, rain and mist the trees began at last to draw back from the path and we saw the sun above again where there had been only the darkness of leaves and branches. And truly I think this journey may be an emblem of life and our wandering lost in it and our coming out onto the plain an image of that other life we are promised. The Hibernian turned aside to a hostel for travellers as soon as we had left the forest but I ordered our tents to be set up and an early start in the morning for I was anxious now to be done with the journey. Before he left us he said that he intended to visit the monastery at Prum and perhaps Echternach founded by our own Willibrord when he came to work among the heathen Frisians and where his body lies in a marble sarcophagus.

Once out of the wilderness we made faster progress and knew that we were nearing our journey's end by the numbers of travellers, merchants and people of all kinds on the way which had become wider and rutted by many feet of men and horses and the wheels of cart and carriage. Then as we got closer to Aachen we heard the noise of tools on stone and voices of workmen and traders raised in a great din after the silence of the forest. We camped outside the city and I sent Aelfwin to see what we should do to present ourselves and our letters and gifts.

When he came back it was with the news that the Queen would receive me after the midday meal and would then take me to the King. I prepared myself and my gifts and made my people comb themselves and put on their finest dress before we entered the town and made our way to the palace. Everywhere men were building what seemed a heavenly city and Aelfwin pointed out to me the walls of a great cathedral which were beginning to rise, and told me that the King had permission from the Pope to send to Ravenna in Italy to take stones and pavements from there to decorate it.

The new Queen is very young and was educated with the King's children in the palace school. She kissed me kindly and then led me into the hall where the King had just finished dinner and was being read to while eating grapes with a cup of wine. He is tall and strong, thick-necked with a head of curling white hair and is dressed in linen shirt and drawers under a tunic fringed with silk, and long hose after the Frankish fashion. The Queen led me by the hand and he motioned us forward until I could kneel before him. 'You have come from my dear sister?' he said. 'Have you brought me a letter?'

I answered that I had and Aelfwin presented it to him. He opened and read it. 'She says that you are wise and clever too and have made her gift of a book of Scripture in your own hand, and that you have come to take up rule of the house that belongs to your family in Thuringia, the Abbess Switha being lately dead. This I will grant even though I am angry with your race for their murder of Kings and neglect of God's Church.'

His eyes which are large and glittering stared at me fixedly like an unhooded falcon's and I did not dare to answer.

'Yet they are punished for it,' he went on, 'for their sins the Holy Island of Lindisfarne and the monastery of Bede at Jarrow are destroyed by the heathens. It is lucky for you that you are not from Northumbria or I would take away your rule and give it to one of my own people and put you under her. Nevertheless because of my love for some of your countrymen I will watch and see if you govern well.'

I had not expected to be treated so rudely but I held my tongue in humiliation until the King signalled to the Queen that we should withdraw. She took me to her own apartments, which were hung with richly embroidered stuffs, and ordered me refreshment. 'I am sorry that you should find him in an angry fit,' she said, 'but he has many cares and bad news from every side.'

By this time I had recovered a little and was able to answer that his chastising of us was just, for in all the kingdoms of Britain there was violence and evil living, incest, adultery, regicide and murder as all the world knows and that these are like contagion. When they infest one country they may spread to its neighbours but that now in Wessex we have a wise King Brihtric and the people are quiet. Then I gave her the things I had brought in the hope of pleasing the King: among them the two woollen cloaks from you, a green silk cope embroidered with gold and silver thread and, for herself, a silver stylus and *The Life of St Boniface*. At this she took me in her arms and kissed me.

'Let us two be like Queen Hildegard and the blessed Lioba: Queen Hildegard was a second mother to me and I was there in the court where Lioba came to say her last goodbye. I remember her words as she kissed the Queen first on her mouth, then on her forehead and then on her eyes: "Farewell for evermore my dearly beloved lady and sister, farewell most precious half of my soul. May we meet again without shame on the Day of Judgement for nevermore on this earth shall we enjoy each other's presence." Though you must go away to the North I shall send for you after and you must keep a place always ready for me both in your heart and in your home,' and she had me shown to a chamber in the guest house. 'Now rest,' she said, 'for the King always undresses and lies on his bed for two hours after his dinner, according to the Rule of St Benedict, and you should do the same.'

Later I was awakened by a great noise of people and when Aelfwin came to receive my orders I asked him what it meant. He said that the King with his sons and attendants had gone to the great bath that receives the hot springs and were bathing, laughing and shouting almost a hundred of them altogether like schoolboys. At night I kept to my chamber and began the writing of this to you but I could hear from the distance singing which reminded me of your hall at home and the old songs of kings and warriors that some say are of the devil. The sound brought me a longing for home and you, and a sadness at the sea between us for you have been father and mother to me, both. I woke in the small hours and I said Prime and then lit a candle to read until there should be light enough, and just as I had snuffed out my candle I heard a great noise of horses and opening the shutter saw that the King was riding out to hunt with his sons and daughters, a golden-haired girl beside her father on a white horse and the smallest princess, a pretty child, at the back and I understood why the Queen had asked for my love because her mind is more attuned to reading and discussion than to hunting and the distractions and luxuries of the court. And I am glad, father, that when I was a child in arms, after your wife died in

—32—

giving me birth that you took me, sickly as I was, and laid me at the foot of the stone cross where the people come to pray on our estate and dedicated me, if I should live, to this life of prayer and study.

Pray for me my dearest father as I do for you. By the time your letter returns to me I shall, I trust, have reached our house in Clingen. Farewell in Christ.

Hetty looks up with a sense of loss. Her own books lie on the table but she doesn't pick them up. Instead she turns to the index to the volume of transactions unable to believe that there's no more. And she's rewarded. There's another later reference which she quickly tracks down. It's a letter in the next number from a vicar in Colchester claiming to have seen writings under the same name among the archives in Frankfurt, 'which do not as far as I am aware appear in any published edition, even the *Bibliotheca Rerum Germanicorum* of Ph. Joffe (Berlin 1873).' She knows now where Jack will tell her the conference is being held. She gathers up her books, has them stamped out, and drives herself home through the faltering sunlight as if past and present were bound in a silken web.

And so they are, Hetty thinks as she dips a late radish in salt and crunches through it, inspecting the remaining half for the dark full stop of rot at the heart of the coconut white flesh that will tell her to spit out the segment in her mouth before it flushes with the earthy flavour of corruption. But the little globe in its red skin is sound, and the piece that's left safe to follow its other half. Hetty pursues it with a piece of smoked cheese, savouring them both as she hasn't done since Jack, that gash in the calendar from which everything has had to be dated New Style. Now she must recast her time again, not in Old Style though. That's gone. Like Galileo, just once she had seen through a previously darkened glass and the nimbus had vanished from about the moon. Nothing could ever bring back that world where she had thought that his sun went round her moon and she had simply to sit still in the centre and pay her toll for the right to admire.

The whole 'sensible appearance of things' had suddenly been restored to her. Tetta's little devil fox had come to her door that morning with a noose around it and a key in its jaws. She still doesn't believe in omens, portents but she knows that there are holes in time where coincidence pokes through and she understands the urge to touch wood, cross fingers, even spit for luck. Her mother would never wear, or furnish her house with green, mix red and white flowers in a vase, wash clothes on Christmas day and all these superstitions, as she had called them in her innocent teens, she sees now as an attempt to explain what common sense couldn't: the entry of a mysterious symmetry that might bring light and darkness into human affairs, a random patterning that could only be combated by fatalism, the numbered shell or bullet or bomb of two world wars, or by irrational ancient rituals. One day we may find an explanation in the infinitesimal patterning at the heart of chaos or the uncalibrated shock waves at the root of time and be able finally to uncross our fingers. Meanwhile Hetty opens a book on the unclothed wooden table and begins to make headings about the Grand Tour, the French Revolution, the Napoleonic Wars, the Chartists, the banging up of our island fortress into a Dickensian hulk moored off the continental shelf; punctuating these with cheese and celery, more radishes that drip an occasional reddened tear on her reporter's spiral bound notebook, and at last a bunch of raisinous Italia grapes that seem to hold the Umbrian sunlight in each smokey green fruit. Then there's the Empire that convinced us for a time we were quite apart and didn't have much

—34—

in common with them over there, unlike the Colonies which we could mould in our own image of suet duff and India Pale Ale. That will have to go in.

Hetty can see that it's still light outside and she goes to the French windows to step into the evening. The sky as she climbs the brick path opens in an opalescent shoal over her head where small plumed islands float, pink shading through pale to duck-egg blue and finally green, visionary yet vulgarly unpaintable except by those English mystics Samuel Palmer and John Martin for whom such sunsets were steps to an improbable Paradise. She's aware of the fox in the ground under its marquee of chestnut leaves and turns away from it, catching at the incense of night-scented stock. In the plough beyond her garden hedge where she sometimes walks, there are stones in the chalky earth like bones, knuckles, fossil vertebrae, dinosaur carpals and tarsals, constantly poking up into the day as the soil is eroded by man and weather. Should she go back to her note-making or down into the village to The Wheatsheaf as she sometimes does for the noise and voices and warmth from other bodies? She turns back into the cottage, takes a striped blue and red blazer from the hook behind the door, slings her bag over her shoulder and goes out into the creeping dusk. Two bats trapeze past her as she walks along the narrow path, glancing at the lit windows of that cottage, twin to her own but curtained and letting out a faint mechanical murmur from radio or television.

Going out alone at night always makes her a little breathless; not afraid quite. She mustn't admit to fear or she would be imprisoned by the fall of darkness. She walks in the middle of the road as she was taught to do as a child in town streets, briskly, her bag knocking against her hip, her hands in her blazer pockets, the heavy door key gripped hard. Tonight it isn't quite dark yet and shadows drained of colour lurk behind trees that overhang the lane. The cottages lie back behind their gardens. She passes the long high wall of a handsome house she has glimpsed through an open gate, shut now. Where she turns left downhill is the church with its ancient bone yard toothed with illegible stones, and its lychgate fringed with layering cedars, navy-green in the twilight.

This part of the road is vaulted with the branches of high old beech trees but it's downhill and she can go faster, almost at a trot until the light from the pub's car park turns the lane ahead into a stage set with black painted beams in the red brick walls and an heraldic inn sign standing sentinel over the Volkswagens that have come to dine, and the Fords that have come to drink. Hetty will slot herself between the two, at the junction where there's a slip bar that serves as off-licence, with a couple of small round tables and wooden armed chairs. A group of diners are catcalling to each other in the restaurant while from the public bar she can hear the deep burr of the local dialect, distanced to unintelligibility.

Hetty orders her half pint of bitter, comments on the weather and takes the glass to a table. Tonight is the landlady's night out with the Licensed Victuallers' Association. Joyce Bates will have gone off, smart as her polished glasses, in patent leather and pearls. Sometimes Hetty chats to her, admiring her shrewdness, her grasp of her own life, recovered from the wreckage of a car crash that had killed her husband and threatened her tenure of The Wheatsheaf.

'When you're on your own as we are,' she often said to Hetty as a refrain, 'you have to give eye to yourself,' drawing her into a conspiracy that was both bracing and desolate. Her lieutenant, Mick, a thin balding man with the white cheekbones of a Dublin waif, prefers to lean on the bar in the public and take part in the gossip of neighbourhood, sport and television that's passed round to munch on with the packets of crisps and pork scratchings.

The absence of Joyce makes Hetty determined to finish her drink and go. She takes her notebook out of her bag and studies the headings she has made earlier but they don't engage her attention now. They are merely a blind to disguise her solitariness and she wishes she hadn't come. She is staring hard at the scrawled page when she hears the door open.

'Ah now that's a relief; a bit of intelligent conversation tonight.'

Hetty looks up at a voice she knows and knows is for her. It's the man in the donkey jacket, as she thinks of him since they've never exchanged names.

'Let me get you another half.'

'That's very kind. I was just going. . . .' She lets the sentence trail and drop not wanting to offend but not knowing whether she wants to be seduced into a session.

'Oh don't go just when I've come, as the bishop said to the actress.' The man in the donkey jacket laughs showing perfect half-cobnut teeth in a juicy red mouth. His hair is slightly long in dark curls. Her mother would have marked him down for a gipsy. His voice is soft and liquid with a slight Southern country tang. Hetty knows he hires himself out with his monster digger to anyone who needs them. He brings his own pint and her half across to the table and takes a long sup that leaves his lips gleaming.

'Ah I needed that.'

'Been working hard?'

'Over at Cheddle Pixcombe. Bloke with money burning a hole in his pocket wants a swimming pool now the summer's over. Stupid git. World's full of them nowadays. Not the sense they was born with. Have to have everything alike. Sheep. Got to have a pool because Charlie he goes up to London in the train with every morning's got one. In a few weeks when the weather breaks it'll fill up with rain and leaves and the sides'll all wash down if he hasn't got it lined by then. I told him: "Best wait till the Spring." "Anyone would think you didn't want the job," he said. "Not if it's wasting my time and yours," I said. "Surely I'm the best judge of my own time," he said, going all red in the face. So I done it for him. Dug it out, levelled the spoil. Nice tidy job. You should have let me do your bit of digging.'

'But I didn't know you then.'

'You don't now.' He laughs and drinks again.

The cottage, when Hetty had bought it, had had no lavatory or bathroom. She supposed the old man who had died there had emptied his pot in the garden that she had had to destroy to put in a septic tank and land drain. She had thought she would be worried by the image of her own effluent gathering in a huge onion chamber under her feet as she poked in bulbs and scattered grass seed but she found she never thought of it lying there like a chambered vault at Mycenae, secreting her seething dead that had to be sucked out and carried away for reburial on some farmer's fields once a year. Perhaps the old man's way had been better. She has noticed that the lungwort thrust up their fleshy spotted leaves and purple flower spikes most profusely in a rich dark patch under the hedge by the front door where the old man could most easily have thrown his night soil.

The garden had been left lunarscape when the builders had gone, with only its hedged fringes intact and the chestnut holding up its empty branches stark above half an acre of no-man's-land. Hetty is proud of her restoration and grateful, for in mending the garden's great wound she first began to stitch her own.

'No-one knows anyone else really do they,' the donkey jacket is saying. 'We talk to each other, but we don't know what's going on in the other one's head.'

Hetty agrees with this, she has to, and he goes on, 'The people round here they don't understand that you might want something different. You understand me. You know there's more to it than this, that a man might have dreams he couldn't mention to this lot.' He gestures with his eyes sweepingly at the two separate wings of the pub. 'You're not a prude. I can tell that. You've been about and seen a bit of the world.'

She wonders how this false information shows but she smiles as if in agreement, though questioning silently whether that, after all, is the secret of the 'Mona Lisa' and if her enigmatic gaze is just the posture women have been taught, by example, to assume while men assail them, and if she was really wondering how much to leave out for the milkman. Hetty catches sight of herself in that mirror of ourselves we carry in our heads, smiling and bending, encouraging because she doesn't want to be thought rude, or worse dull, even by the stranger in the donkey jacket. She must extricate herself with dignity. His glass is almost empty. She stands up firmly. 'Let me get you a refill.' She takes it from him as he drains the dregs, avoiding contact with his hand and carries it to the bar. When she comes back he's rolling a cigarette.

'Can't stand tailor-mades. D'you want one? I'll roll it and you can lick it.' He sees she only has one drink in her hand. 'Aren't you having one?'

'I've got to go. Expecting an important phone call.'

'Just when we were getting comfortable.'

'That's life.' Hetty drains her glass. 'Nice talking to you.'

'Nice talking to you.'

'See you.'

'Why not.'

She heads for the door quickly. She's afraid he might follow her and hopes the fresh pint will keep him there. In the lit car park she's tempted to run but holds herself to a fast walk. There might be other people about who would wonder to see her ungainly, because unpractised, attempt at a jog that Hetty knows she could only keep up for a minute or two before her heart would be thudding and her side in that stitch she remembers from running as a child. If only she had come on her bike or in the car. The two halves of beer slosh about inside her as she forces herself uphill. Now she stops to take a deep breath and look back. The road is empty behind and the stage set lies like a toy theatre before the cardboard puppets are pushed on.

Her neighbour's insistent broadcast murmur is a comfort as she turns up the drive. She lets herself in with the big iron key and pours herself a glass of red wine from an already open bottle, listening for any sound that she might have been followed, wishing as she does from time to time that she had a dog. Gradually her heartbeat and her apprehension subside enough for Hetty to begin to analyse, rationalise as all her work and training have taught her to do. Why should she flatter herself that the man in the donkey jacket wants anything more than a friendly chat? Perhaps it's all her imagination, or perhaps he's as bound by the convention of how men are expected to behave towards single women, especially those alone in pubs, as her responses are conditioned in their turn.

By the time she's ready to go upstairs to her sloping bedroom under the eaves Hetty is calm and a little drunk. Up there, with the small cottage window open on a night, starred between the leaves, she feels the room is an ark afloat on a dark sea, the double bed Jack never shared with her at its heart. She decides it's too hot to wear her pyjama bottoms and struggles out of them under the sheet, letting them drop in a heap beside the bed.

The sheet is a cool touch on her bare legs and she slips a hand between her thighs. In the time of Jack she had always thought of him as she caressed herself but now she feels she must learn to empty her mind and let the purely physical sensation fill it, uncoupled to any image. Above all she must keep the donkey jacket away from her thoughts. To let him in would somehow be conniving at her own rape. She comes quickly, deliciously, the tingling orgasm flowing into her belly and down her thighs, arcing her body with pleasure and forcing little cries out of her mouth, cries she keeps low enough not to alarm the neighbours, until it has drained away leaving her relaxed and sweaty. Hetty gives the springy moss of her pubic hair a final pat. She remembers a scribble she had read with amusement and approval in the public lavatory on Waterloo Station: *Don't knock masturbation – it's only having sex with someone you love.*

Does she love herself, she wonders. Has she loved herself in loving Jack too much? That nun Tetta would have been forbidden to touch, even to look at her own body. Nuns, she had read somewhere, bathed in their shifts even in the twentieth century and so did the girls in their care. Were they allowed to wash between their legs and soap their breasts? Hetty runs her hands with pleasure over her own smooth skin, warmly plumping out the pyjama jacket. Tonight she has given her own flesh back to herself. She doubts as she drifts into sleep whether she will ever be able to give it again to someone else, or whether anyone, as it ages and dries and winkles, will want it enough to take it. If

Hetty were a man the idea that a younger, even much younger girl might find him sexually attractive would be perfectly thinkable, a pursuit he might contemplate not only with dignity but with society's nudging approval. In spite of the fashionable talk of toyboys, Hetty knows her likeliest pursuer will come after her at a geriatric hobble, determined not to recognise himself in the mummy mirrored in the glass at the turn in the stair. Cherie, the Rose Cavalier are, if they come at all, brief summer signals the first frost despatches.

There's no messenger at her door when Hetty opens it next morning, and the sky is dryly overcast with a grey wind so quickly does our island weather change. But she refuses to become a centre of depression even though she hopes that Jack will ring early and get it over with.

She doesn't want a re-run of those many prevaricating times when he had said of course he would call and didn't.

'Well, what have you decided?' It's the morning coffee break and she has only had to wait for a couple of hours.

'You did say all expenses and a small fee?'

'Ticket and hotel are already booked.'

'Well it would be a pity to waste them.'

'That's brilliant. Bob will be grateful, and me too of course. I'll put the ticket, with all the details, in the post and a pack of the new bumf we've had printed about St Julian's. You can drop it on the chairs; it might drum up a bit of business.'

'Not if I make a hash of my paper.'

'But you won't. I've always had a great respect for your work you know. I hope you're doing more of your own thing now that you've got more time.'

Hetty smiles a little as she remembers how often she has listened dutifully to Jack's theories of history and education, a monologue she wasn't allowed to contribute to. His version of female emancipation had stopped short at a woman's right to share her body but not her mind. She, and Hetty supposed, his wife and the others there had surely been, had always had to share his. At the depth of her bitterness and depression only

—41—

Bob's unfailing kindness and natural courtesy had stopped Hetty tarring all men with the same brush. She would leave leaflets on chairs for Bob and St Julian's, not for Jack.

'And if you could let us have a brief report when you get back, for the files. . . .'

Perhaps, Hetty thinks, I won't come back. I'll do a Mr Polly, a runner, take a powder. She feels light and free, untethered as a cloud.

'Of course I could drop the stuff in. I could make a couple of hours this afternoon. . . .'

Hetty has hardly been listening, off on her own tangential thoughts, but this sudden danger sounds an alarm that has her wide awake. It's the vacation. She's forgotten. There are no students about. 'I shan't be here I'm afraid and the letter box might not be big enough. Safer to put it in the post.' She knows she isn't yet strong enough for any confrontation, especially alone in the cottage with the bed ponderous over their heads.

'It would have been good to see you; have a gossip.' His voice is becoming softer, full of concern, almost pleading.

She must steel herself and cut this short before he slips into his lost boy suit and comes tapping his need at her windowpane. 'Sorry, there's someone at the door. Must go. I'll let you all know how it went.' Hetty puts back the receiver, shaking. It has been a close one and now she must find a reason to be out for the rest of the day just in case he should after all be just passing by and drop in. She will go back to the library and make a photocopy of the letter, order some Deutsche Marks from her bank, perhaps even buy herself something new to travel in and not come back to work on her paper until she's sure Jack is safely home again.

Hetty is in flight. She knows the miraculous lightness of travelling alone unburdened by guilt or anxiety. She doesn't have to look forward or back only out at a shifting cloud-procession of images: an elderly woman cleaner in iridescent sari wearily pushing a grey mop over the marble floor, a moustached young immigration officer who checks Hetty's passport unsmiling, the buffed elegance of the airline staff in their blue school uniforms invested with the glamour of prefects to a third former, the Dachau commandant security guard who feels her up for gun or bomb. She waits for her flight in the Euro-lounge that's somehow already divorced from mother earth, beside her the duty-free yellow plastic bag heavy with treats that she wouldn't normally buy and that are identical in airports all over the world: the names and shapes of bottles, the smells and tastes and opiates in their glossy packaging so that Arabian princesses and Bow hairdressers smell and sip the same.

When her number is called she funnels herself down the plastic tube to the caterpillar that engorges her into the plane, moved along by a brilliant stewardess smile. Hetty stows her coat, sinks into her bucket seat and belts herself in, noting the nearest emergency exit just to satisfy that inevitable rush of anxiety; takes the soothing in-flight magazine from the net in the chair-back in front of her and settles as a million others do every day to be bussed forward to the end of the runway, to gulp as the engines are given a burst of power and the plane begins its run against the wind and probability, to unstick from earth, to lift us out of our element and carry us above the highest bird until what she sees passing, sinking like bath foam below are the clouds themselves, where only saints and cherubs once aspired, looking down on the rest of us earthlings. Hetty feels the inevitable surge in her stomach at parting from the ground, the jolt as the wheels are locked up, the moment of no return, of the improbable miracle that has become the commonplace of the human refusal to be confined.

In the magazine are maps showing how the airline nets up the countries and continents, and Hetty can trace the nun's arduous way, her weeks of travelling to the point Hetty will step down at in two hours. She sees time as a straight line that has given her the shortest distance between two points but cyclical too, a lapping outwards of ripples, a convolute repeat pattern like those she designed as a child in the art room to be made, or rather never made, into improbable furnishings and dresses as an examination task.

Beside her are a couple holding hands and suddenly Hetty doesn't envy them and is no longer afraid; that is, she corrects herself, she no longer cares whether she lives or dies.

Oh of course, she thinks, if there really was an emergency, and the pilot's calm cut-glass accents handed down from Second World War RAF officers announced that we were about to crash, there would be the reflex flow of adrenalin into my bloodstream, the panic flood to be fought, the sheer fell horror; but that's different, just an animal instinct to survive, to escape pain and mutilation. This feeling is quite separate and it's not like the darkest Jack hour either when I longed to be dead, 'to cease upon the midnight with no pain'. This is just an airy indifference, a floating free, a waiting.

She looks out at drifting cirrus and down at a sea wrinkled for the birth of Venus into silver wavelets with one fishing boat in position to haul the fallen boy angel Icarus from the waters that drag at his wings. When she is brought her plastic lunch box Hetty orders a bottle of dry white wine to toast her flight, impervious to the muttered warning of the male of the couple to his wife that: 'Alcohol in the air has double the kick.'

Who else among the plane-load is headed for her conference, she wonders. Well she'll soon know for the cigar-shaped body is tilting downwards though there are still twenty thousand footsteps for them to descend before she can see the mock-up of rivers and hills, model trees and houses dotted neatly about the landscape as they let down through afternoon sunshine and the wheels touch, grip and the reverse thrust of the engines powers them to a bone-shaking halt. 'Welcome to Frankfurt Airport ladies and gentlemen . . .' begins the chief stewardess, getting more attention for her news of temperature and travel than for the doom-laden safety instructions with their accompanying grotesque mime that everyone had studiously looked away from at the beginning of the flight. Hetty gathers up her things. That brief suspension of anxiety and responsibility is over. She must be ready to smile and enquire, meet strangers and perform against the grain of the last solitary months.

She feels a positive sensation of pleasure at the passport control she heads for, marked for EEC citizens, and as she smiles and says 'thank you' for the return of her passport after scrutiny, for being let in and not turned away, wonders whether it's her lifelong study of the Age of Reason as it used to be dubbed that makes her glad to be shut of the guilt of empire, of that dark satanic Britishness that followed the bloody drowning of enlightenment in Marat's bathtub. She plucks her suitcase from among the revolving baggage, watched by anxious faces of all shades of pink, yellow and brown. She will be met, the invitation had said so, and there indeed is a beefy young man in cotton trousers and yellow T-shirt holding up a handwritten placard saying *Europe Conference*.

Hetty steps forward.

'You are for the Europe Conference?'

'Yes indeed.'

'We wait. There are more to come.' And they are joined by three assorted males Hetty hasn't time to take in before the young man leads them through the automatic doors and out into the warm sun towards a minibus labelled *Georg Wielen Centre*. The young man puts their suitcases and bags in the boot, waves them up into the seats with a: 'Please!', slams the sliding door and infiltrates them into the orderly autobahn traffic. The road is sparsely wooded on either side with delicate deciduous trees, maple and lime and beech whose leaves tremble constantly as if invisible hands are setting them spinning. They look fresh and unsullied by the motorway fumes and dust, and untarnished by acid rain. Road signs loom up with names and towns and cities that are completely familiar to her as if she has been here before but she realises that they are remembered from wartime wireless broadcasts, dimly understood above her head that nevertheless have left this residue of knowledge at the bottom of her memory. The parents of the boy driving the bus perhaps hadn't even been born when she was a child absorbing these names, and the association of his fresh face and yellow shirt seems an impossible anachronism against that dark half-remembered tapestry of her early childhood when she and her foster parents had trembled night after night at the crump of bombs searching for the nearby railway line that led to the marshalling yards, just as some child was doing here Hetty thinks as Darmstadt rides up on the gantry and falls away behind.

They are driving across a plain with mountains beyond. 'Taunus,' the boy says gesturing, 'and this the Main river.' *Taurus*, Hetty thinks, like a bull lying down chewing the cud in a water meadow. The boy skirts the city leaving it behind for wooded suburbs and then at the point where it seems they will go on and on towards the mountains, he swings the bus across the road to come to rest in a gravelled forecourt in front of a modern two-storey complex like a motel, or college or monastery in brick and metal and glass. 'Georg Wielen Centre,' the boy says, switching off the engine and jumping out.

'Too late to run for home now,' says a dignified man in, Hetty guesses, his early seventies, hoisting himself out of his seat. She smiles back wondering why an American, a Bostonian she decides as she follows him down the metal steps, has come to a conference on the idea of Europe. In a diffident group they make their way with their bags across the forecourt and into the glass foyer. The boy has already jumped into his minibus and driven off spirting up gravel with his tyres, to collect another gaggle of arrivals.

A first glance as she goes towards an obvious reception desk, shows Hetty that the centre is handsomely modern, internationally tasteful. Earlier arrivals are deep in low leather-look armchairs talking quietly together and glancing out through long windows to where others are sitting outdoors around a pond in the middle of a cloister or quadrangle or better, Hetty decided, fixing a smile and preparing to announce herself to the elegantly forbidding girl behind the small glass pane, an atrium, that Mediterranean design for living that spread further and lasted longer than the Roman Empire itself. She signs her name, fills in her address and occupation and in exchange is given a name tag and an oblong of plastic and pointed towards the lifts.

Hetty has read the obligatory campus and conference novels and should know exactly what to expect but life disconcertingly doesn't always precisely imitate art or rather, by the laws of psychological relativity, the point of observation, Hetty, is bound to affect her perception of reality and she finds herself, in spite of the literature, completely at sea. Even the lift is an adventure. Does button six take her to the desired sixth floor? Will the door open automatically or must she push another button? Does she turn left or right as the lift door swishes, almost soundlessly but inexorably, shut behind her and the lift whispers away leaving her with two stretches of uniform, narrow corridor from which to make her existential choice. Then her blinding anxiety clears and she's able to read the two sets of room numbers and make an informed decision instead of merely tossing for it. She sets off left, turning corners, reading numbers from identical doors until she comes to '636' and puts down her suitcase.

In the dim light from opaque windows and recessed bulb she stands outside her door in the empty corridor. No sound reaches her from beyond, above or below. She looks at the piece of plastic which she has understood is a key. Then she looks at the grey lock in front of her which has no keyhole but a horizontal slit. Again she looks at her plastic card and finds an arrow among the cabalistic etchings. Nervously she puts the plastic tongue in the slot mouth. Nothing happens. She will stand here forever until somebody comes or she will have to toil down to reception and ignominiously ask for help. She pushes harder and feels a slight give. There's a chrome handle which she grasps desperately and bears down on. With a small miracle the door opens, flooding her with relief and light.

Lugging her suitcase inside Hetty extracts the plastic card and closes the door behind her. The room is a hot airless box and she crosses at once to the window and finds she can open it to let the heat out and the noise of traffic in and a stir of breeze. Then she turns to take in her surroundings. There are three doors: the one to the corridor, one to a wardrobe and one to a sealed but private bathroom, tiled cleanly in pale blue. She enjoys the release of a pent-up pee, washes her hands and face, returns to unpack her case and hang her clothes in the foreign wardrobe, dispose of her washing tackle in the bathroom and her duty free bottle of Scotch on the desk, and collapses on the narrow bed with the conference agenda and a glass of whisky and water. Tonight there's a dinner; tomorrow she must give her paper. She finishes her whisky. She is falling asleep thinking about the plastic card key. What will become of fairy tale and that potent symbol of the heavy key, like that she has in her handbag to her own cottage door, turning in the lock, when children know only the electronic button or coded message to unlock the future? That perfect joining of key and keyhole that opened the girl's thighs would be replaced by an oral image, the vertical by the horizontal, cold thrusting metal by neutral plastic.

When she wakes her mouth is furry and dry. She goes to the window and looks down on a junction of broad tree-lined roads where no-one is walking, only cars and lorries come and go as if by remote control. She has been safe up here in her box. Now she must take herself out and down. How dressy will the dinner be? She changes into a patterned green silky shirt and a white skirt above bare legs and this year's fashionable sandals the shoeshops describe as 'Attic', puts on some scent and agate earrings, brushes her hair, dyed a new chestnut last night, pins her name above 'that left pap where heart doth hop', puts a selection of papers in her bag, along with the key, and goes out into the hushed corridor in search of the lift.

As the door opens to let her out she hears the pre-overture, muted and indistinguishable seashell roar of voices. In the foyer two tables with white cloths, bottles of wine and glasses have now appeared with bartenders behind them, male and female in white shirts and black trousers. There's to be a welcome, a *Wilkommen* by a dignitary, that official the British don't admit to, a Minister of Culture.

A glance around tells her that most of the delegates are

men in suits, which accounts for the deep-sea timbre of the conversation, with here and there a conspicuous woman. Looking at her tomorrow's audience Hetty feels a wave of stage fright threaten to shipwreck her small confidence. She hesitates, not knowing how to plunge into this masculine tide where she can now pick out several different languages making exchanges above her head. Perhaps she should sit down in one of the chairs and wait for something to happen to her since she knows no-one. At this moment she hears behind her a voice she has at least heard before.

'Can I buy you a drink?'

'I don't think they're open yet.'

'We could try and force them, at gunpoint if necessary.'

'Do you have a gun? I don't.'

'The old Raymond Chandler routine with the finger in the pocket, if you haven't a banana, might do the trick.'

'Or we could try willing the corks to fly out of the bottles.'

'I don't think that will be necessary. I think what's needed is just initiative, the pioneering spirit to go over there and make them tilt a bottle over our glass.'

'What are we waiting for then?' Hetty leads the way towards the table with the elderly Bostonian following. Suddenly as if by secret sign or charm the bartenders come to life and begin to pour.

'Red or white?' Hetty asks over her shoulder.

'My doctor says white, unfortunately. White or whisky.'

Hetty picks out a glass of each colour from the neat ranks on the cloth and forces her way back to him through the incoming tide, holding the drinks out in front like weapons that part the waters before her. Her Bostonian is in conversation with a red-cheeked moustached young man. As she gets nearer she's able to read his name: Dr Jan Dorff of the University of Cologne, and her American too she can now give a name to: Professor David Tucker. She feels their eyes lighting on her name badge and flicking away as she holds out the glass of white wine.

Tucker bows as he takes it and then straightens, twinkling at her like Walter Pidgeon in old age, a practised twinkle that's meant to charm and disarm, but she lets herself be seduced in penitence for having upstaged him by getting the drinks. Young Dr Dorff bows and extends a hand.

'I very much look forward to your paper tomorrow.'

'Thank you.'

'I will get myself a drink and then rejoin you if I may.'

'Please do.' He bows himself away.

'Well, here's looking at you kid.' Professor Tucker raises his glass. Hetty lifts hers.

'*Pröst*, isn't that what we should say?'

'*Pröst!* That's the full extent of my German.'

'Mine too.'

'It looks like they're about to wheel on the minister.'

There's a respectful flurry going on beside the door. A non-descript rather short, middle-aged man in a dark suit is being ushered forward to the microphone to be introduced by his suited identikit. Hetty has never realised before how the male suit has become an international uniform parallel with the equally ubiquitous denim, making between them a world of bankers and cowhands. At least the denim is unisex and admits of more variety she decides, letting her eye rove around the audience and participants as the minister drones unintelligibly through his speech of welcome. Then it's over to a polite obligatory clap and the arrangements for dinner are announced in English.

'Shall we go?' Professor Tucker takes her arm and Dr Dorff falls in on the other side. After years of pursuing Jack, and a staff common room where there were twice as many women as men, Hetty finds herself with rarity value, an object to be prized and shown off to those groups who haven't managed to secure themselves a female figurehead to breast the way into the dining room where great tables are groaning under a multicoloured spread of dishes that belongs to earlier ages, to banquets and feasting.

Several glasses of good red wine and plates of food later, Hetty hears herself talking fluently about the illusion of historical progress and realises she's quite drunk. She feels brave, witty and free. They are sitting in little cubicles, half a dozen to a table. There's a great din of voices, a babel of tongues loosened by the wine. If she drinks any more she'll wake dull and overhung and she has to give her paper. Hetty gets to her feet with what she hopes is dignity.

Her room when she reaches it through the hushed arterial corridors seems at first a haven where she can leave off her sandals and drop her skirt. Opening the long wardrobe door with its narrow glass she unbuttons her shirt and holds it away from her body with arms akimbo on her hips. Her white skin is moist and supple still. Only her neck shows the beginnings of furrow and pouch. Her breasts are firm because no child has drunk there. She turns away from her image.

'Mirror, mirror on the wall . . . I mean on the door, but that won't rhyme with fairest of them all.'

Murmuring Hetty folds the long glass back into the cupboard. Not feeling quite brave enough to sleep naked in a strange place she puts on her pyjama top and cleans her teeth. When she lies down the walls drift towards the ceiling so she sits up again and arranges her pillows to prop up against the headboard. A couple of hours later she wakes still in the same position with the light on, goes to the bathroom, drinks a glass of water and gets into bed again to fall asleep almost immediately as soon as the light is out, thinking how horrible she's going to feel in the morning.

Surprisingly, when she wakes she doesn't feel too bad and is able to go down for a large breakfast of scrambled eggs and thin slices of mild cheese which she wouldn't, couldn't, eat at this hour at home. She's pleased by the little foil-wrapped butter pats and neat dwarf pots of jam with idealised fruits on their lids that are the size of old pennies. She thinks of her own sticky jar of crystallising marmalade, and enjoys the freedom to choose from honey, redcurrant, apricot, black cherry.

'This condemned man or rather woman ate a hearty breakfast. May I join you?'

Hetty would rather finish her meal alone, free from the obligation to converse, and able to look about at her fellows and speculate but she knows she needs friends for her paper, her own claque to applaud and pat her on the back. She gets herself another cup of coffee to be sociable and wards off his probings on what she intends to say that afternoon until she can decently leave him with an excuse about needing some air before being shut indoors for the morning. Hetty steps through glass doors into the quadrangle where goldfish are loitering their lazy fins and tails in and out of the succulent, water lily stalks. She picks her way along the edge of the pond and under a brick arch, down steps to a sunken lawn. She can't hear the voices any more. She has suddenly gone through one of the invisible barriers that divide worlds from each other. Thrushes run their mottled breasts over the shaggy grass. Trees and shrubs shut in the lawn and flank the path out of it. Each is new to her and each one carries a label on its trunk. Some of the bushes are tipped with small pinkish flowers. She identifies an escalonia from her garden at home.

Somehow she has to get into the city and try to track down the letter from the nun. In the newness of everything she's almost forgotten that's partly why she's here. She could skip the first lecture and go now but that might be noticed so soon. Better to get her own over with and then she can concentrate on finding a way. It would be kept in a museum, an archive. She must enquire from someone since the guidebook she's bought doesn't offer much help. Now it's time to go back, to look interested, perhaps even ask a question or two. She is interested. The lecturer is Jan Dorff and his subject: *New Horizons. Towards Refederation*. A hundred miles to the North-west is Clingen where Tetta had told her father she was going, in that old East Germany, near Erfurt and Eisenach where the English had founded monasteries for men and women, beyond those hills or mountains she had seen as they drove in.

Dr Dorff is clearly nervous which Hetty finds both endearing and comforting as she shuffles on her uncomfortably modernist chair. He is carefully aligning his papers while the audience settles. Then he looks up and clears his throat. 'What I have to say in this first lecture of the conference, dear colleagues, will perhaps not please everyone.' Hetty's thoughts drift a little over the problem of why he has chosen to speak a foreign language instead of his own. Then as she refocuses her mind on what he's saying she realises that it gives him an objectivity that his own language couldn't. She remembers the crowds as the Berlin Wall was breached chanting *Deutschland* and *Vaterland*. Young Dr Dorff is speaking about not just the reunification of the two Germanies which his listeners might want to hear, but a reconstitution of long vanished empires: Ottoman, Carolingian, even Roman, but as a free federation, not he insists a United States of Europe. 'How far should it stretch?' he asks them. 'A few months ago the twelve member states of the European Economic Community seemed hard enough to bring together. Now the goal posts have suddenly shifted to bring in the possibility of a hundred nations or more.'

He's sweating a little. They listen without fidgeting.

'What has once been an idea in the collective human mind may be so again. In history nothing is irrevocable, nothing is, in the words of a famous Cold War film, nothing is forever. I thank you.' He bows, gathers his papers and they applaud him, the hands making muted percussions of politeness, except for Hetty's which are slapping each other hard.

'You seem to buy that,' Professor Tucker whispers to her. 'But would Middle England?'

'If they don't they'll be left behind on the fringe of the civilised world.' She remembers the image of Europe she had conjured back in the cottage which seems through this end of the telescope merely cosy and quaint. A hand goes up in the audience.

'*Vous demandez la fin absolue au nationalisme?*'

'*Oui.*' His answer is unequivocal.

Tucker's hand is up. 'But nationalism is essential to capitalism, a collective individualism that fosters the necessary greed and competitiveness. And I don't see any decrease in it in Europe, rather the reverse. Back in the States we had to invent it with the War of Independence. The reason the Soviet Union will fall apart is it's a young federation and people are still strongly, regionally patriotic: Ukrainians, Georgians, Latvians, Armenians. . . .'

'We cannot go through another hundred years of European wars. A way must be found. There is a point where pride in one's community, a communal identity, becomes simply tribalism. We cannot return to that in the end of the twentieth century. If I cannot convince such a distinguished gathering of minds that this must be made inevitable then what hope is there for the future except new wars? We are packed too tightly in Europe and yet too fragmented for it to be otherwise without some new political structures.'

Hetty finds herself clapping and calling out: 'Hear, hear!' The chairman gets up from the front row to rescue Dorff with the announcement of lunch, the only thing now that stands between Hetty and her own ordeal.

'Luncheon,' says Tucker, standing up.

'I have to do a Garbo,' Hetty says. 'I'll see you later.' She hasn't faced an audience since leaving St Julian's and she fears an attack of stage fright, of stuttering to a halt. She heads for the drinks table and takes a glass of white wine, just one, finds a place alone at a table, eats a little salad and then goes up to her room, to pee and stare in amazement at her lecture as if she has never seen it before. Can she have written these alien pages? The time drains away. She picks up her briefcase, obsessively combs her hair and drinks a little water, repairs her lipstick and lets herself into the corridor. In an hour, she thinks, it will all be over and then I can really relax.

From the lectern she looks through her reading glasses across the dark bank of suits with the white blobs that are faces. They are the bull which will carry her away and trample her.

'Mr Chairman, ladies and gentlemen,' Hetty begins. 'I want to start by tracing for you the British retreat from Europe, in the hope that by examining first the positive images that the British have had and then the negative we may arrive again at the positive. For that I need to go back to the time of the first Queen Elizabeth. Britain as you know tends to throw up strong-willed women rulers, perhaps because of our belief that "Nanny knows best".'

There's a frisson of laughter as the simultaneous translators in their glass cabinet above the audience catch up with her and she is riding the bull with its curls held tight in her grasp and the great haunches rising and falling under her as the air streams past and the hills, rivers, meadows drop away under its polished black hooves. By the end of forty minutes they are all breathless. She has poured the music of Italy into their ears in the English madrigal, coached them over the Alps to filch paintings, bronzes, marbles, replaced Shakespeare's made-up boys with actresses after the mode of France, and grounded them in revolution and nature with Wordsworth and Coleridge. And then the long retreat.

Hetty has wanted to call it 'the Dunkirk of the British soul' but discretion prompts her to the less provocative 'dark night' as she sketches the withdrawal to draped parlour and public school under the gaze of the imperial icon, 'Nanny with orb and sceptre putting the black, brown and yellow children to school and to purge,' as her own, lard-white, ran mudlarking barefoot in the streets or flashed their innocence for the new picture-maker while their parents flattered themselves they were better than all the frogs and wogs put together. But the other coloured children grew up and wouldn't take their medicine any more until Nanny was left with only her indigent own 'whom you can see begging in the subways of London and sleeping in cardboard boxes like discarded kittens.' Hetty draws to a close, bringing them down with her to a dark archway under the bombardment of trains passing overhead, stinking of piss and slopped booze. 'Ideas matter, images *are* powerful. The ideal of Enlightenment, of Light itself has to be revitalised for and by all of us. Thank you.'

Her legs are trembling. The audience is clapping, really clapping. She looks down in embarrassment and picks among her papers. Now the questions. A hand is up. She must stand there, take off her glasses so that the faces can come into focus. It's a woman's voice but Hetty finds it hard to pick her out in the row.

'Would you say, Professor Dearden, unlike some of your country women and men, that you are a European?' There is laughter and a couple of handclaps.

'Yes, I think I would have to admit to that.' They laugh again. Hetty remembers herself as a student on her first trip abroad, after a long night hunched in the corner of a darkened carriage as the train crept through the Alpine tunnels, coming out into the dawn and Domodossola, opening the corridor window to let in the sweet smell of Italy and the cry of the man with his tray of drinks slung round his neck: *'Caffè, caffè calde, arangiata, birra!'* and the hot dark richness of the coffee filling her mouth.

There are no more hands going up. The chairman comes forward to release her, asking for more applause but Hetty can hardly hear because her head seems to have become detached from her body and her ears have gone deaf as if she has come down too fast in a jet plane. She wants to get away to her room or to walk about alone in the garden among leaves and grass but she knows she must mingle a bit first, sip a cup of tea or coffee she doesn't really want and show she isn't proud or afraid.

'That was quite some Grand Tour you gave us there. I had some questions but they weren't really concerned with the main theme so I kept them to myself but that encounter of the British with the Continent, that has an American parallel in, for example, Henry James encountering England.'

'But ours has gone on so long, hundreds of years and yet in some curious way in our heart of hearts we go on denying it.'

'Do you see the package tour as the logical democratised successor of the Grand Tour?'

'I'll have to think about that one. Can I get you some tea or coffee?'

'I think I must take my old bones off for a rest before the pleasures of the evening. In my experience boat trips are draughty and uncomfortable.'

Hetty has forgotten that they are offered a river cruise tonight with dinner on board. She waves goodbye to Tucker and turns towards the cups laid out on a white cloth.

'May I say, please, I think your lecture was brilliant.'

Hetty recognises the voice of her sole questioner. She sees at once why it was hard to pick her out. She's small and slight in jeans and a dark short-sleeved shirt, the hair cut close around a pointed face. It's an elf, Hetty thinks, still a little light-headed, come in from the garden.

'Thank you. I'm glad you enjoyed it.'

'I think perhaps you write books. Tell me the titles and I will look for them.'

'No,' Hetty answers her. 'I've never written a book, just articles from time to time as we all do to keep our jobs.' But the elf has touched an old pressure point. Once upon a time Hetty had aspired to write a book and then she had seen the academic treatises in book form produced by ambitious colleagues, and her desire had faded. That wasn't the sort of thing she had wanted to do. She had wanted to evoke, to recreate. Then Jack had come along and she had felt that to write anything now would have been in competition with his own popularising studies all beginning with the heartstopper 'After': *After Renaissance*; *After Revolution*; *After Empire*.

'You're a great teacher, much better than I am,' he always told her, meaning that she should stick to the spoken word. He was currently working on *After Hiroshima*.

'And what will you do then?' she had once asked him.

'Go back to the beginning and start again. *Before the Neolithic*.'

'Oh but I am sad for all those lost books.'

'Perhaps there are too many books. . . .'

'Can there ever be too many, too many voices . . . ?'

'If they have nothing new to say.'

'You are after all English,' the elf laughs.

'Yes,' Hetty admits, 'I suppose I must be. Does that disqualify me completely?' What from, she wonders to herself. What am I really asking?

'Oh no. You qualify, you qualify beautifully and brilliantly. Are you coming on the river trip tonight? Shall I see you then? The Main is very beautiful at night and I think the dinner will be good.'

'Oh yes, I'm looking forward to it.'

'I will see you on board then.' The elf bows and is gone before Hetty is able to get the identity label in focus against the dark shirt that outlines the nipples topping small mounds of breast. With a shock Hetty realises that her eyes have been drawn to them, an experience she remembers only from adolescence. Since then she's noticed the chest works of her female colleagues merely to compare them with her own, usually unfavourably. This has been different. She has been intensely aware of the nipples naked under the clinging shirt. Her eyes have sought them out, almost caressed them as she has been speaking. At the same time she knows or thinks she knows that she has been subtly courted, chatted up. I'm imagining things, Hetty thinks. It must be the strangeness and the tension of speaking. Upstairs in her room she kicks off her sandals, opens the window and lies down to fall asleep at once.

The coaches come for them at six forty-five. Hetty finds herself seated between Jan Dorff and a restored Tucker. There's no sign of the elf who must be in the second coach.

'Will we hear the Rhine maidens singing do you think?' Tucker asks.

'I think it's the Main.'

'Rhine, Main, schwein. Don't all rivers have maids, Lorelei to lure poor men to their watery grave?'

'What about poor women?'

'That's a different story.'

Hetty has grown fond of Tucker, of his dry indomitable stance. Waiting in the entrance hall for their coach in their little group of three he had called her Hetty for the first time and they had all moved on to first names. He's old enough to be her father and Hetty hopes that he won't spoil their delicate relationship by pouncing on her. She knows she must always contrive not to be alone with him and ward off all gallant offers to see her to her room.

The river cruiser is a glass fly skating the water.

'I'm old enough to remember paddle boats on the Mississippi,' Tucker says as they go down the gangplank.

'Things move so fast these days that isn't unusual.'

'Please ladies and gentlemen,' the chairman, Dr Sommer, is calling them to attention, 'refresh yourselves, eat, drink and be merry.'

Waiters stand smiling above trays of champagne and orange juice. As Hetty stretches out her hand she sees the landing stage falling back, and a strip of churned water like flawed crystal widens between the glass boat and the bank. Through the curved bow window she can see the full stretch of the river shot with flickers of dancing light.

'You can't call this draughty and uncomfortable,' she says as they take their drinks to the padded leatherette benches that divide the lower deck into conversation-sized cubicles with a table down the middle.

'"The barge she sat in like a burnished throne
Burned on the water. . . ." Do you think that was really Cleopatra or was it really Elizabeth the First?'

'A bit of both I should think.' The champagne has bubbled agreeably fast into Hetty's bloodstream and she feels easy and clever as she leans back against the red sofa.

'What about another glass?'

'I will get them.' Jan Dorff gets up quickly. He has been very silent as if something is worrying him. 'What will you have? More champagne?'

'I'll help you.' Hetty follows him towards the stern where a big oval table is covered in the kind of feast she has never seen before with, because they are on the river, dish after new dish of every kind of crustacean, eel, salmon, smoked and poached, flanked with trout all afloat on beds of salad.

'Jan.' She touches his arm. 'You seem a little quiet. Are you not feeling well?'

Dorff looks about him nervously. There's no-one in earshot. 'It's nothing really. You are very perceptive, Hetty. Yes, I can tell you. After your lecture today I went into the city. I found an autobus. It's quite a long ride. I wanted to buy a present for my wife and daughter.' He pauses and takes a quick drink. Hetty takes one too. 'There were signs everywhere painted in black on the walls. What do you call them?'

'Graffiti?'

'That's it. Graffiti. Saying "*Auslander* Out". You understand? With the swastika and a drawing of a soldier in a helmet.'

'Who are the *auslander*?'

'The Turks, the foreign workers. These people don't change. It is so deep down it could all begin again.'

'It's always there to some extent in most countries,' Hetty says carefully.

'But here more than most. You see my wife is half-Jewish, an American. I met her in Amherst. That means our daughter is a quarter-Jewish. I see things perhaps that others don't. But I'm a coward too. I don't know what my father did in the war. I didn't ask him. I only know he was in the army before I was born and before that perhaps in the Hitler Youth. I don't tell him that his grandchild is a quarter-Jewish.'

Hetty wants to reassure him, to tell him it couldn't happen again but the words stick in her throat.

'Europe has to learn to be multiracial, and that includes Britain, otherwise we shall be a white, a Caucasian enclave.'

'That is how some people see the European Community; that's what they want.'

'Then it's back to Orwell and the three warring empires. Surely we haven't got rid of the Cold War just to fall into all that.'

'You saw how they received my paper.'

'Yes but they didn't shout you down, and as long as you, and me too, and others keep our heads and our courage. . . .'

He shakes his head but he is less tense Hetty can see. 'Let's take Tucker a drink or he'll think we've fallen overboard.'

'Down there is the biggest spread you've ever seen, so vast

my puritan British stomach feels quite faint at the sight of it. Nevertheless a couple more glasses and I shall fall on it like a vulture.'

'I haven't said how excellent I thought your paper was this afternoon. I expect you have had many compliments.'

'Oh not enough. The ego is quite insatiable in its need for flattery, for buttering up.'

'"Buttering up"? Yes I see. English has so many good expressions. Kind words butter no parsnips.'

'But they do of course, all the time.' And suddenly Hetty thinks, remembering Freud's question: What do women want? that what they really need is praise not for their faces and their figures which only puts them in the power of the flatterer and reduces them to an object, a toy, but praise as men give each other or withhold for achievements, without the belittlement of praise for physical appearance that's merely the dress they go in.

'I haven't added my widower's mite to your heap.' Tucker holds up his champagne glass. 'But I have to be allowed licence of age.'

'Well I took your remarks to be noises of approval on the whole.'

Outside the windows, river and sky flare and flush with sunset. Hetty looks about at the other delegates enjoying the sensation of freedom from responsibility. If I were in love now all this would look different. But I'm not. I'm no longer in love with Jack. And she signals her freedom to herself by standing up and saying: 'I'm off to try the feast.'

Tucker and Dorff have become involved in a discussion about the future course of multinational capitalism and look up and smile without seeing her. She's glad to see Dorff easier and decides to leave them to it. Suddenly Hetty is restless. She needs movement, novelty. Passing a waiter she swaps her empty glass for a full one and heads for the oval table where men and women are circling, stabbing and scooping to heap their plastic plates. All at once she feels sickened by the elegant symmetry of death against the white cloth, the open boiled eyes and the flesh being broken by spoon and fork. She takes a radish, a tomato, a stick of celery. Child of austerity, born just before the war and adopted into Sunday meat and two veg and told to eat it all up, she finds it hard to be even an authorised glutton. Out of her foster mother's vocabulary rolls the word 'gourmandise' with its coarse and yet oily syllables pot-bellied on the tongue. She wishes she could lunge at the bright red shells of shrimps and the silver rollmops.

'You are a vegetarian?' The elf has appeared at her elbow.

'Not really so. It just all seems too much. Or perhaps I've drunk too much.' The glass hull is noisy with the rising voices. 'It would be nice if one could go on deck.'

'But it is possible. Over there where we came in it is possible to go up and up again. What do you call it?'

'I think it's the companionway if you're being strictly nautical.'

'Delightful. Companionway! Let us take it up to the sunset.'

Hetty hastily munches her radish, puts the tomato in her jacket pocket and with her stick of celery and the wine held dangerously in one hand follows the girl towards the stairs. The neat buttocks in black denim climb above her, round a corner and up again and then they are both out on deck, able to walk to the rail and look out over the arrowed wake to woods and trees and a turreted castle on a rock against a backdrop of painted technicolour sky. 'It's the castle in *Snow White*.'

'But of course. This is called the "Fairytale Route". That's Schloss Rumpenstein. If we go that far the next town down river is Hanau where the Grimm brothers lived. And if we went further we would come to Fulda but we shall turn back before Hanau I think. If we go to the front we can look that way also and see another castle Schloss Phillipsruhe and then Wilhelmsbad where there is an English Park, very Romantic, of the eighteenth century.'

'What was the first castle called?' It had fallen away from them and become an ink drawing of black caps on the paling sky.

'Schloss Rumpenstein?'

'Like Rumpelstiltskin.' At the top of such a tower, Hetty

thinks, the princess spun straw into gold for the dwarf. They walk towards the bows with the river a wide band ahead that seems motionless and then churns away in white water either side as their arrowhead cuts through it. The engines pulse under their feet and through her body. 'Did you say Fulda was down there? How far away?'

'About sixty kilometres from Hanau.'

Mentally Hetty divides by one and a half. 'Forty miles. Not far.'

'An English foundation of St Boniface. But you know this.'

Hetty isn't willing to confess how recent her knowledge is. 'There's something I'm looking for that might have been there once. A letter, written about 786. I wondered, I mean I've seen a reference to its being in Frankfurt at the beginning of this century.'

'I don't think it would be there now. It would be in an ecclesiastical archive if not in a private collection. The tombs of Boniface and Lioba are still at Fulda.'

'Lioba.'

'It means beloved doesn't it?'

'Her name is in another letter I have, from the same person as the one I'm looking for.'

'If you will give me the details and your address I will look some more for you when the conference is finished and I will write to you about what I find. Who is the writer of the letter?'

'She's an English nun who came here and sent those letters, this letter, home to her father. But, something that's been puzzling me ever since I saw the reference in England, why should one of her letters be here?'

'Perhaps it was never sent. Perhaps there was a copy. If it is still here in Germany I will find it for you.'

It's darker now and lights are coming out along the banks here and there, and among the trees where there must be houses hidden. The river air is cooler as they lean over the rail. The boat shudders a little and begins a wide sweep. 'We're turning back. What a pity!' Voyages, Hetty thinks, journeyings are all images of history and of personal history except that usually you don't turn back, you go on, events go on to an end. 'No!' she says.

'Pardon?'

'I've just caught myself out in a piece of self-deception.'

'Excuse me . . . ?'

'I was thinking the romantic cliché that voyages are like lives and like history: they go on to an end; they don't turn back as this one does. But that isn't true is it? Lives go on to a finite end which is death but history can turn and turn, back on itself. It doesn't stop, at least not in any time scale we've discovered.'

'One day the universe must end if it began.'

'Yes, but within that stretch of time there can be circlings and repetitions. Jan Dorff is right.' Hetty laughs, 'Nothing, but only nothing is forever. Even if this universe ends with another bang, falling in on itself, something will emerge when the dust settles again.'

They have turned their backs on Fulda and the wind is stronger, blowing Hetty's hair about so that she's worried that she'll look too dishevelled in the light below deck. For it's time to go down. She fakes a shiver. 'I need some more wine. Shall we go down?'

'Of course.' At the foot of the stairs they pause. 'I must find a colleague,' the elf says. 'Perhaps we shall meet later or tomorrow you give me your address and the details.'

'That would be splendid.' For a moment Hetty looks directly into the other face a little below hers. The girl, woman, Hetty can't guess her age, knows only that she's somewhere between late twenties and thirties, is looking full into her face as if willing her to look back, smiling a little, almost Hetty senses as if they were about to kiss. She feels the symptoms of love and fear breaking out in her body, the shallow breath and thudding pulse and turns away into the saloon. The noise and heat stagger her. She finds her way to the big table with its scattered fragments of flesh and bone, the picked skeleton of the huge salmon, the crumbled rolls and wilting salad, and takes a glass of red wine to where Dorff and Tucker are still sitting.

'Did you feel the about-turn? We're on our way back.'

'We were about to mount a search party,' Tucker says, probing.

'Did you know this is Grimm country?' Hetty asks.

'Grimm as in Walt Disney?'

'That's it.'

'As a child,' Dorff says, 'those stories frightened me so much.'

'They terrified us all.'

'Is it a good idea to give such dark things to children? And yet how can you keep them away? My daughter loves them.'

Hetty doesn't see the elf again that night. When they reach the centre she finds she's tired of performing, of smiling and talking. Declining a nightcap in the bar she goes up to her room, pours herself a whisky and leans out of the window to let the breeze seek her hot skin. She must find out the girl's name. She looks through the list of conference participants but can't decide. If the worst comes to the worst she will simply have to ask her. And who was the colleague abandoned for so long while they sailed the glass boat into the dark? It seems strange that Wordsworth and Coleridge should have come here, to these woods and castles so peopled with the nightmares of childhood, for Enlightenment and Reason among the philosophers of Leipzig and the solitudes of the Harz mountains. And the nun Tetta, who had been on her way north too, had she ever come south to Fulda and Lioba's tomb? Perhaps the elf will find out.

Hetty lies in bed in the morning with a delicious feeling of freedom. She has nothing to do but enjoy her last day. At breakfast she finds the other participants bowing and smiling. Two members of the queue for tea or coffee offer their congratulations. 'I am going into the city again this morning,' Jan Dorff stops by her table. 'Would you like to come?'

There's a pleasurable sensation of wickedness about playing truant, with him as guide and cover for her lack of the language. The tree-lined boulevard runs for twenty minutes before more and more streets begin to fan out from it until it comes to rest in the city centre. 'You should see the cathedral,' Dorff says, 'and then we could have a drink in the Hauptwoche.'

The cathedral is tall and dark red. Sandstone, Hetty decides. Inside is crammed with memorials and altar pieces hard to make out in the shadowy light but when she does Hetty begins to recognise facial types from the streets they have walked, knotty, knobbly faces in the crowds in the Garden of Gethsemane and about the Cross. Out in the square they settle at a table. 'All this had to be rebuilt after the war,' Dorff says. Compared with London on her last visit or even the local cathedral city, it appears clean and spacious to Hetty, the wounds healed over seemingly without scars. The waitress who takes their order has the tip-tilted little nose and doll prettiness of the madonnas that had seemed impossibly chocolate-box in the cathedral, in contrast with a clutch of staid stout matrons who are suddenly disgorged from a coach in the square.

Are there any conclusions that can safely be drawn or is the pursuit of history the chase after marshlights through mist and darkness, and if so how can we ever order the future, Hetty wonders, unsure how much she can say to Jan Dorff who's too young to remember the *terror-fliers* who were the brave boys of Bomber Command.

In the glossy shopping centre Dorff buys his presents while Hetty gazes at an opulence, a patina of wealth on buildings and passers-by that she's never seen before. The presents are elegantly wrapped and ribboned, not dumped in the ubiquitous British plastic carrier bag. 'Perhaps we should be getting back for the final lecture.'

'You didn't miss much,' Tucker tells them. 'I nodded off once or twice. Now it's time for Ole Davey Tucker to sing for his supper.'

As Hetty takes her seat next to Dorff she's scanning the room for the elf. 'Who's that?' she whispers when she tracks down the neat head.

'Who?'

'In the middle of the third row. The girl, woman . . . with the short hair.'

'That's, I think, yes it's Dr Ebbesen from the University of Saarbrucken.'

'Doctor' means nothing of course. Anyone who's here must be a doctor if they're not a professor. She herself has been elevated to 'Professor' on her name tag, continental style. But it means she's an academic, a lecturer.

Tucker's hands with their veins like old root systems are gripping the sides of the lectern. 'I want to put it to you as my first proposition that the whole of the Cold War has been an illusion, a monstrous paranoid confidence trick practised by the rulers of the West and the rulers of the East against their own peoples and the rest of the world. There never was any Cold War in the sense of a real threat to world peace. It wasn't necessary. In these days of the predominance of cinema as an art and propaganda medium the appearance, the shadow is as powerful as reality. We have spent the last forty years at a non-stop picture show of terror and violence that has kept us glued to our seats.

'I am probably the only one at this conference who could voice such a devastating thought because I am an American, and also I am very old.' He laughs and the audience laughs with him in relief and gratitude. 'We have seen the first results of closing down the movie house of fear on one of the protagonists: the immediate upsurge in the demand for democracy, however interpreted and we can talk about that later, and for national autonomy in the eastern parts of Europe. What we haven't yet seen is the effect that must come on the other protagonist, what Gore Vidal has called the ailing empire of capitalism, on the United States of America and its colonies, among them Western Europe and Japan. I want to propose a scenario, a working premise, that what we shall see is a return to isolationism in the States, once the Middle East question can be solved or shelved, a withdrawal from world affairs into the direct business of making money and attempting to address its own internal problems, principally the problem that will arise when the hispanic and black minority becomes by demographic process the majority and whether what is still essentially a white Western Protestant culture can accommodate this shift. Let us accept as given that this is the way things go and return to the theme of this conference. Most speakers have concentrated on the origins of the idea of Europe. I want to look into the future, a future which it is unlikely that I shall see except in my crystal ball.'

She had grown up under the bony menace of a third World War, Aldermaston-marched while a student, picketed the American Embassy as if her young life depended on it. Hetty and her friends had believed that every year might be their, and the world's, last and that if they were to be blown away in the storm of flame it was better to burn, crying out that they had tried. Then she had begun to doubt. As they'd danced on their own graves through the 1960s affirming creation, the threat had shrunk. It was still omnipresent in doleful backdrop but as the decades had passed it'd had to be put in its place: they'd had to begin to refuse to believe with that first intensity. What was Eliot's line about humankind only being able to stand a little reality? Something like that. And now they were to accept that it had been simply a monstrous shadowplay to frighten the children.

Hetty had driven past the women's peace camp at Greenham from time to time and had pictured herself stopping the car, getting out and going over, crouching down to drink bivouac tea and chomp thick sandwiches, but she had driven on though her heart ached to join in, because she no longer believed in the reality of the threat. Yet she did believe in what the campers were doing: in the reality of protest itself, in the necessity for someone to be always saying an unequivocal 'no' but this was a time to leave it to the mercenaries who were paid in coin of comradeship and their own rightness. She would have been merely an unwilling conscript. Again she half remembered a line of poetry about the best lacking all conviction, even though she certainly wasn't setting herself up as 'best'.

She's missed a big slice of Tucker's lecture letting her thoughts carry her away. 'What has to be admitted now,' he's saying, 'is that it follows that naked capitalism is outmoded too. If Europe is to survive it has to find a middle path between these two opposites, and to hold the balance between the rising priorities of Asia and Africa which include the new or renewed dimension of tribal or religious monopoly. It may be that the whole world now has to undergo the same process that we have seen played out in Europe in the late twentieth century before it can grow up, in which case the new Europe may become the pin that keeps the whole works from flying apart. That, ladies and gentlemen, will be nothing less than your task.'

'I thought you were on the other side,' Hetty accuses him as they head for the bar.

'I was being devil's advocate. Stirring things up a little. I think Jan is quite right. What I said just now was by way of an exhortation. It doesn't mean I necessarily believe the Europeans can pull it off any more than the preacher believes his flock will give up liquor and fornication. Well here's to us.' He lifts his glass and Hetty lifts hers in response.

'What are we drinking to?' Jan Dorff has joined them.

'We're drinking to us, to Europe and to the human race,' David Tucker says, lifting his glass again.

'May I join in that?' The elf is there beside them with a glass raised.

'Dr Ebbesen,' Dorff says by way of introduction. '*Pröst!*'

'*Pröst!*' They all down their drinks.

'I was afraid of missing you, forgive me,' the girl apologises.

'Dr Ebbesen has very kindly offered to do a little research for me that I haven't got time to do before I leave.'

'Please call me Helge. We're democrats now.'

Why do I have to go back tomorrow, Hetty wonders, half-way through dinner, looking round at the flushed talkers. I should like to become a wandering scholar, going from place to place listening and talking without responsibility.

After dinner they take their drinks out to the tables beside the pool. Hetty longs for night-scented stocks and tobacco plants to complete her pleasure. 'Have you seen the garden?' she asks the girl she can't yet call Helge even in her head.

'No, no I haven't.'

'Everyone come and see the garden.'

'Ah the English passion for the garden,' Dorff laughs but doesn't move.

'It's too dark. I might break a leg on my last night.' Tucker declines.

So Hetty finds herself setting out under the stars alone with the girl. 'Do you have a garden in England?'

'Yes. I've had to make it from nothing. I'm rather proud of it. Do you have a garden?'

There's a smell of dry crushed grass from underfoot.

'No, I live in an apartment in the city.'

'Look at those stars. They're so bright tonight.'

'Tell me about your garden.'

'You must come and see it,' Hetty hears herself offering.

'I should like that very much.'

They wind their way under the dark branches until the path brings them back to where they can see the lighted windows and the terrace where the others are sitting as if on stage. Hetty waves as they come closer and Tucker waves back.

'I think my old bones have had enough of this hard chair and want to be put to bed. I'll see you at breakfast no doubt.'

'I too must go. I have an early start in the morning. It has been so interesting to meet you both. If you are ever in Köln here is my card. Please do telephone me.'

They all move towards the lift. Dorff and Tucker get out at their floors. 'Which is yours?' Hetty asks. 'Mine is the sixth.'

'Mine too.'

Outside the lift they walk along the empty corridor, Hetty leading the way. She pauses at her door and takes out her plastic key. 'It's the first time I've used one of these. I'm still not sure that I approve of them.'

'I wouldn't like not to be approved of by you. You can say this in English?'

There are moments, events in the lives of individuals and societies when something takes place which can't be reversed or forgotten without a grave violation of truth. Hetty stands quite still. 'Yes, you can say this.'

Slowly the girl puts up her hand with the forefinger a little curved towards the palm and with this crescent she smooths the curve of Hetty's cheek. Hetty still stands, not flinching, not knocking the finger away as she feels a hot tingling begin very precisely in her pursed lower lips and spread over the mount of Venus into her belly.

'Goodnight,' the girl says. 'If I don't see you before we leave I will write to you very soon.'

My dearest father,

I could not write to you before because I have been all this time on my journey and there was no-one I could spare as a messenger to bring this to you. I wonder that Aelfwin has not returned with news from you. However perhaps by now he has reached the court and will follow me. Now I thank God I have arrived at our house in safety after so many dangers and wearying journeyings where I find there is much to do to restore proper order and the worship of Christ, for the people are frightened and until I came, ran about this way and that with no-one to govern them.

Before I left the court there came news of a second great victory over the people the Franks call the Huns or Avars. Duke Eric had taken their stronghold and seized much treasure and a young prince of their nation has come to the court with the wagons full of booty to receive baptism, their Khan being dead in the storming of the stronghold. Gifts have been sent to his Holiness Pope Leo from the vast horde. They were intended for Pope Hadrian but he died on Christmas Day last as you know. It is said here that gifts for all the bishops of Britain from the King were already in the envoy's hands where the word came to him of the slaying of King Ethelred in Northumbria and in his anger he took them back and threatened the Northumbrian people with destruction, only Alcuin pleaded with him to spare them but he, it is rumoured, will never return to Northumbria again but retire to an abbey the King has given him in Tours. So the sins of the English are known throughout the world and surely God must punish us for them.

The prince of the Avars was baptised before the whole court with much ceremony and after this sight of such magnificence I was weary of that life and determined to set out for our house when I could find a party going eastwards towards Erfurt, and such there was, in the company of the Archbishop of Köln visiting his bishopric, for he is a great friend of the King having been formerly his chaplain and employed by him on many embassies and therefore has a dispensation to be often away from his see. I knew that in his party I should be safe as far as Köln where I would find another company, I was sure, travelling to the monasteries of Eisenach or Erfurt and so I did. Archbishop Heribold was very kind to me giving me much advice and his blessing before I left.

Köln is a walled city of many people, built by the Romans, and with many churches where I went to pray but particularly at the shrine of our Lady Ursula for her protection. From Köln we set out towards the great forest of Thuringia that clothes the mountains with dark pine and fir trees for miles on miles. At night we would put up our tents in a clearing while a man kept the fire blazing to drive away the wild beasts, wolves and bears and mountain lions we could hear all around us in the darkness, making sleep hard with their howling and roaring, though my servants were even more afraid of elves and demons. By day it was pleasant enough when the sun shone and the little birds sang but when the rain came and the wind blew it was very hard. As we went I tried to gather herbs and roots that I recognised would be useful, for I intend to make sure that there is an infirmary where the sick can be tended.

Some of our party, even monks, passed their days hunting as we travelled along, leaving the band in the morning to range and returning later with their kill. Their excuse was that we must have fresh meat which I did not deny to my servants but I myself ate none, for I remembered the words of the fathers and also of my namesake Tetta against much eating of meat which can inflame the blood, and against all forms of hunting for sport which draws men's minds from God to follow the chase, even the coursing of hares and digging of foxes which the novices love to the neglect of their books. After ten weary days on horseback we arrived at Eisenach where we rested. Then the others went on towards Erfurt and my party set out alone northwards with a local man as our guide, and passed safely through the mountains when we came to a wide river valley where riding was easier and we made fast progress until we reached a place where two rivers meet and turned northwards again. At last on the side of a hill above the river with woods all around it we saw our house, in a place of such peace and beauty that I got down from my horse and pressed my face into the warm grass in thankfulness.

It is stoutly built of the trunks of great trees which give off a sweet smell of pine so that it is hard to believe that there could be any sickness there but they tell me that in the winter it is very cold when the winds blow down from the North and that many died of the cough last year but I have a recipe for that which was always successful for your cough, my father, and so I remind you of it now lest you should forget when winter comes again, and that is that infusion of horehound in water, drunk warm. The water here is very good to drink and the river wide enough for boats to transport our needs. Therefore I hope one day, if God preserves me, to bring stone from some place where it is quarried and to build the chapel again in stone with perhaps a cloister and a scriptorium so that the work of copying can go in the worst of weather. At the moment there are windows open to the air so that sparrows and other birds nest in the chapel which reminds me of those words of Bede that man's life is but the flight of a bird through a lighted hall, from darkness into darkness. I do not think that I can yet put glass in the windows.

Something there must be, for the birds foul the altar itself with their droppings and twigs as they do in all the buildings, but horn makes them dark which brings on blackness of spirit where clear or coloured glass lifts the soul which the people here have need of.

Our house is not far from the lands of the Saxons who in spite of the many years of warfare still rise in rebellion against the King, deny their baptism and return to the worship of idols just as in the time of the Blessed Boniface. Every year the King goes on campaign against them, removing thousands of families, killing others and putting Franks into their place. I have heard some say that this is too harsh and that people come to God easiest with gentle leading, and that Alcuin himself has dared to suggest this to the King. However at present the Saxons feel great resentment and bitterness because of the harsh laws they have to suffer so that even when they are quiet the people have to live in constant fear, not trusting in God to protect them, but ready to flee into the hills at any rumour. This unease makes for great neglect and disorder. The monks are afraid to work in the fields in case they are surprised by a raiding party. Even at prayer I see that their minds are distracted, and the work of copying and tending the sick is done without proper attention. The singing is out of tune and time and all the vestments are dirty and ragged. If there is any thing in the way of books or furnishings that you can send me you will have the prayers and thanks of us all. I am like the Israelites in Egypt forced to make brick without straw and from whom should I beg since I am a stranger here?

I have written to the Queen to tell her that she cannot come to me until things are in better order. I should not be afraid for her safety for she would be well escorted but I would not want her to see everything so dirty and neglected. With this letter to you I shall send one to the sisters at Wimborne asking them as I do of you for books, an English embroidered altar cloth and even cloaks for I can see that we shall need them when winter comes and the clothing of everyone is patched and thread-bare.

Since I arrived I have ordered an inventory to be made of everything and of all things that need to be done to put the house in order. The people here are suspicious of me and have become used to idle ways but I hope that with kindness and firmness I can win them over as Lioba did in her time. To this end after Mass I took a basin of water and a towel and began to wash the feet of the mistress of novices according to the usual custom. I could see that they were very startled by this but, with some reluctance, she in turn washed those of the almoner and so we proceeded down to the very youngest novice who returned to me. Then I said that now we were all bound together in one chain of love to tread in God's ways and that all thoughts of uncharity and all backbiting would be removed from us by this washing, and I ordered a little extra wine to accompany our evening meal. I thought that after this they all went more cheerfully to their work and there was not the sharpness in their voices I had noticed with pain before.

Then I took my basin and towel and went to the cell of a very old sister who can no longer rise from her bed. Her name is Eanfled of our race and I was told that she had been here many years and is sometimes blessed with visions. I had not spoken to her before because when I first came all was confusion and for several days I was unable to go into every part of the house nor was there any reckoning of all the people both men and women which I have now caused to be made.

She was lying in her cot and seemed to be asleep when I entered. I said, 'Mother, I have come to wash your feet,' and put down my basin.

She turned her head towards me and said: 'Why do you call

me "Mother"? You are Mother here but the Lord does not permit me to rise and wash your feet.'

'Therefore I have come to you if you will allow me.' She said nothing so I laid back the coverlet and exposed her feet which were much swollen, and washed and wiped them as tenderly as I could and put back the coverlet. Then I said, 'I have a recipe for swelling of the feet if you will let me try it.'

She turned her head and looked at me with very bright clear eyes and said: 'It is not the outward symbol but what lies in the heart. When the Magdalen washed our Lord's feet it was with her tears of repentance. You are Berthgyth's brother's daughter and this is your family house but it belongs to no man only to God.'

I felt my heart quicken. 'Do you remember her?' I asked.

'Yes, I remember her. Very well. But do not ask me now. I have spoken all I can.'

'Will you drink the recipe if I send it to you?'

'You want me to be strong to answer your questions but perhaps God does not wish me to.'

'Nevertheless I shall send it to you. The rest is in His Hands.' And I left her.

I went at once with a basket beyond the fields where the men were working and attended by the youngest novice, a child called Adela, a Frank. There I showed her what leaves to gather of mallow, horehound, plaintain, mugwort and betony. We returned to the infirmary still, where I showed her how to pound and beat them and then to mix some together with milk and water to bathe the swelling, to mingle mugwort with oil to eat, and to make a salve of horehound in lard to smear on the feet.

'Now,' I said, 'you must take these to Mother Eanfled and use them exactly as I have shown you. Why are you hesitating?' For I could see she was reluctant to go.

'I am afraid of her; she is so old and they say she is in league with the devil to show her the future and into men's hearts.'

'And what is in your heart that you are afraid that she will see? God knows it all already so there is nothing to be afraid of. If she can see things that others may not it is because He gives her the power not the devil. Go now. Go in with a light heart and she will be glad to see you.'

So she went and in a while came back saying that Eanfled had blessed her and asked that I should go to her again the next day.

My dearest father I laid aside my letter yesterday in the hope that I would have more to tell you but now I hardly know how to write it especially since you must read it when I am not there to comfort you. When I went today I took a drink with me which is good for the spirits, that is betony in sweet water, and I found Eanfled sitting up. She put back the coverlet and showed me her feet and that the swelling had gone down. I gave her some of the cup to drink.

'Come now,' she said, 'and I will speak in a whisper in our own tongue so that no-one shall understand for I have kept this secret a long time.'

So I sat beside her while she spoke and sometimes she fell silent so that I thought that she was asleep or dead but when I moved as if I would go she would open her eyes and continue. And sometimes I gave her to drink out of the cup and then she was stronger to go on. I wrote down what she told me as soon as I had returned to my own chamber, in great haste so that I should not forget, and therefore you must forgive me the many mistakes in translation.

She said that she had come to Frankland many years ago in the days of Boniface when he sent back to England for helpers, men and women. She came from the Abbey of Eadberg in Thanet. 'I was only a novice at the time but I begged to be allowed to go in the party, saying that my youth made me strong and that I had no family to weep for me. Both my parents had died when I was a child and the Abbess had taken me in because although my parents were only freemen I was quick to learn, and God gave me the grace so that by the time I was six years old I could read and sing parts of the service in Latin although I could not of course understand the words themselves. When we reached the land of the Franks, Boniface himself came a long way to meet us for we were a large party, both men and women. It is strange to think now on the different fates of us all, for some God raised up to the highest rank in his service as Bishop Lul and the Blessed Lioba and some laboured as the parable says all day in the heat of the sun but with only the day's wages and others were cast down and lost to sight.'

I felt my mouth go dry at her words so I gave her the cup to drink and she continued. 'Of the women who came here then, Tecla was sent to Kitzingen, Lioba and Waltpurgis were sent to Bischofstein, Chunitrud went to Bavaria. Those are the ones that I remember. Cynehild and her daughter Berthgyth were sent to be teachers and heads of the house in Thuringia, for they were very learned in all the liberal arts and I went with them to be their attendant.'

You can imagine my dearest father how moved I was to hear her speak of your mother and sister but I said nothing that I might not distract her. It was strange to hear all these names that I was accustomed to read in our Book of Life at Wimborne and to pray for, especially our cousin Lul. She continued. 'We were happy in that place until we heard of the martyrdom of Blessed Boniface. Then Cynehild seemed to lose all desire to stay longer in this vale of tears. She grew steadily weaker and the year after she too followed her master. At her death a dispute arose as to who should succeed to be head of the house. Many said that Berthgyth was still too young but this was out of greed and malice for although she was only twenty-two years old she was very learned and I have known some of very young age become heads of houses and rule them well with God's guidance. So when we saw it was not to be, we removed to this place with one or two slaves and one of the brothers who was ordained priest and built this as a hermitage to be at peace apart from the world. Lul had procured us the land that, as he said, God might be moved by prayers on the edge of the Kingdom to extend His grace among the heathen Saxons, and he began to send us gifts and more people so that the society grew and we were no longer at peace. Being still young Berthgyth was often lonely and longed to see her own kin again but she could not leave this place for she had great fame for healing the sick and the people came to her daily in great numbers with every kind of disease. She was blessed too with nightly visitations from God urging her not to leave this place and people.'

Then I remembered my father the letters from your sister which you showed me together with the copies of your replies in which you spoke of patience under God so lovingly, and of your sorrow that you could not go to her, but I did not speak of it to Eanfled who continued:

After some years Berthgyth grew more content. Her people respected her, great improvements were made to the buildings, more fields were cultivated and Lul and others continued to send us valuable gifts while those who were healed and went away rejoicing also gave us money, furnishings, clothes and animals. Sometimes in memory of home and to cheer her we talked together as we are doing now in our own tongue and then her face would glow with a hidden light. Although there were only four years between us she seemed much younger than me and with a great sweetness of countenance.

One day we had set out together to search for a plant which the country people had told her of and which had great powers in healing, for like you she preferred to gather her own herbs saying that the right words must be spoken as they were gathered or they would not have the same efficacy. Yet I never heard her speak the words aloud so she must have said them silently in her head for as she once told me the words might be misused by those with evil intentions if they were overheard.

We had strayed a long way following the directions of the country people in search of the herbs. It was a beautiful morning of birdsong when we came to a little valley with a bright quick stream which we thought was the place and got down from our horses to wander along the banks. We were laughing at some mistake a novice had made in reading the Scriptures at breakfast when suddenly we were aware of a group of men who had come up silently on horseback and were watching us. Our own horses were a little way off browsing. 'Let us walk towards our horses,' I said, but as soon as we began to move, the men quickened their pace towards us and got between us and them. I could see now by their clothing they were Saxons and said so to Berthgyth.

Then their leader drew level with us and stood still looking down and addressed us in their tongue which is so like our own that I understood him to say: 'Which is the wisewoman?' I knew then that this was no chance but an ambush.

'I think they are looking for you,' I said to Berthgyth in Latin.

'Yes I understood too,' she answered.

'We will pretend it is me,' I said but she forbade me.

'They would kill you as soon as they found out and then they would come to the house to find me and kill all within it.'

'Better that than that you should be defiled among the pagans.'

'That is in God's hands. *Fiat voluntas suas.* Be it unto me according to His will.' So she said clearly and slowly in our tongue: 'It is I you seek.'

I heard one of them laugh and say that it was good that it was the young one. There was some discussion which I could not understand clearly and then the leader indicated that Berthgyth should fetch her horse and mount which she did. Then I cried out: 'Shall I never see you again my dear sister?'

At this the leader rode over to me and took out his sword and raised it as if he would cleave my head but Berthgyth said: 'If you kill her I will tell you nothing.'

The pagan put back his sword and motioned me to my horse. When I was mounted Berthgyth called out to me in Latin: 'Come to this place as often as you can and I will try to come or send a message. Pray for me always.'

Then the pagan leader struck my mare with his reins so that she started and bolted forward carrying me away. I tried to look back but by the time I had the reins in my hands the valley was empty and even then it was long before I could control her for she ran on and on until we were both exhausted and lost. I was cold and hungry and fearful. When the stars came out I found the way I must go the next day towards the South and put my back against a tree for safety with the rein in my hand so that the mare could not wander and as soon as it was light and she could see to put her feet I set out again until at last I came to the hut of a slave who by chance had once brought a sick child to us and they gave me milk and bread, what they had, for the child's sake, and led me on my way.

When I reached the house I told them that Berthgyth had been carried off by Saxon raiders and that I had hidden and escaped. As often as I could I went in trembling alone to the place where she had been taken and one day while I waited a single horseman appeared. I could see he was only a boy. He approached me where I waited on my horse, reached in his tunic and brought out a leather purse. I took it and without a word he turned and rode away. Inside was a piece of fine white cloth on which Berthgyth had written her message.

'If you would save my life make a copy in secret of my recipe book and bring it here in a bag which you shall hang from the tree which stands beside the great white rock by the stream. Tell no-one. Do not try to look for me or to rescue me. Pray for me always.'

I was then copying St Aldhelm's *De Virginitate* and was able to slip the recipe book inside its pages and work on it when no-one was near. When it was finished I took it to the clearing as I had been instructed and after covering it with tears and kisses I placed it in the leather bag and hung it as high as I could reach from horseback where I hoped it would be safe from wild beasts. I wanted to stay and see who came for it but there was nowhere to conceal myself and I was forced to leave it hanging there. Although I returned to that place several times more I never heard from Berthgyth again, and in any case the following year, angered by the constant raids and evil deeds of the Saxons, the

King began his long campaigns against them which although he was not able to defeat them until now drove them, for a time, further away. I believe that they took her with them.

Now began a difficult time for this place for there was no-one of your family to rule and the sisters elected one of their number, the widow of a Frankish noble as their Mother Superior. But because she did not have Berthgyth's skill in healing the sick the gifts soon ceased to come nor did we any longer have Lul's protection and gradually we declined into that state of neglect in which you find us.

Then from under her pillow Eanfled took a little book with a purple cover and letters of silver which she put into my hands. 'This is Berthgyth's original from which I made the copy, the mother of that child I sent to her. All this time I have kept it in secret. Now I give it to you and my soul to God. I do not know whose sin it was that brought such sorrow to us and to this place but I have prayed constantly that God in His Mercy would lift it from us and this I see now fulfilled in your coming here.'

'God will take you in His own time,' I said, 'but first you must show me the place where you last saw Berthgyth and so you must rest and gain strength.' And I left her.

My dearest father all this will be a marvel and a piercing to you. We had hoped that if she was dead I might find her place of Christian burial where masses could be said in her memory. Instead I have only her little book.

Hetty has been let down through the bronze exhalation that lies over London and gives it a dingy patina that distresses any building within weeks of it being cleaned. The plane sank through it as if below peaty bogwater to rest on the bottom of the Heathrow runway and disgorge Hetty and her fellow travellers into a hazy afternoon. The cottage when she reaches it is reproachful, full of dead air, and the corpses of flies smudge the windowsills. The low-beamed ceilings oppress her. She opens the door into the garden and sees she must get out the hose, and water. A tang of burning comes to her from farmers who are still setting off clouds of ash and umbrous smoke into the air. She climbs up the brick path to the top of the garden where she can look over the hedge to fields flowing away until, she knows, they reach the sea with its flotsam line of hotels, car parks, amusement arcades. She feels the island imprisoning her like a frog on a waterlily leaf whose legs have atrophied.

The telephone calls her back into the house to Jack's voice. 'Ah, I reckoned you might be back by now. How did it go?'

'I was a great success and the whole thing was ... quite fascinating. It seems strange to be back. ...'

'You sound a bit low. Shall I come over and cheer you up?'

'No, I'm fine,' Hetty says hastily. 'And I've got so much to do.'

'You won't forget the report will you. Did you get a chance to hand out the brochures?'

'I left them on display at the Centre for people to take away.' Only when she was trying to repack her suitcase had she remembered St Julian's publicity material and hurried downstairs to stack it in the glass rack along with the notices of concerts, exhibitions, courses promising pleasure and enlightenment worldwide.

Hetty dumps her dirty clothes in the washing machine; checks the fridge for rancid butter and gelatinous milk. Then she bikes down to the village shop, glad to be out under the leaves, her wheels hissing on the road as the pedals turn them with a regular metallic grunt. She feels a return of that lightness and airiness she had known cycling as a child, feet off the pedals, letting the bike run away with her downhill, and then standing up so that her weight thrusts down left and right up the hill again on the other side until her lungs are bursting and she is sailing down once more with the air rushing past. I'm too old for this, Hetty thinks, and answers herself at once: No I'm not!

She had chosen the village as well as the cottage itself because of its pub and shop, smelling antiquely of cheese and firelighters. It's a long narrow slip, end on to the road. As well as groceries the back part sells wool and knitting patterns while the front is a post office with a rack of newspapers. Outside bags of coalite are propped against the wall in winter and boxes and pots of seedlings in summer. The woolshop is also an off-licence with British flower wines sold loose from kegs as well as the usual bottled booze. All needs are catered for. Hetty leans her bike against the pillar box and lets the door announce her entry.

Picking up a wire basket she begins to trawl the shelves, aware that Mrs Cousins the proprietor, in obsessive whispered conversation with a customer, hasn't seen and acknowledged Hetty's good-day nod. 'Driven around for hours so she didn't know where she was,' Hetty overhears as she brings her basket to the till. The two women cease their conversation and look at her for a moment without recognition.

'I've been away.' Hetty hoists her shopping on to the counter. 'Is anything wrong?' There are always the usual alarms of rural life. Will the county council ignore the parish council's letter rejecting the by-pass, the mains drainage, planning permission to convert the derelict barns into executive dwellings, a rise in the school bus fares? Who's dead? Whose house has burned down?

'You won't have heard then?'

'No. I haven't heard anything. I've just got back from Germany, half an hour ago.'

'There's never been anything like it, you'd never expect it in a village this size where everyone knows everyone. . . .'

'Must have been someone come down the road off the motorway. . . .'

'Then how did he know where to take her back to . . . ?'

Mrs Cousins turns to Hetty eager to explain. 'Mrs Plaswell's eldest daughter Caroline who works at the tax office in Sarnford, just got off the bus in broad daylight when a man pushes her into a car, drives her off with a blanket over her head and a knife at her throat, drives her round until it's dark, rapes her in a barn somewhere, drives her back and dumps her down by the roundabout.'

'She's lucky to be alive,' the other woman chimes in.

'Only seventeen. Nobody about; all indoors having their tea. I'd cut it off that's what I'd do. He wouldn't do it no more.'

'Some judge'll give him probation and she won't ever get over it. Not really. That's if they catch him. She says she never saw his face.'

'She said he smelt of animals or the blanket did.'

'Who can say how that'll affect her, a young girl like that.'

'A dark blue car that's all they've got to go on and he'll have got rid of that by now.'

Hetty pays for her shopping and puts it into her bicycle basket and begins to pedal home. She doesn't know the Plaswell family but she can imagine the girl's pain and humiliation, how she'll feel them all looking at her with a prurient concern when she's fit to wait again at the bus stop in the morning, the men wondering what it would be like and the women too and if in some way she'd provoked it, until she begins to wonder herself. And suddenly, half-way home and passing the pub at the steepest point where she's sometimes defeated by the slope, and has to get off and push, as she does today because the sharp shock of knowledge makes her lose momentum, Hetty knows who it is. The man in the donkey jacket. She even thinks she's seen a dark blue car in the pub car park when he's been there.

At the same moment that she thinks this or a tick afterwards she realises she has nothing at all to go on, not, as you might say, a shred of evidence, that shred being presumably a hair, a fibre of blanket or donkey jacket. There's nothing she can do with what is only a deep instinctive knowledge and to accuse someone of something so terrible on this alone is impossible and wrong.

Or is it? Unchecked 'he' might, almost certainly *will*, do it again. Other women will be terrorised, injured physically and mentally. Someone older, more resistant, less frightened than Caroline Plaswell could be murdered. The sunlight is muted like the bird calls, filtered through the mesh of a girl's pain and terror and Hetty's dilemma that overcasts the day. The cottages lying back in their gardens are the abodes of witch and goblin, of Red Riding Hood's wolf with the glittering bloody eyes. 'Once upon a time there was a young girl called Caroline who was very beautiful. She lived with her mother and father and brothers and sisters in a neat little cottage and every day before she left home in the morning her mother would tell her to hurry back and not to talk to strangers. Well, one day she was walking home when all at once. . . .'

The village is shamed too. They will look at each other and wonder while trying to shift the blame on to an outsider: 'someone off the motorway.' There's a police car parked in the lay-by in front of the wicket gate that leads to the church. A young policeman is sitting at the wheel reading a newspaper. Hetty could go up to him and say: 'I know who it is.' The village would be relieved of its burden. Donkey Jacket lives in another hamlet, not here. He's an outsider who comes to Mereton because of the pub. It would be safe to accuse him, but instead Hetty remounts her bike and pedals away from the car until she can prop her handlebars against her own front wall, let herself in and shut the door.

She remembers the other time the police were seen in any number in the village when Arthur, who'd been a jobbing gardener until his wife left him for someone with regular work in the electronics factory, clean and light, and a light, clean bungalow on an estate outside the nearest town, had shot himself messily with the gun he used on mallard and hare. The village had been shocked when the wife had come brazenly to clear the cottage, taking away anything of value in her fancyman's pick-up and dumping the rest pathetically in the front garden where the rain and wind soon began the work of dissolution on worn carpets and a drunken kitchen chair missing a rung.

Would Donkey Jacket show himself at the pub? Hetty remembers his contempt for the conformist, a contempt that could turn people into things; Caroline Plaswell into an anonymous piece of female flesh, as the Victorian gentleman did, seducer of servant girls, milkmaids, seamstresses. Shall she walk down later to see whether he comes? What would she say to him? How might it show in his eyes? Or perhaps he will tell her boldly, exultant at being unfettered by the rules, with the presumption that she will condone. Thinking all this, Hetty is nevertheless at the same time preparing to go and get out the hose on her parched garden. She looks forward to the arch of shining water she'll erect with its bead curtain of droplets, each one an opal prism in which all the colours of the spectrum are caught.

A face peering in at her through the front window makes her heart thump until she realises that it must be, *is*, Mr Powers who will have seen her bicycle and always peers inside as a kind of courtesy before going to the back door. As usual Hetty opens it and waits for him to make his way round.

'You'm back then, safe and sound.'

'Yes, the wanderer returns.' Hetty finds herself dropping into the gnomic idiom Mr Powers always inspires in her. He smells of the earth, of the grave Hetty has sometimes thought, for as well as one or two other gardens, he maintains the churchyard, mowing and strimming around the stones in summer, gathering and burning the fallen leaves in autumn, pruning and mending fences so that the place clings to his black clothes, the shiny stained suit he wears for work and the clumping black boots. Yet he can conjure grass out of rubble, into a fine lawn, and fat cabbages, bloody beets, glistening onions, lettuce and lacy cauliflower into perfect globes.

'You look after the flowers. I'm no good with they little delicate things.'

Now he goes on: 'I bin up once or twice whilst you was away just to check like.'

'That was very kind. I was just going to water.'

'Ah we haven't had a drop of rain.'

'Would you like a cup of tea?'

'I thought you'd never ask. You put the kettle on. I'll just check how much petrol you'm got for the mower. Grass'll need doing again tomorrow.'

When he comes back Hetty has spooned the square sachets out of two cups and opened the tin of biscuits she keeps for him. He brings his graveyard smell into the low room and sits gingerly on a kitchen chair to sugar his tea. 'Have 'ee heard the news?'

'Some of it.'

'They'll never catch un. They're going round all the houses and all the blokes under fifty got to see the police doctor. You know what I mean. I'm glad I'm too old for that lark.'

'Why under fifty?'

'The maid reckoned he was youngish. Not more than forty. Her could be wrong. It was dark and she never see him in spite of all he made her do.'

This is a new trapping to the story and one Hetty doesn't want Mr Powers to elaborate on. She can imagine what it must be and sips hastily at her hot cup in order not to gag on a too vivid image of the fleshy gobstopper and the warm slime gushing into the throat. She had always known with Jack that that was what he would have liked but although she had been happy to lick and caress his prick with lips and tongue, she had never been able to do more than take it into her mouth although he had sighed and groaned for her to go on. She found she couldn't stomach the final gush of insemination. And she had loved Jack and desired him. Without that it would be intolerable; worse than forced buggery where at least you could comfort yourself with sticking your arse into someone's face.

Hetty wrenches herself back from a path she hasn't wanted to go down but which, like the low parapet above the sheer drop to the vertigo sufferer, has drawn her to look over the edge in horror, to shudder, almost to jump. Mr Powers is brushing biscuit crumbs from his knees and standing up.

'I'll be away then Hetty or the old gal'll think someone's run off with I. I'll be up tomorrow afternoon same as usual.'

'I don't know. . . .' Hetty begins.

'If you're not here don't matter. I'll just carry on.'

They had made the garden together after the builders had left it that no-man's-land of mud and flints. He had rotavated, going up and down ceaselessly like a ploughman from a Book of Hours, himself statuesque clay against the dun ground until the earth was level enough for her to crouch over, picking stones that seemed to be replaced by others as fast as she cleared each layer, as if great auks or rocs or a flock of dodos came in the night to deposit their lopsided fossil eggs. Then Mr Powers had sown, broadcasting the needles of grass seed, the wind pulling at his clothes making him a ragged raven against the sky as his hand dipped and flung.

When he's gone Hetty goes outside to look at their handiwork and try to recapture her sense of pleasure in the achievement of something out of nothing, the greening and ordering of a bit of barren wilderness where she's also planted saplings that will take the place of the old trees when they fall, an oasis of copse in the surrounding plough, protected by its old hedge of beech, thorn and box, burrowed by voles and fieldmice and colonised by small birds. But today her usual delight in all this microscopic life eludes her. The hedge of dusty leaves seems brittle and deserted, the grass harsh and thin, her projected play with the hose mere self-indulgence.

Later she cycles down to the pub but Donkey Jacket doesn't come and after slowly downing a half of bitter Hetty leaves. In the next four days she writes and posts her report, fending off Jack's repeated offers to come and collect it, and refurbishes the garden. Donkey Jacket doesn't appear again. When she enquires offhandedly about the man with the digger as if she might want to employ him, Joyce Bates, the landlady, says she hears he's got a job in the North. Does she suspect anything, Hetty wonders, but can't ask. Has she also put two and two together to make five? But Joyce gives no sign and the gossip dies away leaving Caroline Plaswell to remake her life as best she can.

The letter with its enclosure has come on the fifth day by

express post: 'I think by the German description of the document that this is maybe your person. There is more which I have found a reference to in an ecclesiastical library. I must come to London for three days at the beginning of October. Is it possible to meet and I will bring it with me and tell you of anything else I have found? I have enjoyed so much to meet with you in Frankfurt.'

There are several pages of grainy photocopied print which Hetty's relieved to see are in Roman not Gothic type. The Latin will be hard enough to decipher by the light of her rusty knowledge without the added difficulty of a Germanic or even, Hetty suddenly thinks, a Frankish or Old English script.

Cursive, minuscule, uncial, half-uncial, insular, and behind them linear 'A' and 'B', hieroglyphs, cuneiform, ideograms, runes, the history stretches back and back from the pages in her hands, broken, patched together, lost, reinvented, the substances and forms constantly changing, scratchings on wood, stone, paper, skin; letters, diaries, accounts, invocations, narrative and lyric, a scrawled babble of need and aspiration. She gets out her old school dictionary, thickly bound in ink-blue cloth with an oxblood spine and inscribed in the front: 'Henrietta Dearden Form IV', and begins the work of transformation, elucidating the opaque words into a running meaning, cracking off their shells to get at the kernel. *My dearest father . . . Pater carissime mi. . . .*

As she works at the kitchen table in the cottage she finds herself drowning in a rush of remembered smells of ink and paper and other children, of her own hair and fingers, of coarse school soap, of the sweet rank gym, of girls in menstruation, and soup like sick with throat-gagging islands of mashed potato, and then of her own chill bedroom where she did her homework while her adopted parents listened to the wireless, in the prim sitting room below that she had striven to get to university to escape from. Latin had been the key to that escape. The old instructions come back to her: *ut* with the subjunctive; ablative absolute; 'add *super, subter, sub* and *in* when state not motion tis they mean'. 'The battle having been won the general destroyed the town that he might subdue the people by hunger.'

Tetta's is a simpler language than that of Caesar or Livy; her vocabulary more ornate but her constructions less convolute. Hetty finds that if she doesn't struggle too hard a meaning unfolds itself as long as she lets go of the ordered English march of subject, verb, object and is prepared to float among the words, matching them together by their endings, their correspondences. The more she lets herself be carried along the easier it becomes. Even so it takes her three days to catch up with the story, three days in which she can put off the decision on whether to meet Helge Ebbesen in London.

If she goes where will she stay? Hotels must be very expensive; only for the visiting foreigners to whom alien money seems unreal since currency is just a floating symbol and what we would spend abroad without a qualm is unthinkable extravagance at home. She could stay with Sandy who every year writes on the bottom of the family Christmas card: 'When are you coming to stay?' It was to Sandy she had gone to talk about Jack, to the double-fronted Edwardian house on the edge of Wimbledon Common where they had walked avoiding the dogshit, the joggers and ball players, coat collars turned up against the wind, discussing what Hetty should do. It was Sandy who had made her face the hard truth that she must get out, retreat, retire in order to survive. So, without deciding, Hetty's decision is made now. She writes a thank-you note to Germany asking for precise dates and giving Sandy's telephone number, and when her own telephone calls her running from the evening garden, vowing to buy one of those cordless phones tomorrow, she can put down that heart-in-the-mouth sensation to having had to run so fast while she listens to the voice she hardly knows giving her the when and where of their meeting.

'Thank god neither of the children will be here and Bill's away bidding for a hospital in Saudi Arabia. We can have the place to ourselves. What's up? No don't tell me now, let's wait for all that till we meet,' Sandy's voice is sharp with curiosity.

She's been watching for Hetty's arrival and opens the front door with its leaded-glass sunburst and lilies before Hetty can ring the bell. 'You look wonderful, quite over the dreaded Jack. Come in. It's lovely to see you.'

Hetty is embraced, cosseted by a warm flow of words that wash away the anxieties she's been building up ever since she left home. Here with Sandy she's safe. However much Hetty neglects her, falls into long silences between letters or phone calls, Sandy remains just as she was when they were students together. They begin always exactly where they left off as though they had last met the day before: Sandy deliberately energetic and eager, overwhelming Hetty's usual reserve, the reserve that had so miraculously been suspended in Germany, with an almost maternal warmth so that it's as though there's a great difference in their ages and Hetty is much the younger, yet they're the same to within a few weeks.

'Now a big drink and then we can talk. Where have you been? What've you been up to?'

Hetty tells her about the conference, enquires about Sandy's away-at-university children and Bill's latest project.

'He's a director now. One day they'll stop sending him all over the world chasing contracts and he'll be at home all the time, and I really don't know how we'll manage. Neither does he. So I've made myself a job that takes me out a lot in case we start falling over each other's feet. I'm using my history at last, in a way but it's rather a strange way. I go round to auctions buying props for TV and film companies. It's the ultimate recycling, recycling illusion, history. How about that? What would old Burroughs have made of that? Did you see he's died by the way? All that purity of intention: history as recoverable truth and I end up as a faker.'

'It probably puts you in the mainstream of current historical theory. You know: all Hamlet and relativity: "There's nothing good or ill but thinking makes it so." Anyway history's always been concerned with re-creation, only now we know we remake it all in our own image.'

'You are over Jack! You've got your mind back.'

'And nowhere to exercise it.'

'Maybe you'll think about a book again?'

'I don't know. I want to do something. Ever since I came back from that conference I've wanted to do something but I veer about so. One moment it's a book but what on? Next I want to run a home for battered wives, then I want to save the world. You know, part of my trouble. . . .'

'Tell me your version and I'll see if I agree.'

'I went straight from being a good girl at grammar school to being a good student, then to being a good teacher. I've lived a rather monastic life in spite of Jack. I've never really got away or broken out.'

'You marched.'

'Yes but I think it was really because you and everyone else did. For me it was another conformity. I had five years teaching in a girls' grammar school just like my own and then I went to St Julian's. I've taught the Enlightenment without ever really thinking or trying to fit anything together. I've never inspired passion in any of my students so that they wanted to take something I'd taught, on further and write their thesis about it. They passed in my period and then they passed on.'

'It's a hard one to make appealing to the young.'

'Excuses. I've loved it myself but I've never known how to make them love it.'

'Sounds like the end of an affair.'

'Maybe it is.'

'Tell me about tomorrow.'

'I'm seeing someone I met at the conference. She's been doing a bit of research for me in German archives that I didn't have time to do when I was over there. It's really just an excuse to come to London and of course to see you, all part of this batting about I'm doing at the moment.'

'You should have been Head of Department at St Julian's. If you hadn't got caught up with Jack you would have been, instead he is.'

'Bob mightn't have wanted to appoint a woman. He's very nice but a bit of a head-patter.'

Sandy gets up to refill their glasses. 'Anyway I'm one to talk. I've done nothing except have two kids and keep the home fires burning like any Victorian wife whose husband was away running the Empire. I used to tell myself there was nothing else I could have done but now I'm enjoying myself so much I wish I'd done something years ago before the Big Five-Oh pushed me into it, that and Bill's looming return. Is that awful?'

It's rare for Sandy to ask Hetty's advice and she realises that a subtle shift has taken place in their positions. 'Don't we all feel that: whatever we're doing we ought to be doing something else. I don't know whether men have the same problem. Maybe not in quite the same way.'

'Bill's never had any real doubts that he ought to be doing what he does. He explained what it would mean when he was offered the job after we'd been married a couple of years and we had Jamie. I said I understood, and to go ahead, and as far as he's concerned that permission was once and for all. I don't think that he's had a moment's anxiety since or any feeling that he ought to give it all up and get a home-based job. And a bit of me must have agreed because I've never asked him to. He's always come back when there's been a real crisis, illness or death. But he's really had as much freedom as if he'd been single.'

'And I've had the same freedom and never used it. A part of me's always been looking over my shoulder to see if I ought to have been married and had children, even though I'd have made a hopeless mother.'

'You don't know till it happens. I always thought that, and now looking back, I really don't think I've been any worse than anyone else. Anyway the kids don't seem to think so or, at least, they're polite enough to hide it if they do.' Sandy laughs and Hetty can laugh, too, knowing of old that the two big sons ring up constantly and bring home their washing, and girlfriends for approval.

'I still can't work it out in terms of that history we both

studied,' Sandy goes on. 'I can understand the feminist urge to rewrite it all, to re-emphasise, bring out the things that women did and were but nevertheless there is a whole area of women's lives that isn't susceptible to history of the kind we were taught, that old traditional history of heroes and sages. Women didn't *do*. They simply were and that way they're like the majority of men who simply were: anonymous, obscure lives.'

'Each in her narrow cell forever laid
The rude foremothers of the village sleep. . . .'

'What's that?'

'Gray's *Elegy* as it could have been written. This piece of research I'm doing: I'm pursuing a nun. . . .'

'A nun?'

'An eighth-century English nun who went to convert the Germans.'

'It's a bit out of your period isn't it?'

'That's rather what I said to Jack.'

'What will you do with it?'

'I don't know. Do we always have to do something with everything? Isn't that a masculine, a capitalist way of looking at the world?'

'You're equating masculine and capitalist? Doesn't that make socialism equal feminine? The comrades in the cloth caps wouldn't thank you for that.'

'But the match girls, and the women in clogs and shawls going off early to the mill might have. Maybe that's what went wrong with revolution. It got taken over and pressed violently out of shape into a male mould when it was meant to be freer, more flexible.'

'Tell that to someone like Mrs Thatcher.'

'My point exactly. Lots of people argue, looking at her version of the business suit, that she's been pressed out of a male mould.'

'Since when have you become so political?'

'I think it's since we started this conversation.'

'Maybe all revolutions begin as female like humans and get the equivalent of an added chromosome that pushes them towards violence.'

'How do you mean they begin female?'

'Well most of them start with what could be seen as very feminine requests for better food, and homes and shoes for the kids. What tipped over communism was its failure to deliver the goods when it looked as if democracy could do it abundantly. Economics. Political protest rode in on its back.'

Suddenly Hetty is reminded of Europa. But surely that's a reverse image, she thinks, and then hears herself saying: 'I think I must be quite drunk to be banging on like this.'

'I love it. It's just like being a student again when everything seemed to matter and everything was possible.'

Reluctantly they abandon their discussion and go to bed but Hetty can't sleep when her light is out. She's aware of the big oblong of window full of grey washed sky where a piece of moon is drifting among clouds: Diana raped by a rocket and rubberised men gambolling weightless in their heavy boots. What can we fill the universe with, Hetty wonders, now that the goddesses have packed up and gone away. Will black holes and cosmic dust be enough not to plunge us into despair?

In the morning she feels ragged and unsure. 'I don't know when I'll be back. It might be quite soon.'

'Take the spare key and then you can come and go as you please.'

The walk to the station reassures her a little. It's an autumn morning of gauzy sunlight with a faint smell of bonfires from suburban gardens where Michaelmas daisies are thrusting their lilac and blue banks between heavy-headed late roses that scatter blowsy petals on the neat patches of shorn grass. England seems caught in an eternal St Martin's summer before the two World Wars as Hetty goes downhill to the station where the Wandsworth crowds come up to meet her, urban and multicoloured, washing her along like tumbling shingle down to the platforms, and pressing her among them into the train where some retreat into their own heads with paperbacks or earphones, plugging out the world while others rap as they strap-hang in the sing-song creole of cockney crossed with Caribbean, a code only penetrable by aficionados. These're more consciously natty than their white fellow travellers, Hetty decides. One young man who's alone stares straight ahead. His tall slim body in its fashionable baggy suit is topped by a polled head that has the bony elegance of Benin sculpture. An Asian girl further along the carriage has hair falling in skeins of black silk round a serenely beautiful coffee-cream face. Hetty feels blotchy and rubbed in her pink skin.

The lift at Russell Square Station is packed with its usual freight of tourists clutching maps in assorted languages. She's retracing the steps she used to take with Sandy when they came to inter-college lectures on Wednesday mornings to be carried away by M. R. Ridley sweeping them along with epic grandeur or Helen Gardner sugaring them with Elizabethan sonnets. Hetty turns left and crosses over Tavistock Street into the garden in the middle of the square where they had eaten their sandwiches on fine days. The same benches are there screened by dusty bushes behind the high iron railings but occupied by blear-eyed tramps talking in short broken phrases and nursing half-empty bottles. On one a boy in ragged dirty clothes is drawn up like a foetus on his side asleep. Hetty feels humiliated that these are the scenes of London life, like something from the pages of the Victorian Mayhew, that the tourists have to pass through. She crosses the little park diagonally, by paths flanked by beds of florid tea roses, coming out at the far corner opposite the side railings of the British Museum and makes her way past them until she can turn right, along the front to the main gates where the crowds throng in and out all day. She hasn't been here for years and it's much more populous than she remembers. Once it had seemed somehow privileged to come here at all. Now the hordes are cheerfully matter-of-fact and there are ice-cream vans and hotdog stands. Yet the Smirkes' great colonnaded portico is as impressive as she remembers and she can see among the groups of people waiting on the steps a figure she recognises (with relief because she had been afraid she wouldn't) as Helge Ebbesen, dressed like a student in blue jeans, white trainers and some sort of red shirt under a denim jacket. Hetty sees her scanning the advancing crowds and puts up a hand to wave. She's been seen; Helge waves back and begins to come down the wide stone steps towards her. She looks appallingly young.

'Hullo,' Hetty says. 'I hope you haven't been waiting long.'

'Not at all and it is such a beautiful day it doesn't matter. Where would you like to go. I hope you have a little time?'

'Oh I've lots of time. Maybe now we're here we could go inside. I haven't been for years. It must have changed so much.'

It has and yet it hasn't, Hetty decides quite quickly. The greatest change is the sheer number of people and the glass cage in the entrance hall with a crater full of money of all colours and denominations, an open begging bowl for Smirkes' shekels. But the temple itself, for that's what it is, is unchanged, the Assyrian sculptures as monumental as ever.

'We should look at the manuscripts perhaps?' Helge laughs. 'Or no, look we should visit our ancestors.'

'Our ancestors?'

'The Anglo-Saxons. There is a special exhibition.'

They climb the stairs and pass through Roman Britain, to the *Early Mediaeval Room*, past Merovingian, Slavic, Viking, Byzantium, the Lombards through Celtic and Germanic to the barbarian treasures of Raedwald, lost pagan King of East Anglia, sailing into the seas of the dead in his longboat with his Byzantine silver dinner service and Swedish armour, his lyre for singing Hel to sleep and his drinking horns for the eternal carousing to while away the night.

'It would be fun to live like that do you think?'

'Only if you were the King.'

'Now we should see the manuscripts?'

After the glitter of gold and silver, enamel and semiprecious stones and green glass, the intricacy and variety of ivory, crystal inlay and engraving, the books seem at first subdued under the hushed lighting until, as their eyes become accustomed, they too begin to vibrate with colours and shapes while the elegant painstaking scripts assemble into lines and columns of meaning.

'Look here is the oldest piece of Saxon poetry. It says the letters show traces of Anglo-Saxon influence. *Heliond*: the Saviour. And it is here in London.'

'The spoils of Empire I expect. But then look here, it works both ways. The finest copy of this manuscript from Northumbria is in Italy.'

'But it says it was a present to the Pope.'

'These leaves had been used to bind an account book. There's a moral there.' But underneath Hetty is thinking that these were the kind of things Tetta looked at every day.

When they come out into the sunshine again Hetty finds it hallucinatory in its brightness as if her eyes have been opened, from blind, and people, trees and buildings shimmer, dissolve and remake themselves in front of her.

'Have you time for some lunch?'

'Oh I think so. I'm quite hungry aren't you?'

But she isn't. Her heart seems to be permanently in her mouth and she feels a little sick and light-headed. 'There's a pasta bar. What about that?'

When they're perched at the small round table, have ordered and are sipping their first glass of wine Helge takes an envelope from her shoulder bag and passes it across the table.

'Here is another letter for you. I think it is from the same writer.'

Hetty opens out the now familiar photocopy which begins like the last one: *Pater carissime mi. . . .*

'Is it right do you think?'

'I'm sure it is. I'm very grateful.'

In return she offers Helge her translation. 'I brought this along in case you'd like to read it. But maybe you didn't need to. Maybe your Latin is better than mine. . . .'

'Not at all. I haven't studied it. I should like very much to know what it is you are pursuing.'

Hetty thinks suddenly that she would like to know too, and that if Helge asks her why she's so interested she won't be able to answer. Instead she says, 'Tell me something about yourself. There wasn't time to ask you at the conference.' She's aware of the clumsiness of her question.

'I am at the University of Saarbrucken, a very junior lecturer. I try to alter, no I mean adjust I think, the balance of history a little in favour of women with the study of social change. I have an apartment in the city.'

'You live alone?'

'Yes, now I do.' The question and its answer hang between them like smoke from a shared cigarette, that discredited erotic symbol from a thousand movies.

'When are you going back?'

'In two days time. And you?'

'Oh I'm quite flexible. I'm staying with a friend I haven't seen for a long time. I don't think she'll turn me out.'

'So perhaps we could meet again tomorrow?'

'Yes, yes we could.'

'Perhaps there is a concert or the theatre you have not seen?'

'I haven't seen anything. I live a very quiet life in the sticks . . . the country.'

'In the sticks. The country? I like that. Sticks are pieces of wood yes?

'Twigs, small branches or wood for lighting the fire, kindling. I think it was probably an Americanism or Australian. Anyway that's where I live.'

'With your English garden.'

'Yes my garden.' It seems very far away, Alice's glimpsed landscape through the little door she had had to kneel down to put her eye to.

'Do you like to go to a concert or the theatre?'

'A concert would be best. Plays can be an unknown quantity.'

'And for me the language is not so easy.'

'I'll buy a paper and see what's on.'

'Shall I telephone you at your friend's house?'

'Yes, yes do.'

Hetty watches Helge at her spaghetti, the spatulate fingers with straight, cut clean nails deftly twirling the strings into her mouth, and hopes she is eating as tidily, that her lipstick isn't smeared, that there's no sauce on her chin.

'This afternoon I must go to the Museum of Labour and meet a Mr Mackilroy. We are hoping to exchange exhibitions with them. You know this museum?'

'I've heard of it but I've never been there. What time is your meeting?'

'Two-thirty.'

'Then you must go soon. I think it's somewhere in the East End of London, the old docks perhaps.'

Helge takes a typed letter from her bag. 'Limehouse Town Hall. Is that far?'

'Yes it is. I'll get the bill. This is on me.' Quite as if she's used to it Hetty signals the waitress.

'I can't permit you to pay.'

'Why not! You're a guest.'

'They say in the letter I should take the Docklands Light Railway from Tower Hill.'

'I expect that's right. I've got a tube map in the back of my diary. We'll look up how you get to Tower Hill.'

Hetty gets out her diary and traces the route. 'Can you see?' She puts out her finger. Helge leans across. Hetty turns the map around to face her and Helge puts out her hand. For a moment they touch and then look straight at each other, the contact Hetty has managed to avoid up till now, knowing instinctively though without making it consciously precise in her mind what it might mean, what white water she might be embarking on.

'Time was away and somewhere else . . .' she remembers, conscious of Helge's face and their touched hands and of all the world outside holding its breath. 'Do you see,' she manages to ask, 'Tottenham Court Road on the Central Line, the red one to Liverpool Street and then the yellow Circle Line to Tower Hill.' She might have been offering a magic formula instead of directions for Limehouse.

'It's a very old part of London. It used to be the Chinese quarter where the sailors went for girls.'

'But not now?'

'Now it's been gentrified and politicians and television directors live there. But the local council is still socialist, I think. But you must go. It will take you a long time.'

They are out in the street again. 'Until tomorrow. I will telephone.' Helge bends her head forward and quickly kisses Hetty's cheek with a soft pressure of her lips and then is gone, walking briskly up Great Russell Street while Hetty turns away, her heart thudding so painfully she's seriously afraid she might be sick or that her trembling legs won't carry her.

As it is she only makes it to Russell Square where she sinks on to a bench not already populated. She wishes she hadn't given up smoking. She wishes she had a drink, anything that would calm this crazy flux of adrenalin. She knows now she's on the edge of that abyss of being in love if indeed she hasn't toppled down and down already. A song comes back to her from the old Jack days, admonishing, mocking.

> 'I'm not in love so don't forget it,
> It's just a silly phase I'm going through.
> I'm not in love no no. . . .'

Even the three fountains in the middle are stilled as if struck by a witch's hand. On the next bench a boy and girl are talking, touching each other with the intimacy of those whose bodies know the smell and feel and shape of the other and for whom the knowledge hasn't grown stale to that point where the self reasserts its sovereignty. Hetty looks at her watch, calmer now, able to go on, wondering how long she's sat here.

A boy is crouched in the underground tunnel beyond the lift, a piece of cardboard round his neck on a string like a child's bib that reads: 'Homeless and Hungary'. Perhaps it's the same boy from the bench in the square she had seen all those aeons before. She puts a pound coin in his battered trilby hat sitting on the floor beside him. His head is bent and he doesn't look up as her small round of fool's gold plops softly down. He has the turnip pallor of the imprisoned. Hetty would like to pull him up and take him away to fresh air and good food and hot baths but she knows that such an individual act of charity is both pointless and patronising. She remembers the *scunizzi* of Naples, the first time she went there on that student jaunt in the late 1950s, the shock of their spindly persistence, the dirty, clutching, monkey hands, and once, when their group had stopped to rest on a stone seat under the feathered palms overlooking the blue bay, a woman in a tired, rusty black dress cradling a baby as hollowed as herself stretching out a hand that seemed to be joined only to a length of bone. It was impossible to tell whether she was a professional and the sight of a few coins would bring a whole tribe out of the surrounding alleys or whether she was indeed Our Lady of the Destitute in search of an epiphany for her rickety child.

There's no answer to Hetty's ring at the door when she reaches the house so she lets herself in with the key Sandy's given her, grateful to be alone and goes upstairs to her room where she drops off her jacket and shoes, undoes the waistband of her skirt and lies down on the bed to fall asleep at once. She dreams she's Europa being carried away by a small black bull that grows smaller under her as she seems to swell but still rushes her onwards with a fierce energy she can't control.

Sandy is knocking on the door and calling: 'Hetty, I've made some tea.'

Hetty wakes confused. 'Thanks, I'll come down.' She goes into the bathroom and fills her cupped hands with cold water to bury her face in and then goes downstairs to the kitchen.

'The evenings are starting to draw in,' Sandy says. 'I hate it, don't you?'

'Have you got a paper I could look at? I'm supposed to find a concert we might go to.'

'Try the *Guardian*, behind the bread bin. How was your day? Where did you go?'

'The British Museum. I hadn't been there for years. It was full of people.'

'It always is these days. All the world is on the move, inspecting each other's cultural washing: all those combs and hair pins, and buttons and bits of broken china, and deities of course. All over the world rooms full of variations on the same theme, the accoutrements of living. My new job makes me cynical. Sometimes, I can only see history as a series of backdrops put together so the soap opera can go on in front of them.'

'That's one way of looking at it, and probably just as valid as any other.'

'Do you think Bill has affairs in some or all of these countries he's always going to?'

'Do you think he does?'

'I always told myself he hadn't got time but sometimes lately I've wondered. I expect he wonders about me too, left behind. I hope he does. Have you found anything?'

'There's Monteverdi. It seems more neutral than Beethoven or Elgar. St John's Smith Square. Where's that?'

'Just off the Embankment, near the Houses of Parliament. She might not like it.'

'What? Monteverdi?'

'Countertenors neighing in Latin. Not everyone's cup of tea. Oh, take no notice of me. I'm jealous; no not jealous, envious.'

'Envious?'

'Because you're starting something new. You are, aren't you?'

'What do you mean?'

'Come off it Hetty, I can see. Have you done it before?'

'What? Done what?'

'Had an affair with a woman. I've sometimes thought I might. It wouldn't be such a betrayal of Bill. But then that's nonsense. People are people. You're very much in the fashion. There's a lot of it about, especially in the media world.'

Hetty is shocked, unable to answer as Sandy goes on. She

hadn't thought in those terms, hadn't thought at all. She had just gone along, responded. Suddenly she's required to embed fragile things in concrete or amber, engrave them on crystal so that they're set fast and can be observed, appraised by others.

'I've never thought of it. I don't know that I'm thinking of it now.'

'Why haven't you thought of it? Didn't you think about us? At Queen's I mean.'

'Did you?'

'In a way. That is I thought about what other people would think when they saw us always together.'

'But there were the boys, Derek and Evan. We were a four-some.'

'No we weren't. I never fancied Evan. Nothing happened between us. I know you went to bed with Derek but that was just trying it on for size if you'll forgive me. You weren't in love with him. You and I were closer.'

Hetty can't deny this, partly because to do so would seem rude and possibly give pain, and partly because it's largely true. Instead she says: 'I don't think I knew such things were possible then. Did you?'

'Yes, yes I did. You see I'd had a friend at school and was in love with. We never did anything physical about it.'

'Oh, I had crushes at school.'

'This wasn't a crush. It was real.'

'I think I thought that it was just a phase you went through at all-girls' schools, you know: falling for prefects and favourite teachers, until you met boys and then that was the real thing. I was very ignorant. I had to learn about sex in biology lessons and from *Lady Chatterley's Lover* and those talks you and I used to have. My parents behaved as though sex didn't exist. Maybe that's why they didn't have any children of their own. As for homosexuality . . .' Hetty brings out the word, tonguing its syllables deliberately, facing it.

'Sodom and Gomorrah! They were religious weren't they?'

'Chapel. I've never told you, I've never told anyone; when the legislation went through that said adopted children had the right to know who their natural parents were after they came of age, I wrote to the society I was adopted from and asked them if they had any record of my real parents. I didn't want to do anything about it, didn't want to trace them, I just wanted to know, like settling a historical fact. They told me my mother was a bus conductress in Southampton and my father was a Free French sailor. So technically I'm half-French. I never told my adopted mother I'd found out. It didn't seem kind.'

Hetty remembers the fortnightly visits to the old people's home where the mother who'd brought her up had wandered in and out of lucidity as through a maze that sometimes opened into a half circle with a seat where she could rest and sometimes lowered its hedge to show a distant prospect, clear and open which she could glimpse but never reach, before enclosing her with its dark narrow lanes again.

'Anyway technically I'm half-French and maybe if I'd known that from the beginning it would have made some sort of difference.'

'How do you mean?'

'Well, it's somehow liberating, less conformist.'

'Knowledge is power. That sort of stuff?'

'That's it.'

'We've strayed from the main point,' Sandy is saying firmly when the telephone begins to call and she puts down her teacup and goes out of the room. Hetty stands listening to the silence when the receiver is picked up and is ready, heart pounding again, when Sandy comes back saying with a smile and raised eyebrows: 'For you.'

Helge's voice is very collected. If her heart is thudding it doesn't make her speech shaky. 'Hello. Have you found something that we might visit?'

'How do you like Monteverdi?'

'Oh very much indeed. There is a performance?'

'Tomorrow, yes. In a church.'

'How interesting. Where shall we meet?'

'Outside the west door of Westminster Abbey? The main entrance. That should be easy.'

'At what o'clock?'

'Seven? The concert begins at seven-thirty. Unless you'd like a drink beforehand?'

'That would be good.'

'Okay then. Six-thirty at the Abbey. How was your day? Did you get to the meeting in time?'

'I was a little late but it didn't matter. I have to go again tomorrow and then all will be settled. Have you translated the letter yet?'

Hetty laughs. 'Good god no! I need a dictionary and several days' hard work.' She realises she must end the conversation and go back to Sandy but she doesn't know how, and in any case she isn't eager to meet Sandy's penetrating examination and knowing smile. She's let off the hook by the sound of the pips, followed by a falling coin.

'I have only ten pence. I must say goodbye. Until tomorrow six-thirty at the Westminster Abbey. Sleep well.'

'And you.' Renewed pips cut her off. Hetty puts down the receiver. When she gets back to the kitchen Sandy has replaced their dirty cups with glasses of whisky.

'I thought you'd need a pick-me-up.' She lifts her glass. 'Here's looking at you kid,' she too toasts Hetty in the words they always used. 'And here's to your French *papa*. I think you're going to need his patronage.'

'I don't know,' Hetty says uneasily. 'Probably nothing will happen.'

They change the subject then and talk of other times and people, easy with each other now, an old unmarried couple and this night Hetty sleeps soundly and wakes in the morning able to tell herself she's been 'imagining things' which was her mother's formula for dealing with the potentially untoward.

She spends the next day browsing and window shopping in the King's Road with Sandy, stopping to lunch in The Markham Arms on a plate of salad and a glass of beer.

'It's been such fun having you to stay,' Sandy says. 'And now I'm going to lose you again.'

'Why should you?'

'Because if I'm right it's inevitable. Now I must go and pretend to do some work. I'll see you tonight or tomorrow morning as the case might be.'

When she's gone Hetty sits for a bit finishing her drink, watching the other customers and the passers-by through the windows, speculating on lives and relationships. Out in the street again she drifts with the crowd into the glass emporia of domestic goods and gifts, thinking that she might buy a present or two.

She had bought very little for the cottage. The things she had had in her flat had been almost enough to furnish it, with the addition of the double bed that had failed to entice Jack. Mostly she buys things for the garden. So she's surprised, almost shocked by the Aladdin's caves of furnishings like some imperial ware-house of colonial stuffs, carpets, painted dishes, she compares to the drab rooms she had grown up in, devoid of ornament or comfort. Was it only the War that made her childhood memories so dingy or was there a real change in the way of looking at the things we surround ourselves with so that now everyday life has to be visually resonant? What her mother would have described contemptuously as 'needing everything that opens and shuts'. Those bedspreads and cushions from India in the colours of a Mughal miniature, those cachepots and vases in millefiori would once have seemed pretentious and materialistic and were now the commonplace desires of every household. There's nothing Hetty can think of to buy Sandy that she cares to carry with her to the concert. She wanders out again, looks across the road wondering if she might cross and sees a banner slung across a classical façade announcing an antiques fair. That might provide something.

Hetty pays her pound entrance fee and goes into what she realises from the decoration must have been an opulent monu-ment to Victorian civic pride, an Old Town Hall whose council chamber is now fringed with stalls displaying the clutter of the last two hundred years. Here surely where there's everything from a hatpin to an elephant's foot she'll find something to buy for Sandy. Helge too. After all she owes her something for all her research. . . .

In the end she settles on a Victorian oval brooch of black stone with a snowdrop inlay for Sandy. Helge is more difficult. What might she wear from among the jewellery? A ring is too intimate though it's these that draw Hetty to peer into case after case, imagining the dead fingers they've clasped. Then she comes upon the lacquered papier-mâché glove boxes, just right for desk tidys for pens, pencils, paperclips. One's a polished chestnut with an inset of romantic landscape around a castle that reminds Hetty of the rivertrip on the Main. That will do.

She's been dawdling, unwilling to commit herself to the meeting and now it's nearly five o'clock. The stallholders are beginning to pack up. It's time to find a public lavatory where she can wash and comb her hair and try not to dispirit herself by looking in the mirror before she sets out for Westminster. She retraces the length of the King's Road a little weary and apprehensive, waits for what seems forever on the platform at Sloane Square until an Asian voice distorted by the address system announces that because of an 'incident' earlier involving 'a person on the line', they are 'experiencing delays'. Hetty can see it too clearly: the end of *Anna Karenina*, the moment's horror as the train hurtles down. 'No, no, I didn't mean it!'

The metallic taste of fear is still in her mouth as she comes up at Westminster into the square with Big Ben striking half-past six and hurries towards the Abbey where of course Helge is already waiting. She'll think I'm always late.

'I'm sorry. The train didn't come. There'd been an accident. Let's find somewhere for a drink. I could do with one.'

'I have found the church and there is also a bar.'

'In a church?'

'In the underneath.'

'The crypt.'

'Yes. The crypt.'

They thread their way through the old streets behind the Abbey until they reach Smith Square and the handsome classical building which is its centre and join the queue down into the dark crypt where the performers in evening dress mingle with the audience, and they eventually find a table where they can lodge their plates of sandwiches and glasses of wine.

'This I like very much. It has atmosphere like a bierkeller but with culture.'

Hetty laughs, relaxing. 'Should we get tickets?'

'I have them.'

'And I have a little present for all your research.'

'Please it is nothing.'

'It certainly is not and I should be paying for the tickets.'

'You have paid for this.' Hetty indicates their glasses and food.

'I hope you like it. I thought it was light enough for you to take home without it being a nuisance.'

'But it is beautiful. What is it?' Hetty is aware of the firm squarish hands again, stroking the smooth shiny box.

'I think they were to keep your gloves in. Fine ones.'

'And the picture: it's like our journey on the Main.'

'I hoped it would remind you of that.'

'I don't need reminding. I remember everything.'

Helge has bought seats in the first few rows. As the church fills, Hetty sees her looking around at the audience, who are informally, almost shabbily dressed, in contrast with the performers when they file in, and with the elegant penguin conductor.

And then it begins, the baroque instruments entirely in place in that setting, the voices of the choir alternately soaring and dancing while the soloists weave their arias among them. Suddenly Hetty feels her hand taken as Helge points to the text printed in the programme.

'*Pulchra es, amica mea*. You are beautiful my beloved.'

I am fifty-two, Hetty thinks, and I am holding hands in public with another woman. She lets her eyes slide sideways but their neighbours are intent on the music. Hetty doesn't pull away and Helge doesn't let go. A smooth warmth flows from Helge's palm and fingers into her own, a heat that seems to be carried by the music further and further along her bloodstream and down between her thighs just as she remembers. Only the interval, with the necessity to clap, breaks the spell.

'Let's go outside.'

They sit on a stone balustrade from which they can look down at the pavement below where other concertgoers are walking to and fro under the stairs. 'Tomorrow I have to return to Germany and I don't know how to go away and not see you again. May I call you? Will you write sometimes? I will look for more letters from your nun but I am a little jealous because I think you are in love with her.'

'Can one be in love with someone dead for a thousand years?' Hetty laughs, trying to keep the conversation within her control.

'Of course. It is very easy. And there are no difficulties. You can't quarrel.'

'The next piece is about a quarrel: the combat between Tancredi and Clorinda.'

'Tancred, the German knight?'

'I think so. He takes on a strange knight in single combat not knowing it's really a woman in disguise and kills her.'

'That is horrible. Why is she in drag?'

For a moment Hetty doesn't understand and then she says: 'I can't remember. Maybe she's an Amazon. Anyway she comes close to beating him but he has to win in the end because you couldn't have the hero going under to a woman in the sixteenth century. I think the conflict, the combat rather, is symbolic, about the relations between the sexes.'

'Or between lovers.'

'It looks as if they're starting again.'

'Look,' Helge says when they've resumed their seats, *'Madrigals of Love and War*. "Each man kills the thing he loves." Oscar Wilde, isn't that so?'

'I hope not. Otherwise where's the point in anything?' Hetty whispers for the bobbing conductor is back, the soloist is poised with open book.

Amico, hai vinto, io ti perdon . . . perdona tu ancora. . . .

It is when this point in the text, the dying words of Clorinda, is reached that Hetty's hand is taken and held, and again she doesn't resist but sits there in a flush of desire, at once relaxing and lustful like being in a hot scented bath. When it is all over they walk back slowly through Parliament Square to the tube station.

'Do you have to go back to your friend? You could come back to my hotel for a drink, a nightcap.'

'I think I'd better go. It's quite a long way.' The charge has drained from her now, leaving her tired and unsure.

'You will write to me?'

'Yes, I promise. I must go.'

'Goodbye then. No goodnight. Sleep well.' Helge bends forward to kiss her but this time full on the mouth and again Hetty knows that remembered surge overcoming the tiredness, the electric charge along the nerves from the momentary fusion of flesh, fiercer than she had ever known with Jack.

In the car, driving back the next day Hetty begins that monologue in her head that she recognises as the obsessive voice of the state of being in love, explaining, involving, admonishing. *You see I've never been here before. I've never even thought about it. I don't even know what I want.*

Yet she's surprised when her only caller that evening is Sandy wanting to be sure she's got home safely, and the cottage seems dull and lifeless. Perhaps she should get a dog or a cat. It's too late to begin translating the new material and anyway her interest has deserted her, the pages hold no excitement only labour. Mr Powers has been, and the garden, 'your English garden', comforts her with the smell of mown grass and the stippled reds and yellows of the nemesia still blazing back at the sunset as if they have fallen from the sky.

It's Jack who rings next. 'Bob thought your report was brilliant and we'd like to publish your paper in *History Now*. I've spoken to Hodgins and he thinks it's just the sort of thing we ought to be doing. And there's something else I want to discuss with you. I'd really like to come out and talk. It's so difficult on the blasted phone.'

'I might be coming into town,' Hetty lies. 'That would be easier for you. Can't you give me some idea what it is though, then I can be thinking about it.'

'Well . . . Alright then. Bob and I were wondering if you'd like to come in part-time, help out a bit.'

'I don't think the terms of the retirement scheme would let me do that, I'm afraid. Not without losing my pension. We're not supposed to take up "gainful employment".'

'We were thinking more of on a voluntary basis, a small seminar group to keep in touch really.'

'Oh I don't think I could take on anything like that. You see I'm working on a project that might mean spending some time abroad, on and off. I wouldn't want to be tied down. The occasional lecture, well-paid of course . . . I might just fit that in.' Hetty laughs to take the sting away.

'Well we could talk about that.'

'Honestly Jack I don't see the point in wasting your time. If you've got a one-off you think I could usefully do, you can always ask me.' It's the first time she's been able to say his name and it signifies that the magic has gone out of it. Naming him she reasserts her strength and freedom. Once it had been a spell she had murmured to herself alone, then a coin she offered him in return for love when they were alone together. It had first become impossible for her to say his name in public, in the staff common room, to colleagues. Her throat had contracted against it. Then it had become impossible to say it to him and finally, after she had left, even to herself.

When this call comes she realises by her disappointment what she's really waiting for. She finds herself unwilling even to cycle down to the village shop in case she misses it and thinks of buying an answering machine, except that she would have to spend a couple of hours going into Sarnford to get one. She loiters among the pots and tubs outside the back door where she's sure not to miss the ringing or props the instrument on the windowsill with the window open when she's forced to weed the front bed. *Il faut cultiver notre jardin*, Hetty says to herself mockingly and then wonders how it could have been a Frenchman not a Briton who had proposed it as a way of life.

She's on her knees with a trowel with her bejeaned rump stuck in the air when she hears a sound behind her – the clearing of a throat demanding attention – looks round and scrambles up. There are two men she doesn't know dwarfing the little front garden.

'Miss Dearden?'

'Yes.'

'We're police officers. Might we have a word with you?'

The rape, Hetty thinks. I've missed the house-to-house enquiries while I've been away.

'Of course. Would you like to come in?' She leads the way and they bend their heads under the lintel of the front door. 'Do sit down.'

'Thank you.' They fill the sitting room with their crumpled suits.

'Now, how can I help?'

'You've been away Miss Dearden,' the younger one says while the other listens.

'Yes.' Should she tell them her suspicions about Donkey Jacket?

'And where did you go?'

'I went to London. If you mean the last two days. Or do you mean last month when I was in Germany?'

'Well, both. We need to know about both occasions.'

'I don't quite see. . . . Anyway I was in Germany of course when it happened so I'm not much use there. . . .'

'When what happened Miss Dearden?'

'Well Caroline Plaswell . . .' Hetty can't bring herself to say the word 'rape'.

'You thought we'd come about that?'

'I'm afraid I don't. . . .'

The older man speaks now for the first time. 'That's a local matter, Miss Dearden. Sad as it is . . . a matter for the local police. We're from London. I'm Inspector Maidstone.' He briefly flashes what looks like an ID card with his photograph on it. 'We believe you can help us.'

'What about?'

'Who did you see in London? Where did you stay?'

Hetty feels her legs shaking with fright and anger. 'Do you have a warrant for these questions?'

'We could have if we needed it. We thought you would prefer to help us of your own accord,' the younger one takes up the thread to wind it a little tighter. 'How long have you known Helge Ebbesen?'

'I met her last month in Germany.'

'And you went to London to meet her again?'

'Yes.'

'Why did you go to meet her in London?'

'She's been doing some research for me in the German archives. I went to collect some material from her.'

'And what was the nature of this material?'

'It was a photocopy of a document, a letter. . . .'

'Could we have a look at this letter Miss Dearden, just to corroborate the reason for your visit . . . ?'

'Oh yes,' Hetty says with relief and goes to fetch it from the kitchen table where she had been giving it a first attempt at decipherment over breakfast. 'There you are.'

'This is it?'

'Yes.'

'This is a xerox. It could be anything, have come from anywhere,' the younger one says. His senior holds out a hand and takes the stapled pages.

'This could have been sent by post. Why was it necessary for you to meet?'

'I wanted to discuss what further material there might be.' Hetty is surprised and a little excited by this lie and her ease with it. Even so she's not convinced by her own words and wonders if they will be.

'This "letter", I think you said, is in what language?'

'Latin.'

'Latin?'

'Yes, it's from a nun to her father.'

'Ah. And when was it written?'

'About twelve hundred years ago, I think.'

'Or yesterday?'

'I don't follow.'

'People have been known to use another language as the basis for a code. After all, it doesn't matter what the words say. They're only the sheep's clothing if you follow me. The words can be a poem or even a shopping list.'

'But it's just a piece of research.'

'You don't mind if we keep it then?'

'Yes, I do mind, actually. I'm in the process of translating it and it's my only copy. I'll get another one made and you can have that if you're so keen.'

'How would we know if you've copied this particular document and not just substituted another?'

'I'll mark all the pages. Here, now, and you can take a note of how I've marked them and . . . and the first and last lines of every page. You can't, I think, remove them without a warrant or my consent.'

'No madam, that's perfectly correct. Although under the Prevention of Terrorism Act such niceties can be overridden. Colin, help Miss Dearden to mark the pages and take a note as she suggests.'

The mention of terrorism has of course struck terror into Hetty's heart as it's meant to do but she tries to appear calm. The young policeman hands her the sheaf of photocopies and a red biro from his pocket. She begins to sign them with a hand she tries to keep steady.

'Perhaps I should tell you a little more about the person you've been receiving documents from, Miss Dearden, since you claim

—116—

not to know her very well. That is when you've kindly finished marking the pages for us.'

Hetty has been signing each page with the biro. 'That's the last.' The young policeman takes them and his pen from her and begins to make entries in his notebook while his senior takes out an identical book, opens it and proceeds to read to her.

'"Helge Ebbesen, born Leipzig 1950. Father fought on Russian Front. Emigrated to West Germany in 1959. Student at Cologne University where known for her left-wing sympathies. Took part in student riots in 1968. Suspected of subversive activities and membership of left-wing International Brigade. Applied to study in USA. Refused a visa. No confirmed activities except for membership of feminist groups since 1975 when post obtained at Saarbrucken University, entailing frequent trips abroad and contact with other nationals." Those are the known facts. The rest is speculation and I won't bother you with it.'

'But that could be anyone's story,' Hetty says, 'anyone of that generation. Any woman I mean.'

'Yes. You were an active member of CND weren't you?'

'So was anyone with a care for the future.'

'Good causes provide good fronts for some people, Miss Dearden. Are you planning to go to London again soon or to meet Helge Ebbesen?'

'I have no plans to meet Dr Ebbesen in the immediate future.'

It's a long time after they've gone before the cottage returns to its rightful proportions and her hands stop shaking. Hetty has just made herself a cup of tea when the telephone shrills.

'Hetty, I'm so sorry I didn't ring you yesterday. . . .'

'The police have been here, asking a lot of questions. They told me, hinted at, all sorts of things about you. Why didn't you tell me you were an East German, that you were refused a US visa, that. . . .'

'Oh Hetty, *liebling*, I am so sorry, so very sorry. . . .'

My dearest father in Christ and in the flesh. It was such a joy to see Aelfwin again with your longed for letter and the many gracious presents. Truly my heart overflowed with happiness at your words and to know that you are well but with sadness too that such lands and seas lie between us. The altar cloth is the finest English embroidery and the people here were overwhelmed with its beauty. I intend next Lordsday which is the feast of St Pelagia the Penitent to dedicate it and place it upon the altar. Also they are pleased with the warm cloaks you have sent for already summer is over here, the nights grow soon dark and the mornings are chill with a cold heavy dew that soaks our clothes and our feet when we go out. But thanks be to God there is already a new order and spirit here and the people's hearts have inclined towards me through your goodness, for they see that I am not alone and that they can expect more support than they have had in the past now that our family house is under our care again.

I send you some honey from our own hives in return for your sweetness. Since I wrote to you I have established the hospice more diligently so that the people come from far and wide for healing and I have also opened a school for both boys and girls who are brought here by their parents to be dedicated to God, so many indeed that we cannot find room for any more until either some are grown enough to join houses elsewhere as novices or we can build more dormitories and draw in more good teachers. Now at last I am almost ready for the Lady Liutgard if she should incline to visit me, and the bed hanging which you have sent with the scenes of Adam and Eve in the

Garden before man's first fall shall adorn her bed if she should come.

All this takes up my time so much that I have little left for the copying of books with my own hand. Instead I have tried to improve the work here by advice and instruction and by sending for good examples from the sisters at Wimborne and also to the Lady Gisela at Chelles who was so kind to me on my journey here; the script is somewhat different from the English style and so I will have some write one way and some another, whatever is most fittingly done.

Of our other purpose in my coming here I have little to report except a strange encounter which you may find interesting and curious. In my last letter I told you of the old sister who had been here in Berthgyth's day and of her story of how Berthgyth was taken by Saxon raiders. I was determined that if I could make her well enough she should show me the very place. Why I wished to see it or what I would find there after all this time I did not know, only that I seemed to be moved in my heart to go there if I could. Therefore after several weeks had passed in which I had treated Eanfled's infirmities and fed her on good broth, under dispensation, to strengthen her limbs, I thought her strong enough to attempt the journey in a litter if she could remember the way, which I did not truly doubt because God in his great wisdom has kept her mind clear.

However because I did not wish the others to be curious about our journey, I said only that I was taking her to a holy place I had heard of where there was a spring of healing water and this was also true, for the country people do say that a certain spring once the abode of a pagan spirit was blessed by Willibrord on a journey north and the spirit departed and God made that water for healing through the prayers of the venerable man. Therefore we set out with only two servants and the child Adela and travelling slowly of necessity, we followed Eanfled's directions and indeed her memory became clearer the further we went for, as she said, she had been many times to the place hoping that Berthgyth would send another message or come herself, and so she remembered the way perfectly even though to me the forest and the hills all appeared alike but she would call out from the litter: 'You see that rock. We must go right about it and there will be a path behind.' And so there always was.

We rested at noon and said prayers for our safety, for those parts are quite wild still and the haunt of runaway slaves and lordless men who live by robbery though the Saxons are quiet this year because of the King's heavy hand upon them, and God protected us. Then Eanfled said that we were drawing near to the place and I felt a great excitement rising in me that at last I should see it. But then I remembered the words of Scripture: What went ye out for to see? A reed shaken by the wind? And I was ashamed and stilled that fierce beating of my heart. At last after more than an hour's journeying she said that beyond this last line of trees we should come upon the little valley with the stream running through it, and so it was. We halted the horses on the edge of the trees and it was just as she had described it. I left the litter in the care of Adela and the servants and rode forward slowly to the bank of the stream. As I walked my horse along it I came to what I had thought from a distance was an outcrop of rock but as I approached nearer I saw it was the work of man's hands, a kind of cairn and I was afraid that this was some pagan altar that the people had secretly built to what they foolishly believed the god of that place as the Saxons do. Then I made the sign of the Cross over it and abjured any evil thing to depart from there.

All this time I felt that I was watched, and I remembered Eanfled's story of how the men had come upon them suddenly and silently before they were aware, for the valley is much enclosed with trees and hills, and I began to wonder whether my urge to see the place was indeed the prompting of God or whether Satan was leading me astray to destroy me in my pride and curiosity, and I fell on my knees on the damp grass and prayed for the soul of Berthgyth and my own too. And even as I was kneeling there a figure on horseback came forward from within a great cleft between two hills leading out of the valley, and I thought that my prayers were now to be strangely answered and he would kill me where I knelt for he had a great sword hanging by his side and wore the dress of the Saxon pagans with gold armbands and torc, which is indeed like that of the Franks but wilder. But then I saw that he approached me slowly and that a child rode behind him with its arms about his waist and I rose to my feet, calling silently on God to protect me and stood firmly waiting for the pagan, for such I believed him, to reach me. He came on until he was only a few yards away and then he stopped and looking down upon me spoke in a tongue so very like our own that I understood him to say: 'I knew that one day you will come.'

I did not answer him. He dismounted from his horse and lifted down the child which I could now see was a girl of five or six years with a crippled leg, and taking her hand led her towards me. He began to speak to me again and as far as I could understand him told me that the child was his daughter and that he wished me to take her and bring her up to the monastic life because he loved her dearly and among his own people she could not marry and no-one would protect her if he was killed. I asked him if he was a Christian and if the child was baptised and he shook his head.

Then I thought that I should baptise her myself before we left that place for if she should die on the way back without baptism, either through sickness or at the hands of evil men, Satan would claim her soul. So I led her to the water's edge and the father too and I said to him that she must renounce the gods of the pagans and be baptised before I could take her, and that she must repeat the words I would say to her, and then I began upon the renunciation of the Blessed Boniface which he used in their tongue: *Ec forsacho diobolae end allum diobol glede, end allum dioboles wercum end wordum, Thunaer ende Woden ende Saxnote ende allum them unholdum. Ec gelobo in Got almachtigen, fadour. Ec gelobo in Crist Godes sunn. Ec gelobo in halogan ghast.*

And when she had repeated it all after me I poured the water of baptism over her head with my hands, made the sign of the

Cross upon her and said: 'I baptise thee in the name of the Father, and of the Son, and of the Holy Ghost.'

Then he kissed the child and said something to her which I could not understand and put her hand in mine and clasped them together with his own. He remounted his horse and at that the child called out: 'Father!' He spoke to her again and she began to weep but did not try to pull away from me. Then he turned his horse's head and went back the way they had come into the dark cleft between the hills and was gone as if the hills had opened to swallow him and closed again. At this it seemed to me as if God had given us this girl child in the place of the sister you have lost and I knew that there was nothing further to do in that place, except that I picked a few white days eyes that were growing there and offered them to God and laid them on the cairn of stones. And when she saw what I was doing, the child picked some too and put them with mine saying: 'Father.'

Then I led her by the hand back to where the others were waiting and said to them: 'God has given us a little sister to take care of, and Adela shall teach her our ways and the ways of God.' For I could see that she shrank back a little from Eanfled and even from me and I thought it might be our black habits that frightened the child whereas Adela, who still wears the white veil, is a sweet-natured girl as well as quick in learning, and she put her arm around the child and drew her under her own cloak and spoke to her in Frankish which she seemed to understand.

We began our journey back then but we could not return directly without visiting the spring blessed by Willibrord where I had decided to spend the night, for the sun was already setting and soon it would be too dark to travel. With directions from Eanfled we retraced our route until we came to a broad ride much used by travellers, where the going was easier and so we eventually reached the place where a little chapel had been built and we prepared to spend the night there, weary from our travelling. The men lit a fire and put up a small hut for me and the two girls. Eanfled stayed in her litter and fortunately the night was dry and not cold so that when we had eaten some of the food we had brought with us, the children took themselves to sleep while Eanfled and I said the last hour of the day. And when we came to *Nunc dimittis* Eanfled prayed with great feeling and afterwards she said to me: 'I hope my Lord will soon call me now for I am weary of journeying. I have waited a long time for your coming and the burden of my secret to be lifted from me. *Fiat voluntas sua.*' Then she closed her eyes and I wondered if she slept her last sleep till we shall all wake, but when I bent over her she still breathed but small like a bird. I found I could not follow her, even though I tried to compose my thoughts to rest in God's hands, but my mind returned continually to the events of the day, for it was clear to me that nothing had happened by accident but all by some design which I did not understand.

Eventually I slept and woke before the dawn and said Prime and went to see if Eanfled was awake. She looked at me with a fierce strength and said: 'Let us go soon.'

I answered: 'First let me bring you to the waters of Willibrord's spring.'

She said: 'They can do me no good now. Nevertheless for the sake of that venerable man of our people, and to please you, we will do it.'

Then one of the men lifted her up and carried her to the grotto beside the chapel where the water welled up in the rock, and I took a cup and gave her to drink and bathed her hands and face, and her feet. She said that the water tasted sweet and that it seemed to carry a soothing throughout her body so I filled several bottles with it before we left.

Our progress was slow because I could see that she was sinking fast but she did not complain. She said that she had no pain and felt a great peace of body and soul but that she would like to die in that cell where she had spent so many years of her life. So we came at last to our house and I made haste to have her brought to her room and sent to the men's house for the priest and gathered the sisters together that we might sing her soul to God. She spoke to them, all who could get into the chamber, and said that she died in complete ease of body and mind, that her pain had been washed away by those healing waters and that she had no fear. We began to sing and never had the sisters sung with more perfection of harmony so that when the priest Fridugis arrived to give *viaticum* her soul parted from its earthly shell even as he spoke. At that, one of the sisters fell down with a sharp cry as if struck and when she came to herself she said that even at that moment she had seen Eanfled's soul going straight up to heaven in a shaft of light. Then everyone began to speak of a miracle but I stopped such talk by leading them into chapel for prayers, for I knew, as Mother Edgyth taught us, that the evil one often deceives us with such tricks which are most dangerous because they appear the work of God.

That was nearly a month ago and the Saxon child already shows herself quick to learn to read and write under the tuition of Adela, and of a sweet and affectionate disposition but a little wild and wilful, and impatient with that affliction God has laid on her. But Adela she loves and follows everywhere. She has told us her name is Gundrada. Adela came to me the other day and said that she had found the child weeping because of her crippled leg and she had told her that she was fortunate that God had marked her out for his own to preserve her to himself in whose eyes all limbs are straight and that deformity exists only in the eyes of men. I know this to be true my father, and yet sometimes I wonder then why it is that men who are marked in some way by the hand of God may not be priests when we are taught that God sees always the perfect soul inside its fleshly dress. And I wish sometimes that I had some wise counsellor to whom I could write for guidance on these and similar matters that vex me, as Lioba did to Boniface, for you my dear father are too dear to me to trouble you often and show you how weak my faith sometimes is alone here and I remembered how you were disturbed by your sister's letters to you when she was cast down with sadness in this place at the great waters between you.

But for your sister since Eanfled is gone I do not know where I must turn for enlightenment, and I am angry with myself that

I did not ask Gundrada's father more before he left, for surely, as I now think, he knew that place of old and perhaps he built the cairn there and knows some story from long ago of the fate of Berthgyth but I do not think I shall see him again, unless I should take the child there to show her to him and how she grows daily in stature in the eyes of God and men. But then how would I find the way without Eanfled? Nor do I see clearly the will of God in all this for surely if we were meant to know He would have shown us and not given us the child instead. The whole matter is very dark to me and I can only trust that in time I shall see the way more clearly.

My dearest father this letter has been held back because last week came the news that the King was coming into these parts to hunt with all the court, as is his custom, and that the Queen would come with him as well as his daughters, and that she would pay us the honour of a visit for one night. You can imagine our confusion of preparation, every room had to be swept and fresh rushes mixed with sweet herbs laid down in the refectory. Our best copyists were set to work to make a beautiful scroll with the *Lux Aeterna* on it in letters of gold and I myself drew the capital 'L' and adorned it as well as I could for the hours of daylight are now so short. I worked as long as I could by candlelight and when my eyes grew weary I bathed them in betony water and so continued. And I decorated the capital with vines signifying life and with the rays of the sun signifying light which is her name: the guardian of Light in our tongue, and in the space between the arms of the 'L' I inserted a picture of the Blessed Virgin.

The guest chamber is of course our finest, apart from the chapel. The walls are covered with hangings and already the windows are filled with glass. The windows of the chapel I have filled with horn for the time being against the winter. The sheets were our finest lawn, perfumed with rose water, her pillow stuffed with down mixed with lavender and the bedhangings, which included yours, of embroidered silk so that when she saw it she cried out that it was beautiful, though she said that she would rather have slept as we did but that the King would be affronted.

We awaited her arrival outside our gates. She came with a strong escort who camped in the fields about. When she saw me she got down from her horse and took me up from where I was kneeling into her embrace, then she told her escort to await her return and with only one maid she let herself be led into our house and placed herself entirely in our care. I brought her perfumed water in a silver basin to refresh herself and a fine linen towel and a cup of wine with sweetmeats, and then she asked to be shown our chapel and that she might hear the sisters sing and as it was by then the hour of Vespers we went there and she astonished them all with her devotion. Afterwards she said that the singing was the finest for sweetness and correctness that she had ever heard and she presented our chapel with a silver ampulla and paten with the words 'When you offer these in your hands every day at the altar, say: "Christ have mercy on Liutgard His humble handmaiden."' And for myself she has given me a beautiful mantle which I think I shall use to decorate the altar.

When it was time for bed she bade me share her chamber so we might talk and the maid slept on a pallet outside the door. I had a bed made up for me at the front of hers and there we lay together in the shape of Christ's Cross. 'Ah,' she said, 'yours is the better life here away from courts and the world, and here I would be, except that I cannot leave the King who is like a father to me. I often speak of these things to your countryman Alcuin who is my father in God, but he tells me to be patient and obedient to His will Who will call me in His own time, and that meanwhile I have much to do here.'

And it is true father that they say that the King listens to her advice on many matters. Only on the question of the Saxons he hears no-one not even Master Alcuin. Nevertheless it is a great thing for our race that he is so well regarded here, for some say that there is no man of greater learning in all the world and all this first inclined the Queen's heart towards me as she said.

Perhaps also she feels a kindness towards us because she is of the race of the Alemanni not the Franks. We talked long, for her heart was full of many things and I found myself by the Grace of God able to advise her and to speak freely on matters of scripture. And then we fell to talk of poetry and she confessed that she did not like so much to hear the old tales and songs that please the King but more to hear verses of devotion and of the beauties of the earth. She recited some of the lines of Alcuin which so moved my heart that I have determined to try my hand at some verses to send her, for I have always been too busy with practical affairs to attempt such things although I have seen at Thanet some lines which the Blessed Lioba sent to Boniface, and am therefore emboldened to try what I can do.

Finally we slept but I awoke as usual and went to the chapel for Matins leaving her sleeping like a child. I was careful not to wake her when I returned and when I went again to the chapel but at Prime she arose too and kissed me saying that she had had a dream of great peace and sweetness, and came with me into chapel like another sister. Then she was bathed and dressed by her maid and came again to chapel for the Mass and afterwards we ate breakfast in the refectory all together and Adela read most beautifully from St Augustine's *The City of God*.

Now it was time for her to rejoin the King but she would not leave me and insisted that I accompany her to his camp and she told me to bring the child Gundrada with me and so we rode out with Gundrada carried on the pommel of one of her escort. But before we left, when we were alone together, she said that she felt her spirit renewed and asked that she might come again whenever she had need. 'And then we shall be together in heaven where, as Alcuin has taught me, neither sex, nor age, nor rank matters.'

The camp when we reached it was an orderly bustle and of the bigness of a town with many rows of tents and fires and lines of horses and weaponry but it seemed to me that there were more warriors than courtiers if the King was here only to go hunting, and I thought that it was more likely that he was making a show of strength in these parts to impress the Saxons. He was sitting on his travelling chair covered with a fur cloak when we approached, and first the Queen went forward and knelt before him, and when he raised her up, kissed him and spoke to him. I waited some way off, having got down from my horse, with my head bowed and holding the child by the hand. Then the Queen came and led us forward until we knelt down before him and I heard his voice, which is somewhat thin for his great size, asking what she had brought him. Then she showed him the scroll which we had made and when he had admired the work she led us forward. I was afraid to meet him or to look up into his face because of the rough words he had given me before.

Then I heard him speaking to me: 'You have given my Queen a beautiful present, and she tells me that all is order in your house and God is worshipped with prayer and work, and that the praises of God are sung after the correct manner as ordered throughout my Kingdom but very often neglected. Therefore you may ask of me something. Speak up.'

I lifted my head, for I saw, and indeed I have heard, that he is a man who likes those who do not shrink from him and therefore I answered in as large a voice as I could: 'Lord King of your graciousness I need stone and glass for the windows.'

He laughed and his laugh was bigger than his voice. 'I ask the Pope for marble and you ask me for stone. The Pope says I may take my marbles from the palace at Ravenna. Where shall I give you your stone from? How will you bring it into these wild parts?'

'By water, Lord King, by river.'

He laughed again and said, 'If you can get it there you can have it. I will have a letter of authorisation written allowing you to take what you can find. And who is the child?'

The Queen took Gundrada by the hand and led her up to him. 'She is one of your Saxon subjects my Lord who has received baptism and is learning the work of God.'

The King's face had softened for he is very fond of children and especially his daughters but now he scowled at the hated race. 'What is your name?'

'She is called Gundrada like your granddaughter.'

'A Saxon child with a Frankish name. What is your father's name?'

'He is called Ecgbert.'

At this the King's face grew even darker. 'Then you must learn to pray without ceasing for he will surely burn in hell for his many sins against Christ and his warriors if he is that Ecgbert. Is your father a warrior?'

The child answered with a fearful pride: 'Yes.'

And here you can see, father, the quickness of this King that he had asked at once a question which we had all neglected. But even if I had asked the question the answer would have been dark to me for I did not know the names of the Saxon chieftains apart from that Widukind whom all the world knows for his long rebellion against God.

Seeing the King's displeasure I was afraid for the child, and for the stone, but the Queen spoke soothingly to him. 'My Lord, here is one at least saved and who knows what work she will do among her people when she is grown, and under the teaching of Mother Tetta she will learn everything that is necessary. Therefore my Lord you must give her what she asks for making her house strong in the wilderness and beautiful in the eyes of God and the pagans.'

Then the King laughed and said he could refuse her nothing for she had the most eloquent tongue of all his advisers, and then he turned to me and said: 'Do not be afraid, Englishwoman, you shall have your stone.' And I hurried to take the child away before he could change his mind.

My dear father, the winter comes on us quickly now and they say it will be harsh, not as at home among our soft hills. Already the berries have gone from the bushes along with the leaves, and the birds are hard put to it to find a living. It is too cold for copying and so we make clothes and embroider for the cloth keeps our hands warm. Fortunately there is plenty of fish in the river and I have set in hand the building of a pond so that if too many are caught we can keep some fresh for when the weather is too bad. In the mornings the rime lies on grass and branches as if they are painted with silver and now the first storms are over that brought down the leaves, the sky is clear and blue and very cold. The pine trees stand out dark against it and it is easy to understand how superstitious people might see in them the spirit of winter and fall into idolatry, and I am reminded that it was the chopping down of that great idol, called the Irminsul, by the King that caused the greatest rebellion here and that our Boniface himself was forced to destroy a mighty tree called the Thunderer's Oak to prevent the people worshipping it. Therefore I make sure that minds as well as hands are kept busy. We read constantly and I have given dispensation for more speech when it is on matters of faith and doctrine, for in that way it is easier to avoid the sloth and melancholy which Master Alcuin says are the chief vices of our life and are both the children of anger. So I hope I have taken every thought to seal our house against wind and snow, and sickness of body and soul born of listlessness and ungodly sorrow, and that we shall sail out the storms under the hand of God as Noah did the flood.

Gundrada is a great cheer for us and I have allowed the keeping of a little cat which has many pretty ways, and it is a delight to see them together and helps to drive away the black elves. It is a lesson too for in the child we see, as Augustine says, the development of that rational human soul which is the part not shared with the animal nature which is irascible and concupiscible, and I foresee that in summer we shall have to put nets over the fishpond when the little cat is grown bigger.

My dearest father, I pray you are safe and well at home and that no sickness touches you in these winter months. I know that I may not hear from you until the spring breaks the ice and men can put to sea again but know that I pray. . . .

The photocopy finishes abruptly here and, underneath in the space before the bottom of the page someone, Helge, has written: 'This is the end. There is no more.' The words when she reaches them after two days of translation seem to Hetty as stuffed with opaque meanings as the utterings of the Delphic oracle or like a picture, an op-artefact, that can be read in two ways, black on white or white on black.

Yesterday she made her photocopy of a copy, even more grainy and smudged, and left it at the police station as instructed, with the envelope marked: 'For Inspector Maidstone.' Hetty doesn't believe this market town is his real name; as well be called Basildon or Basingstoke. She feels herself suddenly plunged into a world of shadows where the life of Mother Tetta has more reality than her own and so she steeps herself in that buried life, finding the passage from Latin to English comes more easily the more she does, yet at the same time forced to look at the text through Maidstone's eyes as a species of acrostic code she can't decipher. Her own signature on each page is as enigmatic as the rest.

The phone call from Helge had been cut off and not renewed. Afterwards Hetty had felt bereft and betrayed, by herself as well as Helge. She hadn't known she was going to burst out in an accusation like that, and she's shocked at her own reaction. There had been no time for explanations before the line went dead. Hetty had no number to call back, even if she had been inclined to do so.

She wants to tell someone about it all and last night when she got a little drunk she rang Sandy and then was unable to say anything as though to speak would be another kind of betrayal. Hetty finds herself practising the reticence of an unhappy marriage where the partners, either or both, present a harmonious public face so that people say after the divorce: 'We never even suspected.' Sandy would love the story, with its *Third Man* hint of underworlds where a zither plucks dark alleys and running footsteps out of a rainstreaked city but she would also imply 'I told you so', in her murmured sympathetic comments, so when she asks: 'How's everything?' Hetty merely answers: 'Fine, fine. How're you?'

Perhaps she was wrong to turn down Jack's offer of a return to unpaid work. The devil finds work for idle hands she hears her adopted mother say from childhood and although she doesn't believe in that devil, so beloved of her mother, the psychology makes sense. She's staring out of the French windows at the last strip of yellow light slashed across the hill thinking she hears a car on the road going away, or is it only the distant motorway slur, when the doorbell rings, making her jump and her heart races with fright as if she's just avoided running into the car in front.

It can only be bad news: Jack come out to hunt her down; Donkey Jacket; Inspector Maidstone. Her curtains aren't drawn yet so whoever it is can see in, see her against the light and she can't pretend she isn't there. Reluctantly she goes into the sitting room switching on the porch light before she opens the front door so that at least she will be on equal terms with the caller, and turns the catch.

It's Helge. 'Hetty you will forgive me? I couldn't endure you not to understand and the phone is. . . .'

Afterwards they can't say who moves first, who is iron and who magnet or if they both move, flow together as Hetty pulls her inside, closing the door, turning as Helge drops the travelling bag from her shoulder, and they are kissing. And it is that first kiss of Paolo and Francesca after which 'they read no more', or that last kiss that never was of Lancelot and Guinevere, kisses that change the course of lives and from which there is no going back until the kisses stop or become just flesh-on-flesh formalities.

'I'd better draw the curtains,' Hetty says as they finally break away because they've reached that moment when there's no breath left to kiss with any more. 'How did you find me?' And then: 'Do you think you were followed? Will they know you're here?'

'I took the taxi. You told me your station in London and also here you remember. But I also looked on the map of England, before I mean, to know where to think of you. I don't know if I was followed. I came to Paris and then across the ferry. It is easier than to fly. You don't have to book the ticket. It is still allowed to travel, at least inside the community.' She laughs.

Hetty feels a chill touch her but shrugs it away. 'You must be so tired and it's cold in here. I'll light the stove. No I'll get us a drink first. Sit down.'

'Please Hetty, can I use your bathroom?'

'I'm so sorry, of course. It's through there on the left.'

When Helge goes out with her bag Hetty kneels in front of the black stove, rakes the silvery ash through the bars and smooths it down in the pan with the poker, lays a firelighter in a nest of kindling, sets a match to it and closes the door to draw up the flames through the spitting wood. Now she goes in search of glasses, a bottle, a corkscrew so that by the time Helge comes back the fire is leaping behind its glass bars and casting fiery eyes into two glasses of red wine. Helge finds her way back to the sitting room. She comes over to Hetty, reaches up a finger to touch her cheek as she did before, outside Hetty's room and says, 'Kiss me.'

They kiss again, this time not straining against each other but long and slow, their bodies exchanging heat even through their clothes, heat that flows down from mouth to belly, to groin. They touch each other's faces and hair, exploring. Then Hetty takes Helge's hand and leads her to a chair, pushing her quietly down and offering her the glass. 'What about food? You must be hungry.'

'I don't feel hungry.'

'I'll make us something later, a sandwich. How long can you stay?'

'A day or two only. I have a lecture on Tuesday. Until then I can play truant, hookey is that right?'

'Another Americanism,' Hetty laughs. 'What do we do if the police turn up, if you have been followed?'

'Can they come in here and search?'

'Not without a warrant. They know I won't let them. I refused before.'

'I am so sorry, Hetty, to involve you in all this.'

'What does it mean?'

'What did they tell you?'

So Hetty repeats Inspector Maidstone's insinuations, half-truths.

'And what did you say?'

'What happened to the phone the other night?'

'I hung up. I was afraid of two things: that I couldn't explain properly through a machine, and that we might be listened to.'

'Tapped?'

'Yes. I think my phone is bugged; tapped you say? Hetty you must believe me. I am not a terrorist. I would never have come to you if there was any danger for you. You don't think it, do you?'

Hetty doesn't want to think, certainly not such thoughts, but there are unresolved shadows across her will to believe that for the moment she's anxious to ignore.

Helge is going on. 'I am political yes. There are things I wish to say and do, things I wish to prevent but I am not what the police say. I am not violent. You must believe I am not a violent person. You do believe that don't you Hetty?' and she punctuates her question by taking Hetty's hand and kissing it.

With her hand held and kissed what can Hetty do but believe what she so desperately wants to believe and she finds herself, without reflection, bending to kiss in return the hand in hers before she gets up to refill their glasses and put more logs in the stove. Later she makes them a plate of sandwiches; later still she says that Helge must be tired. 'Would you like the bathroom first?' Hetty asks.

Helge gets up and puts her arms around her. 'I can sleep with you please?'

Suddenly Hetty is afraid of her body's blemishes, of exposing them to someone else's eyes. 'I'm too old for you. I'm fifty-two.'

'I know. But that is only thirteen years between us. If you were a man you wouldn't even think about it.'

While Helge is in the bathroom Hetty undresses quickly and puts on her clean cotton pyjamas and some scent. Then she goes downstairs to wait for Helge's reappearance so that she can clean her teeth, as she tells herself, but also thereby ensuring that the decision on where to sleep will be Helge's. 'Did you find everything you wanted?'

'Yes thank you. I think I used your towel. I hope that was okay?'

'I'll give you a clean one tomorrow.'

Hetty shuts the bathroom with a shaking hand and begins to clean her teeth. There's a strange spongebag in black and tan stripes and a foreign toothbrush on the soapdish ledge of the washbasin. How much should she wash? How will she get upstairs and into that bed Jack never slept in, on these weak legs. She can't spin it out any longer. She has to leave the safety of the bathroom. She makes a last dab at her armpits with the deodorant, then she switches off the light and begins her impossible journey upstairs.

The lamp on Helge's side of the bed is switched out already. 'Have I taken your place?' she asks, her hair very dark against the pillows.

'No, no. That's fine.' Hetty folds back the bedclothes in a triangle, sits on the space and draws up her legs. The knot in her chest is threatening to choke her with apprehension. She switches off her lamp and snuggles herself down under the bedclothes. At first the room seems very dark, then she can make out the window and the looming bulk of the chimney breast. She feels

Helge move in the bed beside her, reaching for her hand, turning on her side towards her.

Helge's mouth finds her cheek, and her neck, and her throat, in the dark, and then her mouth. Hetty is aware of a hand unbuttoning her pyjamas and slipping under the jacket to touch her right breast, caress the nipple into erection while Helge's mouth moves down to tease the left one with a hot tongue. Hetty finds her whole body throbbing with a desire that lets itself out in little gasps until the hand moves down from her breast stroking her belly and inserts itself under the waistband of her pyjamas and finds its way down between her thighs, to the burning lips that it gently parts with a finger and slips between to stroke her into a pleasure so sharp she longs for it to stop and yet never to end, and then that finger slips down again and deep inside her. For a moment she's held on an apex of sensation, but only for a moment for with the next movement she finds herself falling, her body convulsed, her mouth opening in a long crying she can only faintly hear and has never heard before from all Jack's thrustings. She's aware too, distantly, of Helge's voice uttering the sweet banalities all lovers use and is charmed and comforted by them.

And now it's her turn to give back what she's been given. She's never touched another woman's body before and she's afraid of being clumsy but she's excited too. When she puts out a hand to Helge she finds softness and smoothness over a firm armature. She runs her hand down the silky back feeling each little lump of a vertebra, over the hip and on to the inside of the thigh. Helge's sharp intake of breath fills Hetty with a sense of pleasure and power. Always before she had waited to be taken. Now she knows the delight of dominance, of the mover, the cause. With her touch she makes Helge thrust against her, her body begging not to be left, not to be stranded until she has been completely washed over, drowned, sunk in an irresistible pleasuring that makes her cry out again and again in her turn. And now it's Hetty who holds and murmurs those words that soothe, against that post-coital *tristitia* that afflicts the human animal, as sensation ebbs and reason and angst resume their role. They fall asleep still entwined. Hetty, as she finds herself sliding away prays that she doesn't fart or snore because this is the first time she has shared a bed since she was taken from that mother she knew only from the inside.

Hetty wakes in the morning to anguish. The face on the next pillow looks so young. The cruel daylight will show up every wrinkle in her own skin. She doesn't want to see those, sometimes grey and sometimes amber eyes open on realisation, perhaps to disgust. She slides out of the bed, opens the door as quietly as she can and goes downstairs to the bathroom. She's very conscious of the slept-in smell of her own body. Hetty cleans her teeth and combs her hair refusing to think. She goes into the kitchen and puts the kettle on.

Five minutes later she re-enters the bedroom with a tray. Helge's eyes are open now. 'I missed you.'

'I went to make some tea.'

'English tea.'

'I always have tea in the morning.'

'You are angry with me?'

'Angry? No of course not.'

'Then you will come back to bed? I want you.'

Later that day when they are walking along the narrow verge left beside a field of heavy plough Helge says: 'I don't know how to go away tomorrow. I don't know how to leave you.'

Hetty can't answer. She's afraid of being left, of the doubting voice that will begin when she's alone. While Helge is there she has no questions. She lives very simply from minute to minute so intensely that even a cup in her hand is transformed, its blue stripes seem to pulsate, it becomes a chalice. She's aware of every nuance of Helge's body, the planes where light falls, the hollows, her gestures, each fleeting expression.

'England is so *made*,' Helge says. 'Every piece is grown on, walked over, cultivated. People here have been digging in it, building on it for so many years it feels like.'

In the afternoon Hetty drives them to Wimborne. 'I want to

show you where Tetta came from though I don't think there's anything left of her monastery. The Danes sacked it in 990 something or at least that's what they believe. After that it stopped being a double monastery under an abbess and eventually it became a college for secular canons under a dean. Men only. The whole idea of strong intelligent women in charge of houses seems to die out. Maybe because of the Danish invasions, so many places must have become unsafe especially for women.'

'In Germany they continue more I think. It was the Empire under Otto. There were still famous women, scholars and writers.'

'When we were taught the Middle Ages at school, the daily life of a monastery, that kind of thing, it was always men, as if women hadn't any part in it. Even the illustrations were always of men copying manuscripts, praying, working in the garden. Until recently I hardly knew women were involved at all. And I'm supposed to be a historian.' Hetty is remembering the black and white woodcut figures of robed male insects that crept and chirruped between the text, scratching out their own copy.

'We are all taught about Hrotsvitha who was a writer rediscovered by the German Humanists in the fifteenth century but they saw her as an example of Germanic culture only, another piece of propaganda. I can say that?'

They haven't spoken again of the reason for Helge's visit and now isn't the time because Hetty is picking her way through the little town's traffic looking for somewhere to stop. They find a car park high up on a small hill and follow a narrow lane between the high back fences of gardens down into the town itself.

'It's like Dickens,' Helge says, 'the little shops and houses.'

'There's the minster.'

'We must put our names together,' Helge says when she sees the visitors' entries. 'I shall write: *a beautiful day*.'

'There's nothing left of the old building,' Hetty reads from the guidebook. 'Only a piece of "coarse tessellated pavement" that might date back to Tetta's day.' There's a chained library full of 'old' books but nothing earlier than the seventeenth

—138—

century. Hetty can cull no residual sensation of that other life and she feels almost let down by the visit as if she had expected some revelation.

Outside the square is full of children dancing a ragged morris and stalls with a banner proclaiming a 'Craft Fayre'.

'Teatime I think.' Hetty leads the way into a shop, past a display of highly coloured cakes to the little tables at the back mostly populated by mothers with children or elderly couples. Do they know we're lovers, Hetty wonders? using the word to herself for the first time, but looking round she decides it's unlikely. They will see only two spinsters taking tea.

'What do you think of an English country town?'

'It is very peaceful.'

'Even with the cars?' Hetty laughs.

'It seems unchanging. These people are all. . . .'

'Respectable. Dull.'

'It gives you a strength. You don't march behind banners.'

'Is it strength or complacency? Anyway we riot. We always have.'

'I love you Hetty. I am fallen in love with you. You are strong.'

'No, no I'm not. All my life I've been weak, sheltered, taken the easy way out.' Even her affair with Jack had been conventional, adultery with a colleague. 'What shall we do this evening?'

'You are bored? You want something to do?'

But Hetty isn't bored, only afraid of boring. 'No, I mean what would *you* like to do.'

'I would like just to be with you. Can we do that?'

On the way back they stop in Sarnford to look at the cathedral and the library. 'I must show you the library. That's where it all began.'

Helge wants a music shop. 'I want to buy you a present, some music you can play for me.' She brings Hetty a compact disc of Monteverdi *Vespers*. 'Look this is just right.'

'But I can't play it,' Hetty moans. 'I can only play cassettes and records.'

'Then I will find something else,' and the gods who are kind to lovers provide her with a tape of the *Madrigals of Love and War*. 'Just what we have heard, with the Tancredi and Clorinda.'

Their evening foreshadows next day's severance. When they make love that night it's hard and fierce as if they would tear down their separateness and become one flesh.

'I'll drive you to London,' Hetty has said.

'It's too long for you.'

'I can't just put you on a train here. It gives us another two hours together.'

'I'll let you out at the station, at Victoria. I don't think there's anywhere to stop.' And anyway, she thinks, I couldn't bear the desolation of goodbye on a station platform underlain with all the grief of all the lovers who've ever stood there.

The drive back alone is on automatic pilot.

'I will telephone you as soon as I get back to Saarbrucken, from a call box. That will be safer.'

That has been their only reference since their first night, and now it's too late for all the questions Hetty should have asked and that begin in her head as she leaves London behind on the monotony of the motorway. The cottage is small and empty beyond the front door. She goes upstairs to her bedroom where she left the bed deliberately unmade and buries her face in sheets and pillow to try and catch Helge's scent. Under her own pillow something crackles. There's an envelope with, hastily scrawled across it: 'I love you.'

Suppose Helge doesn't ring what will she do? How can she pass the time until night when she can reasonably expect a call? Hetty gets out her bicycle and goes down to the village shop, seeing nothing of the lanes she passes through or the sky beyond the leafless scratchings of branches. As she smiles and gossips with Mrs Plaswell she feels as if the muscles of her face have stiffened, are palsied and have to be worked by a conscious will. However the trip has passed a little time and once she's wasted more in putting away her purchases and making tea she's able to switch on the television for the six o'clock news. There's no report of ferry fires or train crashes but only the usual roll call of sporadic tribal violence from every corner of a world, caught in the web of wires and beams we've slung around the globe that trembles to every wingbeat, every trapped spasm.

As she watches Hetty is beaten down by images of violence and despair that seem to her more unnatural, more monstrous than ever in the afterlight of the last two days. No wonder religions have always tried to explain life in terms of the conflict between light and darkness however personified, she thinks, as the screen fills again with stumbling figures, gunfire, gas clouds and the dislocated shape in centreframe lying so still. How can life survive the running sore of death, she wonders.

It's late when the phone rings. 'I am safe home. I miss you already too much. I will telephone tomorrow from the university. Do you miss me *liebling*?'

Lovers are saying these things to each other all over the world, Hetty thinks. There's nothing new to be said. 'I love you. I miss you.'

After, she sits by the fire drinking wine, playing Helge's music and replaying last night, unable to think of a future that might not contain Helge yet unable to visualise one with her. Still, she does fall asleep alone in her double bed and wakes knowing she's dreamt but not what carried her away.

Inspector Maidstone and his sidekick Colin arrive just as she finishes making a fair copy of her last piece of translation.

'Ah Miss Dearden, good morning. Might we have a word. We understand you've had a visitor.'

What can she do but let them in to fill up her sitting room. 'We understood you had no plans to see Dr Ebbesen in the near future.' The notebook is consulted. 'That's what you told us only four days ago.'

'That's right. I had no plans to see Dr Ebbesen. She came unexpectedly to see me.'

'And what did you discuss?'

Hetty flounders. 'Tell the truth and shame the devil,' her adopted mother had always said and Hetty has always kept close

—141—

to what she feels is the truth and this has made her congenitally incapable of a deliberate lie.

'We talked about music and the position of women in the Middle Ages.'

'Politics?'

'Very briefly. She admired the English for their peacefulness. I pointed out that we're inclined to riot.'

At this point the telephone rings. Hetty dreading that it will of course be Helge murmurs: 'Excuse me,' and goes into the kitchen to answer it while they sit on impassively, able to absorb every word. She almost drops the receiver in her nervousness but it's Jack.

'Hetty?'

'I can't talk to you now, I've got someone here.'

'What have you been up to? The fuzz have been to see Bob asking questions about your political views.'

'Ring me later.' She puts back the receiver, longing to be able to stop it ringing again but not able simply to leave it off the hook because of the telltale, bossy, recorded voice that will spill out of it admonishing her to: 'Please replace the handset and try again.'

When she returns to her sitting room Maidstone has her translation in his hand. 'We've sent your piece of Latin away to the experts. But perhaps they'd do better with this. Or did Dr Ebbesen bring you some new instruction?'

'It isn't an instruction. It's a piece of research and she didn't bring me anything. I told her about your insinuations and she came to reassure me.'

'And did she?'

'How do you mean?'

'Reassure you. Tell you everything was alright, not to worry.'

'We didn't actually discuss it.'

'But you said, Miss Dearden, that was why she came.'

'It all seemed too absurd. I couldn't bring myself. . . .'

'You must forgive us if that seems a little too hard to credit. Perhaps if we told you a little more about Dr Ebbesen's activities it would help. For instance where she went when she was here before.'

'She went to the Museum of Labour. She was trying to organise a joint exhibition.'

'Leaving aside the possible political colour of that organisation itself for the moment, or some of those attached to it, while it's true her ostensible business took her there, it also provided a convenient cloak for her meeting a group of people in that area, with, it's believed, the intention of setting up an active political cell.'

'What do you mean by *political*?' Hetty asks, hearing Helge say in her head: 'Yes, I am political.'

'I don't think it should be necessary to spell that out to an intelligent woman, a professor of history.'

'If you mean communist why don't you say so? In any case it isn't illegal for someone to be a member of the Communist Party in this country.'

'Ah things are much more complicated these days Miss Dearden. You read the papers I'm sure. We all know that old style communism is discredited in Europe. But leopards do change their spots, into stripes if they want to merge into a new background. We're anxious that nothing should disrupt the new state of affairs, no regrouping under a different banner. That old network of underground agents hasn't just blown away. Those people have gone somewhere. They won't give up so easily. It's a way of life, an ideal, almost a religion with some of them. You say it's not illegal to be a communist in this country and that's true but it doesn't mean society can afford not to keep an eye on anyone who steps out of the norm whether politically or sexually.'

Even though Hetty has been expecting this, bracing herself for it, she feels herself blush with anger and embarrassment as if a Peeping Tom has shown his face at her bathroom window.

'We should like to feel we have your co-operation, Miss Dearden. If Dr Ebbesen is above board, as you might say, she has nothing to worry about. On the other hand perhaps she's got herself into something she can't handle, got carried away or come under the influence of unscrupulous people, and there are a lot of those about. All the upheavals over there are bound to have stirred up the mud and let all sorts of things come up to the surface. We'd like you to tell us if you come across anything that worries you.'

I'm being given the soft soap now, Hetty thinks, but it only fills her with contempt which she immediately realises she must conceal. Maidstone is succeeding, where life has so far failed, in making her crafty, devious, a liar.

'What do you want me to do?'

'Well, just keep an eye open. And perhaps you could let us have a copy of this,' he picks up her translation again. 'Our chaps might see something in it you haven't.'

'But those are my words, my interpretation. Someone else might have a quite different rendering. Translation isn't an exact science like mathematics. There could be several different versions, one for every reader.'

'Still, we'd like a copy, even if just to see what you made of it.'

'I'll drop one in tomorrow.'

'If you'd just mark the pages for me as you did before.'

Colin gets up to take the sheets from Maidstone and hand them to her to sign, forcing her into a meaningless ritual, making her an accessory to absurdity. Anything though, she thinks, to get them out of the cottage.

Jack rings again as soon as they've gone and while she's still shaky. 'What was all that about?'

'The police were here.'

'I told you they've been to see Bob. Wanted to know about your political views. He said as far as he knew you weren't particularly interested in politics but that in any case it was none of his business to enquire into his staff's voting habits. Then they asked him about . . . well shall we say "your private life".'

Hetty feels a surge of nausea that threatens to choke her.

'I felt a bit nervous when he mentioned that, as you can

—144—

imagine, but they wanted to know whether you were interested in women.'

Hetty hears his extravagant laughter emptying into her ear.

'Bob said, "Rather the contrary though I haven't myself been fortunate enough to be the subject of Miss Dearden's affections." He said he was absolutely livid. What's it all about, Het?'

She knows she has to answer. 'Oh it's all to do with someone I met at that conference. They seem to think she's a spy or a terrorist. Something like that.'

'Is she?'

'Oh I shouldn't think so. Historians aren't likely secret agents, at least I can't think of any former colleague I could imagine in that rôle, can you?'

Jack's laugh is uncertain. 'It's funny, Het, you've changed. You seem quite different.'

'Yes, I think I have. I feel much better for it too.'

Yet when he's gone she chafes even more at the impossibility of telephoning Helge, at having to wait passively for a call which in any case she now believes might be tapped at her end. Hetty goes out into the garden which has always in the past had the power to restore her sense of balance. The grass hasn't stopped growing because my world has gone mad, she tells herself. Soon, tomorrow, I'll have to mow again. The anticipated smell of shorn clippings, the rhythm of up and back, striping the lawn soothes her. When she was younger she had despised gardening as anti-intellectual, suburban. Now she sees it as part of the struggle to recycle rather than spend, each shrub and plant as a stitch in the fragile living tapestry thrown over the earth to cover barrenness of rock and desert, and suck the poisons out of the airy tissue of clouded ether. This may be my last mowing of the year.

Beyond the hedge she can hear a concerted twittering from where a telephone line sags under the small black wedges of massed house martins, that fling their spearheads up into the thermals, looping, falling, catching themselves up in an intricate invisible cat's cradle before dropping down again to their gathering point. I could fly away too! There's nothing to keep me here, Hetty reassures herself.

She turns back into the house suddenly dreading the winter to come. Last year the village was cut off for two days when the snow fell, and she welcomed it, the sugary drifts climbing each window pane shutting her inside her paperweight, the sharp bird prints bitten into the flocked white mat that covered the garden and lay against the door. If Helge were here they could shut themselves away from the world, except that Maidstone would come and leave his bootmarks blackly along the path.

When the phone finally rings and it's Helge, Hetty says: 'The police have been here again. They know about your visit. I suspect that my phone is bugged too now; at least I think we should assume so.'

'It's not easy for me to speak what I want because of the switchboard,' Helge says.

'Perhaps we should return to the good old-fashioned letter.'

'Let's do that,' she hears Helge say and finds herself smiling at this suddenly perfect idiom.

'Lots of love. Sleep well.'

'You also, Hetty.'

Can letters be intercepted and read, she wonders after they have broken off. If so, how are they to speak to each other, exchange those crumbs of words and signs without which love starves and dies? Perhaps they can work out some scheme. She could use Sandy's address and Helge would have to find some disguise at her end. Suddenly Hetty finds the whole thing absurd and laughs out loud in her low-ceilinged kitchen with its pine table and blue-ringed china. All this cloak and dagger! Yet she feels a surge of energy and determination. She remembers the scented sweat that filmed their bodies and the musky, seasalt tang from Helge, on her hands and lips, that she didn't want to wash away.

She imagines herself telling Jack, watching his face dissolve as he tries to decide whether to feel scornful or rejected. No, in fairness to him, he would understand better than most. He'd always had an eye for a handsome male student though she'd never been sure how far he might have gone in the curious age of innocence before her fall into bitter knowledge and death. She will ring Sandy and set up what she remembers from Greene, Le Carré and Deighton is called a 'postbox' or a 'dump'. Then she will write to Helge.

Sandy shows no surprise. She's intrigued and, natural iconoclast, pleased to be a means of bucking 'the establishment'. Writing to Helge is harder. Hetty has no experience with love letters. She never wrote to Jack, seeing him almost every day, and knowing that letters are time bombs folded away in wallet or pocket. It takes her half an hour to begin. Dear, Dearest Helge; Darling or even *Liebling*: all have something to be said against them. In the end she opts for caution. 'No names, no pack drill', as her adopted father used to say, meaning, she supposed, that without identification no-one could be punished. 'My darling' she wants to write but *is* Helge hers? It's too soon and there are too many questions. 'Darling', then she begins, the word unsullied for Hetty since no-one had ever used it to her and she had murmured it to Jack only once or twice in her head, trying it out for sound and size. But after she's detailed the second visit of Inspector Maidstone and Constable Colin her pen falters. To ask questions seems untrusting yet they hang around in the cottage bumping against the ceiling. She and Helge haven't enough shared life to be able to fill the page with minutiae, the sketches in the margins that illuminate the day to day, the common coin of daily commerce. Hetty is driven back on: 'Write soon: I miss you; take care.' She feels her letter might be scratched on cardboard or even stone it seems so stiff and unyielding.

She gets out her Philips' school atlas in its faded blue cover inked with messages to the girl sitting next to her as she went up the school. 'Who were you with last night?' 'First smeller, first stinker.' 'Stew and semolina. It's Tuesday,' ineradicable traces of her childhood like the doodlings on the winter chill and Father Columban's temper that survive, interlining gospels and holy lives, treatises on earth and heaven.

The map of Europe shows the old Cold War frontier and for the first time Hetty realises that Tetta's house must have been just over that vanished border. Perhaps now the Wall's down she'll be able to go there with Helge though like Wimborne there're probably no traces left of Tetta's presence, especially if she never got the promised stone for her rebuilding. Now Helge is back in Saarbrucken, Hetty's finger travels the map to find that too. Helge had said it wasn't pretty: industrial, spoiled, laid waste, the continental equivalent of 'dark satanic mills'. A strong red artery runs out to it from Paris which makes it seem closer. Suddenly Hetty is bone-tired. There's nothing more she can make happen tonight. Tomorrow she can post her letter, start enquiries about routes and times. She reopens the envelope inside the one addressed to Sandy. 'I could come to you,' she adds and then almost regrets this admission of need but seals it again quickly before she can tear up the whole thing.

The morning is ghost-grey. Is anywhere other than our damp island so reductive of the spirit in winter? She decides to take the car into Sarnford to ask about travel to Saarbrucken. Helge came so *she* must be able to go. And in Sarnford she has the benefit of the library to make the required photocopy of her translation, and a big central post office with all its anonymity.

Hetty opens her door on the first frost. Her brick path is sprinkled with deceptive icing sugar, each pink oblong outlined with frail crystalline daggers heliographing back the sun. She sets out down the path with the letter in her pocket to where she's left the car at the end of her lane. As she approaches her eye picks up something it can't identify, a strange shape that seems to be sticking out of the petrol tank. She's within a few feet of it now and still her mind refuses to interpret the image it's being offered.

For a moment she pauses and stands quite still focusing on the object. A catface snarls at her, the lips drawn back in a grin of pain and fear, a hideous puppet rearing out of her uncapped petrol tank that makes her catch her breath with shock. It's an ordinary black and white cat. She's seen several asleep on village walls and through windows. She goes a step or two closer, afraid to reach out and touch it, of its spittled rictus and its pied coat, staring in death like the fox's. Her hand reaches forward to see what keeps it seeming to squat, legs adangle over the mouth of the petrol tank, and finds it's impaled on a thick bamboo cane, the sort she uses to prop up too heavy flowers. With a cold nausea she draws the stick from the tank trying not to touch the dead fur and turns back to the house holding the rigid body in front of her like a grotesque talisman.

Hetty carries the murdered creature round the side of the cottage into the garden, collecting a fork as she goes, hoping that last night's frost won't have hardened the ground too much, heading again for the soft loam beneath the chestnut. She must be careful where she digs so as not to disturb the fox. She lays the rigid figure on the grass, digs out an oblong of leaf mould, spoons it in and covers it as quickly as she can. Then she begins to tremble and feel sick.

The fox had dragged itself to her door to die, she's sure of that. This new manifestation is quite different. She wants to mourn for the animal so viciously sacrificed but she can't because the meaning of this hideous symbol thrusts its way into her consciousness and fills her with dread and disgust.

Ding, dong, bell
Pussy's in the well.

Hetty's thoughts rhyme. Someone is trying to frighten her and who else can it be but Maidstone? Suppose she goes to him and complains? He'll deny all knowledge, any involvement and she'll merely look like a silly woman, victim of a cruel joke, the work of some teenage vandal. No, she can't complain; try to challenge him, then. But she needs to tell someone and suddenly Hetty's afraid of her own isolation. Even Sandy will find this hard to believe. Jack would simply think she was ill again, hallucinating. Neither would see the metaphor of poor pussy impaled, run through so brutally. The one person of course who would understand she can't reach. Unless she quite simply packs a bag and leaves.

Yet she's afraid to do as Helge did, to arrive unannounced, afraid of what she might find. Helge spoke of her apartment but she never said specifically that she lived alone, only that she was alone, meaning free to love, now. Perhaps the real reason Hetty isn't allowed to telephone is that someone else might answer. The thought is too painful with its train of suspicion and betrayal and she pushes it down. She will stick to her original plan: post her letter, make her enquiries, wait for an answer. Hetty thrusts the fork hard into the ground and goes back to the lane and her waiting car, retrieves the plastic Marks & Spencer bag she had been carrying from where she dropped it on the shingle, and unlocks the driver's door. Then she remembers the open mouth to the petrol tank and casts around to see whether her night-time visitor has thoughtfully placed the cap where it can be easily found but there's no sign of it.

Was the dead cat their only act? Mightn't they have put sugar or something in her petrol tank? But the car starts after the second turn of the ignition key and Hetty eases out into the road. As she looks right and left her eye registers a car drawn up on the verge a little way down the hill and a figure in it behind an open newspaper. The broad double spread tells her it isn't one of the tabloids. As she passes the village duckpond she glances in her mirror and sees that what she thinks is the same car has fallen in behind and is shadowing her. At least that's what Hetty decides even while part of her mind finds such an idea absurd.

How far will they go? Disinformation, dirty tricks: such phrases only partly understood, from some news broadcast, concerned documentary or half-read article in a newspaper, come into her mind. Would they go so far as to injure her physically? This is England; I have rights; it's a democracy, she tells herself, and then she remembers other snatches of information hardly digested because surely they could never apply to Hetty Dearden:

spinster, lecturer, fond of gardening and member of nothing more sinister than her professional union whose meetings she never attended, and the public library.

The other car is a long way behind on the motorway so perhaps she was wrong. Hetty drives to the central car park, snaking round and round until she can find a place to slot herself into. Leaving the car she feels exposed, naked. She crosses the footbridge over the canal where a few mallard are unfurling their webs against the cold stream, past the brick-clad bulk of Sainsbury's great warehouse. One of their trolleys has found its way, pushed by children or revellers or the wind, into the water and lies on its side, algae and weed beginning to colonise this alien construct. Hetty wonders why no-one has taken it out, cleaned it, put it back into service. She passes through the little shopping mall where she sees with shock the gaudy forerunners of Christmas are already on display. Christmas! She hasn't thought about that.

Now she's in a main street where there are more cars than pedestrians heading for the centre of the city, to be suddenly plunged among crowds in a market-filled square. It's a Breughel morning she decides, when everyone looks vicious and stupid if not merely lumpish and dull. The faces that pass her seem to have come from an earlier age of unenlightenment, and their clothes are either too tight or sag cheaply. She's been so sheltered she hears herself telling Helge. These are ordinary people. I shouldn't feel like this. The *jeunesse* at St Julian's weren't exactly *dorée* but they were silver compared to the lead and plastic moving from market stall to stall filling their rubbed bags with cheap vegetables, seconds of dull cheese, and tinned fruit past its sell-by date. The thick features are anxious and shrewish as they peer at the price tags. No-one laughs or jokes.

Why haven't I noticed this before? Hetty wonders. Is it the cat, a kind of unlucky charm that's bound up my eyes or opened them? She can't decide which. We look poor, mean-spirited, narrow. I suppose when I've walked through here in the past my eyes were turned in. I was thinking about Jack or work.

Perhaps it's always like this in winter, feeling the pinch, and I've never noticed. Perhaps everyone comes alive in summer and puts on colourful clothes and laughs. But she can't believe it. The shop windows with endlessly duplicated artefacts in alloy and viscose, and the international uniform of young clothing in its cheapest version, give no indication that it might be so. Compared to the modish city blacks she'd seen when staying with Sandy, the English descendants of Alfred and Harold seem worn and faded, without pride. They all walk as if their feet hurt, Hetty thinks, deliberately springing her steps. Even the younger people she passes trudge without grace and rhythm, the faces closed; some coarse, some sullen or angry. A girl mother shakes her toddler angrily, a rag doll held by one hand as she tries to manoeuvre a battered pushchair with the other. Hetty couldn't tell its gender but it seems to be crying for everyone when it puts up a meagre wail.

Hetty remembers her adopted parents as neat and dull, respectable. Shut in her quasi-academic hothouse dedicated to attempting to encourage the exotic, she had supposed that other people had gone on changing as she and the students had. The village people she had managed to slot into a rural timelessness when she had moved into the cottage, as inheritors of *Lark Rise*, even Mr Powers himself. There was Donkey Jacket of course but he was quite different, possibly a little mad, certainly not like the people she sees passing her. Even the children are turned into anonymous bundles by their clothes. We're clothed and fed, Hetty thinks, but we haven't much spark. She remembers a couplet from Arthur Hugh Clough's *Decalogue*, that had appealed to her because of its irreverence when she was at school doing A levels.

> Thou shalt not kill; but needst not strive
> Officiously to keep alive. . . .

Her eyes have opened like Miranda's in *The Tempest* but she sees no brave new world full of luminous and handsome people.

I shouldn't feel like this, she tells herself again. These are perfectly decent ordinary people. And yet it's my fault. I haven't really noticed what's gone on in the rest of the world. I've been too absorbed in my bit of it, and I haven't even the usual justification that I've been caught up in creating life, in my children's lives or even my family.

She remembers the relief she felt when her adopted mother had finally died in the geriatric ward of the local hospital and she no longer had to make that painful and depressing fortnightly visit, down the long prefabricated corridor smelling of urine into the ward where thirty wrecks had been beached in various stages of dissolution and from which only one or two escaped alive. She should have seen from that, she realised now, from those frail humps and tenuous intelligences and their anxious visitors, how the world was going. Some of the voices round the beds were too loud with the heartiness of desperation, others cajoled or exhorted. All must have been depressed by the lack of that privacy and dignity they couldn't afford to buy.

Hetty thinks of the efforts of the staff to provide a semblance of Christmas: the troupe of local entertainers, polystyrene beakers of sweet sherry, the attempts to start a sing-song from the repertoire of the music hall and shows of the 1930s. Her mother hadn't joined in. She had liked the carols in the evening better she had said, when Hetty came the next day, and she had never touched alcohol in her life. The thin hair had been washed and brushed and there were balloons tied to the curtain runners round every bed.

If her mother had simply died, in the garden or one night in her bed asleep at home, Hetty would have been shocked, would have felt her own mortality but her mother's dissolution in company with thirty others filled Hetty with horror at how little of her own life was left and how she had wasted so much of it already. And yet until now she had known no way out of the desert she had wandered into, the desolate yet gilded landscape she daily picked her way across.

She's in danger of forgetting the copy of the translation she must make if Maidstone isn't to have an excuse for another visit. She'll go to the library now and perhaps a print shop where they'll do it all for her and she can buy a large envelope to put it in. The back of the shop is full of elegant grey shiny machines tended by dark young men in very white shirts and cloth trousers. This is the scriptorium, Hetty thinks as she waits for her pages. Perhaps they're all brothers and live a monastic life in a tall house presided over by their mother. This time she will post the document to Maidstone, not deliver it in person. She feels since this morning that to go up those steps under the blue lamp is somehow to put herself further in his power. The constable or sergeant, she couldn't tell which, on duty at the desk last time had looked at her strangely and called her 'love'.

'I'll see he gets it, love. Don't you worry.'

The familiarity of it had had the effect of aggression, of a putting-down that left her feeling humiliated, diminished. She didn't want the experience again. 'Stuck-up bitch coming in here like Lady Muck. Old enough to be my mother. Whatever she's been up to she ought to know better.' Hetty can hear the dialogue behind the swinging door where calls and interrogation rooms and records must lie out of public sight, until you're taken through, no longer a member of that public presumed innocent but a suspect presumed guilty. She dreads the moment she fears will come when Maidstone will ask her to 'accompany' him to some place no longer her own ground where she'll find it harder to be brave and resist.

So she addresses the envelope to him in the main Post Office, grandiose as a Town Hall, and puts her name as sender on the back, and posts it, along with her letter to Sandy with the one for Helge inside, and finds a certain ironic satisfaction in the two letters jostling each other through the mouth of the postbox. Now she can make her way back across the market to Thomas Cook's and enquire about ways and means. She comes out of the brightly lit shop with its enticing technicolour posters and brochures offering new worlds, new lives, comforted by how easy it is to cross the world or at least that sleeve of water between herself and Helge. When she'd gone to Frankfurt it had all been arranged for her. Now the girl behind the desk smiles and assures her she could be there tomorrow or even later today, a free traveller. It seems like a charm, as if love does it rather than the travel agent. 'When you've decided just give me a ring and ask for Jane.'

No further excuse to loiter in Sarnford presents itself and Hetty is forced to return home, stopping off in the village at the pub for a sandwich and half of bitter.

A log fire is falling into glowing ash in the grate. Outside the windows the day is sinking towards dusk. In here it's warm and safe. What will she find when she goes home? It's too soon for a letter from Helge. Somehow she has to pass the time until she can go to bed. She would have stayed in Sarnford and gone to a film but for having then to come home in the dark.

'We're paying out the Christmas club tonight. You weren't in this year were you?'

'No I wasn't.' The Christmas club and darts team give the pub a semblance of community to put against the passing trade of the restaurant. The pub will be full tonight, the wives coming too to make sure the savings reach home safely. It signals the start of the winter solstice, that attempt to drive away the dark and cold and bring round the Spring again to our island raft, afloat on the bitter North Sea. Hetty wishes she had an excuse for being part of the evening's jollification but her uneasy position on the fringe of village life, half-in, half-out, would make her presence uncomfortable to everyone. If she had been a part, had come regularly every Friday to pay in her small savings she would have had somewhere to go to, been welcomed, known more people. She drags herself away from the spurious comfort of the log fire, oak beams, chintz curtains, and drives the last couple of minutes, so short it seems, back to the cottage with its unlit windows, cheered by the goat lady, her neighbour's television murmur and the light coming through her curtains. Tomorrow she will ask if she can buy tangy milk and cheese.

The house seems still and inviolate. She stands inside the front door for a moment trying to sense whether anyone has been there. She can feel nothing either good or bad and goes through to the kitchen to make tea. Then she riddles the ash into the pan, lays a firelighter and sticks, and begins to conjure life back into the house. Hetty drinks her tea drowsily beside the fire and soothed by its warmth falls asleep in the chair. When she starts awake it's pitch dark outside. The little dusk is quite gone. Soon she can watch the news and pick out an evening programme or two.

She gets herself a glass of wine and switches on the television. The last minutes of the current soap from the land of perpetual sunshine and tanned smooth skin are unfurling to the fake crisis that will keep the audience cliff-hanging until tomorrow, the electronic equivalent of mediaeval romance and Victorian novel, the pursuit of others' lives to deflect us from our own, as necessary to the human mind as sleep and dreaming. Once upon a time. . . .

The idealised blonde nymphette utters her final question; the theme music unrolls the credits. Hetty puts another log on the fire and clangs the iron door shut. Letters, symbols, the world, humankind fly apart and reassemble in front of her and give way to the news announcers and their careful tones. An African politician is in intensive care after an assassination attempt; commuters protesting at a shortage of trains home have stormed the station master's office, early morning fog is expected to cause further disruption tomorrow; the Secretary of State for the Environment has refused permission for the conversion of former Ministry of Defence property to an industrial estate and designated it an area of scientific interest; West German police and protesters both suffered casualties when two demonstrations clashed in Hamburg today.

Hamburg? Surely that's a long way from Saarbrucken and Helge can't be involved. Yet Hetty has a sense of foreboding as she waits through the other news items as each is fleshed out in its turn. 'Pitched battles broke out in the streets of Hamburg today as West German police struggled to separate the two groups when thousands of demonstrators collided in the area near the Rathaus, the Town Hall. Many were pushed into the canal and police used tear gas and water cannon to break up the fighting. Here is our correspondent Hugh Markband live from Hamburg.' The announcer vanishes and in her place is a fair-haired young man, a microphone slung round his neck against a background of lit night streets with a smudgily distant crowd and the universal symptoms of public disorder: burnt-out cars, smashed windows and pavements, litter and debris.

'The trouble began when a counter march against a demonstration by the neo-Fascist party refused to follow a route designed to keep the groups apart and police were forced to take action to separate the two groups and restore order.'

A series of familiar images replace him on Hetty's screen: of fleeing, scuffling civilians; helmeted and visored police wielding truncheons; figures on the ground; bodies still struggling dragged by arms and legs and hair; the hiss of tear gas; an arm flung up to hurl a reply; people being helped away with their faces muffled; a stretcher hurried jerkily past; blurred shapes; a sudden face in clear focus, dazed, Helge's face, glimpsed only for a subliminal second and then gone so that Hetty isn't sure that it wasn't a trick of her own imagination.

When had it all happened? The sky had been dark behind the reporter but lighter in the film sequences as if the events had taken place earlier in the day. She can watch the next news in less than an hour to try to find out the time and whether the still face of Helge appears again. If it was earlier, Helge might have returned home, might risk the telephone or Hetty might ask the international operator for Helge's number or, and now she's working her way through the international section of the telephone dialling code book, she could send a telegram. But perhaps she was wrong and it wasn't Helge at all but someone who looked like her and whose face Hetty had translated into the one she wants to see.

She must be sure before doing anything. It's the local news now. Hetty watches impatiently with the sound turned down.

Then she changes channels in time for the absurdity of pre-news commercials with their comforting solutions to everyone's daily problems of feeding and filth, the bland assurances that there's nothing that can't be put right by spending money, against which the newscaster's gravity will suggest that most of the world's ills are insoluble.

This time the piece from Hamburg is longer and comes second after the assassination attempt. Hetty finds herself leaning forward in her chair peering into the corners of the picture as it flicks past, and there it is again, that face, taken by a different camera, the angle more oblique, seen an instant and then gone, leaving her less sure than ever.

If she tries to telephone and she herself is being bugged her whole conversation will either be frustrated or overheard. Hetty suddenly understands that some people live their daily lives like this for years and years, and for a moment is almost angry with Helge for breaking her quietude, as the bearer of bad news could once be killed for it or the victim of rape be seen as its provoker.

She can't keep going round and round on this black carousel. She must do something to break what's becoming a circle of hell. She dials the international operator. By the time the receiver is delivering its steady foreign bleep so unnervingly unlike the British couplets, her hands are shaking, she's ready to be sick and wishing she'd stayed passively waiting for whatever.

'Hallo? Bitte?' It isn't Helge's voice.

'Could I please speak to Dr Ebbesen?'

'She isn't here right now. Can I take a message?'

'No thank you. It doesn't matter.' Hetty puts back the receiver quickly, trembling, knowing she's said too much and too little.

It's late when the telephone rings bringing Helge's voice. 'It was you rang me, Hetty?'

'Yes, I'm sorry. I was worried. I thought I saw something. . . .'

'It was on British television; I see. I didn't think they would report it.'

'It was you?'

'Yes.'

'Are you alright?'

'A few bruises and stitches, that is all.'

'Oh God!'

'Don't worry.'

'They'll be listening.'

'Then they will understand that you know nothing, that you are not involved.'

'The person who answered was American.'

'Yes, Christine is American. Hetty darling, I have written to you but we must talk about many things. There was no time in England. Can you come here?'

'Where?'

'To Hamburg? Where I am now.'

'Yes, yes I can. When?' She's ashamed of the pleading in her own voice. 'Are you sure you want me to?'

'I am very sure. I want you.'

'I don't know what that means. No don't say. Not now. When shall I come? How shall I find you?' She's forgotten the listeners, the tape that will be played back in some other room full of men, exposing her need.

'I'll telephone you tomorrow. Bring your Latin dictionary. I have something for you.'

... and our time was made to pass more quickly by the glazier whom the Queen sent us and who reached us before the snows. Because he worked with a furnace he was able to continue throughout the bitter months and it became a favourite pastime to visit him on some pretext or other and the novices among the monks vied with each other for the privilege of assisting him and learning his craft. The child Gundrada too showed great interest in his workings especially in the many colours of the glass which he made while the men were kept busy chopping wood for his use. I myself visited him on every possible occasion to follow his progress and to discuss the designs for the windows of the chapel. I encouraged the other sisters to visit his workshop too. For the transmutation of common sand, of which our river banks yielded a good quality as he said, mixed with soda and lime, by fire into clear and coloured glass, is a kind of parable of this life, both our life on earth where we must be continually refined by fire and of the spiritual life in such a house away from the world.

Gundrada liked best to watch him put together the bundles of different coloured glass rods, fuse a section of them in a crucible and tease it out thin into a flower or a glowing red cross on a blue ground but it seemed to me a clearer lesson to watch the bubble of glass blown up out of nothing, drawn out by the tongs to a cylinder and then the scored cylinders opening out as he heated them again into clear flat sheets, without blemish, for the light to shine through. We celebrated the feast of the Epiphany with all the windows in place in the chapel and he is now working on the main hall. The Queen sent us magnificent gifts for the feast: two ivory book covers for a psalter showing King David playing upon his harp, and that greatest of Holy Fathers, Gregory, who first sent Augustine to our Saxon race, and a crystal goblet delicately engraved which we use on special occasions.

And now my father, I have found my stone or rather Aelfwin has found it for me on his way back from carrying my last letter to Cologne. Night coming upon him suddenly he lost his way and was forced to take shelter in some ruin. In the morning light he could see that there were several stone buildings much overgrown with trees and grass and the roofs all fallen in. He believes that it was built by the Romans for the blocks are finely cut after their fashion and that it was once a fortress protecting the approaches to the city from the Germans and that therefore the stone belongs to no-one so that when it is possible for heavy carts to travel again I can begin to transport it here, and if anyone disputes it I have the King's authorisation.

My father, this letter was set aside for many days by the strange events that have happened here, two days after the first load of stone arrived. We had resumed our work in the scriptorium and I was showing Gundrada how to order a page with a complete design in the English style as I learned it myself, which she already begins to show skill at, having great patience in such things for one so young and a liking for the colours and shapes, when there was a loud noise outside of shouting so that I thought the house must be on fire or under attack. Two young men burst into the scriptorium with drawn swords and by their dress Saxons. Gundrada let out a cry and clung to my habit.

I spoke to them in Frankish. 'Who are you? What do you want? Put away your swords. We are all people of peace here.'

The foremost of them answered, indicating Gundrada: 'I have come for my sister.'

Then I asked the child if this was her brother and she nodded to show it was so. 'Her father, and yours, entrusted her to me.'

'Our father is dead, killed fighting Charles, King of the Franks.' At this Gundrada cried out again and began to weep.

'Why do you wish to take her away when her father gave her to us and to God?'

'I am head of the family now. I say she must return to her own people and gods.'

'Do you have the intention to find a husband for her when she is old enough?'

'No-one will marry her. She will live in my house and help my wife, and earn her bread.'

'She is not strong enough for such work. Here there are many tasks she can do which are suitable for her weakness of body. She would be useless to you and one more to feed.'

'She should be with her own people.'

'Here we are all God's people whether we come from Saxony, or England or the Island of the Scots or the lands of the Franks.

In Christ there is neither Angle, nor Saxon, nor Frank or Scot but only his children. Let us ask the child what she wishes.'

So I took her by the shoulders and turned her to look at her brother for she was still hiding her face in my skirts. 'Will you accept her choice freely given?'

'If you will, and there is no witchcraft.'

'You may ask her yourself.' And I stepped back from her so that she stood between us.

'Gundrada, come home to your people and leave these foreign ways and their gods.'

'I cannot come for I have given my word to God and His Holy Mother Mary and Mother Tetta. I have no mother at home.'

'My wife will be your mother.'

'She cannot teach me to write and draw and sing to God in Latin.'

'Better the songs of the Saxons, of our heroes, of your father Ecgbert.'

'My father gave me to the Christian God to pray for his soul until I die, and if I do that then God will hear me and I shall see my father again.'

'Your father has gone to the halls of the heroes where he feasts among the gods.'

'But our mother is not there. She is a shade, a fylgia who haunts the forest and comes to me in dreams. Her too I pray for. I will not return to be the slave of heathen gods.'

Then her brother could see that his arguments were in vain and I feared he would take her by force.

'Let her stay for now,' I said. 'She is young and her mind is set on it. You know where she is. That she is safe.'

He hesitated. Then he said: 'I will not take her now. They said that you were a witch and I feel the power of your sorcery. But she shall come back to us.' And he turned and with his follower strode out, both with their swords drawn before them so that I heard some of the sisters shriek with fear as they passed along the cloister.

'I will not leave you,' Gundrada said. 'He only wants me as a servant to his wife.'

I tried to reassure her but we both knew that he would return. 'Let us go to the chapel and pray to God and His Mother to hold us in Their hands.'

The rest of the day passed quietly, as quietly as may be that is with the noise of building, of masons and carpenters at work on stone and wood. We sang Vespers in our little wooden chapel and remembered those in our Book of Life, especially Lioba and Boniface and all the English, and I thought that since the windows were put in it is as if the richness of the glass has entered our singing, and who knows how much finer again it will sound when all is in stone and the windows removed to their new places as I have designed.

We said Compline and returned to sleep until Vigil, I to my own chamber for I confess I find it hard to sleep at all where some snore and some cry out, and I think it right too that the sisters should sometimes be without my presence and learn to love in their hearts without my guidance. After Vigil we returned to our rest until Matins and I rose as usual when I heard the bell, for even alone I sleep very lightly, and was leaving my chamber when a group of novices ran up to me, which as you know is forbidden, crying out that Gundrada was missing. I calmed them at once by saying that first we would do our service to God and then I would enquire, and led them into the chapel. By the time Matins was over and I had composed my thoughts, dawn was breaking and I went with the sisters to the novices' dormitory where Gundrada had slept and found her pallet, which was just inside the door, with the blanket folded at the foot, not in disarray, and I concluded that she had risen of her own accord and gone out.

I followed the way I believed she must have taken towards the river, looking about all the while for some sign. At the end of the path from our house I found horse droppings as if a band of men had stood there waiting with their horses but I did not know whether to turn up or downstream until suddenly it was as if an eye winked at me, a point of fire in the way, catching the light of the rising sun and I ran to it and knelt down and saw it was a fragment of glass, and I remembered that Gundrada had a little bag of these fragments which the glazier had given her to play with and that she would arrange in different shapes in imitation of my designs for the windows. I remembered too that only last week I had told her the story from the pagan writers of Duke Theseus and how he found his way to return through the maze after he had killed the Minotaur, that offspring of unnatural lust, by unwinding and winding up the thread which Princess Ariadne had given him and that this was a paradigm of the Christian life, to follow that holy thread of the Scriptures and the Fathers which Christ has given us, which shall lead us through the darkness and twistings of this life safely back to Him.

I offered up silent thanks to God who had surely caused me to speak to her of these things, and determined that after we had broken fast I should try to follow and see if the child had indeed left more signs or if this piece had fallen by accident, for I reasoned that if she had left signs she wished us to follow them, and had not gone away of her own accord whatever the appearance.

When I made my intention known to Aelfwin he begged to be allowed to come with me, saying that you would never forgive him if he let me go into those places alone where the way might lead me. But I told him that God had spoken in my heart that I should trust only in Him and take no man with me and that I should go as Mary Magdalene went in search for her Lord with only the other women, and brought back the news that He was risen. Then Adela asked if she might go with me, as Joan the wife of Herod's steward went to the tomb with the Magdala, and thus it was decided.

So we put ourselves in God's hands and took food and water and two quiet horses and beginning at the river bank followed the path upstream until at a fork where there were two ways I was forced to get down and examine the ground to see if there was any indication of the way we should take, and found another piece of glass just along the right-hand way and we therefore took that. And so it was that we were led forward deeper into the forest and yet I thought I began to remember certain places and said to Adela: 'Was this not the way we came with Eanfled to the place where her father gave us the child?'

'Yes, Mother, I have thought as much for the last mile but could not be sure.'

We continued to follow the trail and at last came out at the clearing I recognised, with the cairn of stone that was like an altar, and on it lay a larger fragment of glass that glowed like a red coal. I took it up and put it in my bag so that no Christian workmanship should rest on a heathen shrine, and Adela and I ate and drank a little and refreshed ourselves. Now I believed that we must follow into that cleft in the rocks through which her father had disappeared and so it proved for Gundrada had left us another sign just inside its dark opening which was like the entrance to Hellmouth itself or that gloomy Dis which Virgil speaks of. We rode between high overhanging rocks until we came to the end and out into the light again where the path continued across a grassy plain towards some low hills covered in trees, with beyond more cliffs and rocks, a place as wild as any hermit could wish in which to praise God away from the temptations of the flesh, and I was reminded of the stories of how when the English first came here in your mother's time they sought out such places in particular, and God guided them to build there so that the wilderness would hear his name, and now they are great places of praise and learning as Fulda and Echternach and Fritzler.

However in spite of the wildness of those parts the path was quite clear as if trodden for many years by men and horses and so we went, north and east by the sun until I judged it was time for None and we dismounted to pray and then continued, with the hills now beginning to rise up around us and press in to end this part of our journey. The ground on either side of the path had become very marshy and in some places logs had been placed on the path to carry it over mudholes, and the grass had given way to reeds and bogworts. Just when it seemed that the way must end at the mountains it entered another cleft and came out into a natural bowl in the hills, at the far side of which there was a settlement, surrounded by a fence of massive tree-trunks above which we could just see the thatched roofs of several buildings. Upon the path to show us this was the right place lay a piece of blue glass, which my eye picked out at once being accustomed now to do so.

As we neared the village or camp we began to hear voices, the neighing of horses and hammering as of metal. The fence was pierced by a high gateway large enough to ride through in which as we approached a man's figure suddenly appeared and disappeared, to be followed a few minutes later by running men with short swords in their hands who surrounded us, caught hold of our reins and led our horses forward. Inside the fence people had gathered to watch as we were brought in. Then we were forced to dismount and pushed towards a square building that was bigger than the rest and made to enter. It was full of smoke from a great fire in the centre, where meat was roasting turned by miserable wretches on big spits, so that at first we were choked and blinded after the sweet air and light outside.

When my eyes grew accustomed to the smoke and gloom I saw that the hall was richly furnished after the barbarian custom with furs and silver and purple cloth from Byzantium as wall hangings and at the far end a dais, covered with the same, on which was a painted and jewelled chair where Gundrada's brother sat with two great hounds at his feet. I thought that he was very young to govern these people and that his youth made him impulsive and therefore dangerous, for he must seem to be strong when he was still but a boy. Beside him stood a cradle. Fastened to a bench by an iron collar and chain was Gundrada who tried to rise when she saw me but the chain was too short.

Behind us a great crowd of people had pressed in so that we were driven forward until we reached the dais.

'Gundrada,' I said to the child, 'why did you run away?'

'They said they would burn the house and every one in it if I did not go with them.'

Then I spoke to her brother. 'You have broken your word. You said you would respect your sister's wishes and let her stay.'

'I have not broken my word. I vowed only that I would not take her then. She belongs here.'

'Nevertheless God has sent me to fetch her back to Him. She was made His by baptism and no longer belongs to you.'

'Your God has no power here.'

'God is everywhere and His power is over all. He is here now. Even your child wears his symbol.' For I had spotted that the baby had a thong about its throat and on it hung, in metal, enamelled and bejewelled, the sign of the Cross, that emblem by which the Emperor Constantine conquered and which is also the name of Our Lord in Greek. (My dear father I can hear your eager question but be patient.)

'How can that be? While he lived and wore it, it protected my father from harm in battle. It was he gave it to the child.'

'Nevertheless it is the sign of Our Lord.'

'Of Charles, King of the Franks?'

'It is his sign too. But it belongs to a greater Lord Who is above him, Whose Kingdom is not of this world.'

'The Emperor of Byzantium is greater than the King of the Franks.'

'This Lord Who is our God is above them both. It is He Whose sign hangs about your child's neck. No doubt your father stole it from some Christian.'

'You lie witchwoman and I will kill you for calling my father a thief. It was left about his neck by his mother when she fled from our people and her husband and child.'

(Then I grew sick and faint for I perceived what must be and why the Lord had led me here that all should be made plain and yet I hardly know how to write it to you.)

'She too was a witch and her curse falls upon the women of our family and that is why my father gave the charm to my daughter in the hope that it would protect her. And then the

—167—

witch his mother sought him out in battle and took him away with her in death. And she would have taken my wife in childbirth but I held her hands and would not let her go.'

'If you will let Gundrada return with me, her power over you and yours will be broken for we shall pray unceasingly for your safety.'

'Why should you pray for us and why should your god listen to you when the gods of our people could not protect my sister from the curse of the witchwoman, our father's mother?'

'Your father's mother belonged to our God but she betrayed Him and that is the reason for the curse. But if you give Gundrada to Him in the place of that one He lost then He will turn His anger from you.'

'How do you know that, except by sorcery?'

'I know it by the Cross about your child's neck which was given to your father's mother by my father, and her brother, on the day before she set sail with her mother for the lands of the Franks. She was a child then but when she was a grown woman she was taken by the Saxons and never seen again. I have come to find her.'

'How do I know if your story is true and not a trick? The Christian god and his people are full of deceit. If she was your father's sister she abandoned her husband and child as my father has told me, taking her god with her, to be eaten by wolf or bear or murdered by strangers. Her husband searched the forests for her but in vain. How can you prove your story?'

'Her name among her own people was Berthgyth. You and Gundrada and I are kin. My God has sent me to lead you back to Him.'

'I will not follow this god who causes a mother to leave her child and has made my sister a cripple. Besides if I should become a Christian my people would fall under the yoke of the King of the Franks. Therefore I will stay with the gods of my father's father.'

'But let me have Gundrada and we will pray together to lift the curse.'

He thought for a moment. 'If your god can unchain her she can go with you.'

Then I approached Gundrada and looked at the halter lock. 'Do not be afraid,' I said to her, 'you shall not be hurt.' And I prayed in my heart that God would guide my hand as I felt among the keys of the abbey hanging at my belt, and as I touched a certain one I felt as though my fingers tingled. I held up the key saying: 'This is the key to heaven,' and plunged it into the lock where it turned as easily as if it had been made for it, the cruel collar fell from Gundrada's neck and she stood as upright as she could.

All the Saxons cried out in amazement. 'Go,' said her brother to her, 'but if any harm comes to me or mine I shall come again and find you, and this time although you are my sister you shall die.'

So I took the child by the hand and led her out of the hall followed by Adela, and the people fell back before us on both sides to let us through as the sea parted for the Israelites. We reached our horses and Adela took the child up behind her and we rode away. My limbs were trembling but my heart overflowed with praise of God and His care of us. By nightfall we had recrossed the plain and reached the cleft in the rocks and the clearing beyond where we rested until dawn, which luckily comes early at this time of year and so in the morning we retraced our steps and reached the house in time for Vespers where we went straight to the chapel to thank God, and truly I could say with Our Lord's Mother that He had regarded the lowliness of his handmaiden and had put down the mighty under our feet.

And now my dearest father I do not know what to think or do. It is clear that your sister has broken her vows to God but we do not know whether by force or willingly, nor what has become of her. It seems to me that remorse must have caused her to run away from the heathen but to what fate? If God preserved her life the first time she was taken it must be that He had some purpose for her. Perhaps that purpose is to be fulfilled through the child Gundrada if she lives. But must we consider Berthgyth utterly lost to you and to God? We must pray unceasingly, of course, for her that her soul be not irrevocably lost wherever her body might be, and that if she is dead to this world that she had the opportunity to beg God's forgiveness, which we are assured through Our Lord and Saviour will never be refused to those who truly ask in His Name.

All this must be bitter to you my father to have so nearly found and now so darkly lost at one and the same time. The next day after we returned home Gundrada came to seek me out and asked me to explain all that had passed with her brother and the meaning of it all. Then I told her how her mother's mother had been the head of this house and your sister, and had been stolen away and made to break her vows of chastity and poverty and give herself in heathen marriage and bear a son, Gundrada's father, and that then she had fled from the heathen and had never been seen again.

'That signifies,' said the child, 'that we are kin as you said. I have a home now.'

'And when I have gone to be with God you shall govern here in my place in our house, if God wills and if you make yourself acceptable to Him and the other sisters through learning and devotion.'

She took my hand and said: 'You are truly my mother now and I will study hard to please you. But you must not go away for a long while yet and then perhaps we shall go together.'

But though I said to her, because of her youth, that Berthgyth had given herself in heathen marriage, this cannot be true, for there can be no true marriage between a heathen and one of Christ's virgins and therefore I should better have said concubine but I would not, lest it should put perverse thoughts into the child's mind and make her question what her youth cannot understand.

Thus my father we have lost one of our family and gained two by blood. One is lost to Christ as yet, though he is young and may return in time if he is not killed. The summer campaigns against the Saxons will resume shortly and he will take his father's place, but how shall he succeed where experience failed and he is pitted against God and the King? So I fear for his life and soul and the more that I saw in him some lineaments of your dear face that made me long for him to be brought to Christ. Therefore we pray unceasingly and you must do likewise.

Dearest father, the Queen is sick and has sent for me and I must go to her, taking what I can of my leechcraft. She has not yet given the King a child but he loves her dearly as indeed do all who know her. I know that she longs for the quiet life of contemplation withdrawn from the world, and yet she loves the King too and he is sad when she is separated from him. I must try all my skill for body and mind, for fretfulness is the enemy of health. If she should die I shall lose a dear friend and protector, and kings are apt to forget their promises when the occasion of them is gone.

And now I long so much to see you my father and put my arms about your neck and kiss you. Do not forget your Tetta who is often lonely in a strange land and at the mercy of strange events in which I try always to see the hand of the Lord but sometimes fail, and am weary at all that must still be done here before I can hope to make the journey home to visit you. I know that through your infirmities you cannot come to me and yet my longing to see you is so strong that I sometimes feel as if my heart will burst, and I echo those words of your sister Berthgyth to you of long ago which she culled from Solomon's Song of Songs: Love is stronger than death, and my soul like hers is weary of life languishing for you. I pray especially to Blessed Cuthberga the founder of our abbey at Wimborne that I may see your face again, and shall celebrate her feast at the end of August if I am spared. You do likewise my dear father Baltheard, and perhaps our prayers will be answered.

I shall take Gundrada with me to court that she may find favour and a protector there for if anything should happen to me I am afraid for her. Perhaps I shall ask the Lady Gisela to take her under her protection so that the abbey of Chelles will receive her if God shall see fit to take me, or perhaps she should return to you and comfort your old age.

As for Berthgyth herself, unless the hand of God guide me I can do no more, for surely search was made for her by those who knew that country well and that was many years ago, so that by now time and the seasons must have covered up every trace of her going.

Hetty is in Helge's borrowed airy flat above a wide tree-lined avenue. Limes, she thinks they are: I am on Linden Lea; I am *Uber den Linden*. She's a little light-headed and breathless still from her flight. Helge met her at the airport and although they hugged, Hetty was suddenly swamped by doubt. Who is this stranger whose arms are around me?

She feels nothing but desolation, a deep sense of loss and reassertion of their divided selves. Yet once they're alone together she hears the ice crack around her heart, a metaphor she recalls from she can't remember what childhood story, senses a sudden rush as of meltwater, and turns to Helge, hoping she hasn't seen that moment of separateness, the loss of faith, tormented that Helge might have felt the same and hidden it too.

Once more Hetty's in danger of forgetting the questions she's come to ask. On the aeroplane she'd resolved that she isn't going to make the same mistake once more, of permitting herself to be what used to be called knowingly 'a bit on the side'. That was all she'd been for Jack, all she could ever be. This time she's going to be firm. Better nothing than that humiliation again, she tells Helge in her head while picking at the plastic food pack and darkening the moisturised wipe (provided so that all the passengers may smell hygienically alike) with the grubby stains of newsprint.

Now that monologue has faltered and dried as their selves enmesh through touch and smell, the chemistry of loving that fuses them hotly into a changed substance until they have to draw apart again. 'Tonight we can go to a little place to eat where the students go. You will like it, I know.'

Being driven back from the airport in Helge's Volkswagen Hetty had looked out at the city searching for traces of war damage, of fire, storm and blast, but there were none. It was, to her eye, completely whole, with a glossy patina and a combination of sleek and comfortable passers-by that made London in memory alternately raffish and dowdy, pranced through by the occasional gilded peacock. If the indigent exist here they are out of sight, not walking the cleanly pavements, and there are none of the traditional burghers in stone-coloured macs and tweed pork pies, like the English pillars of the Women's Institute that Hetty sometimes spots near the cathedral on their way to run a coffee morning or furbish a plant stall.

Light comes in filtered through the branches outside to wash over the houseplants within. There's a handsome Persian rug and old furniture though Hetty's eye is out for deciding its true age. But these aren't Helge's things, an expression of her that Hetty might caress with a finger for greater understanding. They are just lent to us, she explains.

The bruises to her arms and the grazed cheek, the barbed-wire stitches under the short shiny hair, Hetty can touch. 'I don't understand. You have to explain to me.'

'No, better, I will show you. Tomorrow.'

'And Christine?' She hasn't wanted to say the name but there's no way round it.

Helge takes her hand. 'I will tell you that, yes. We were lovers. Not now. We have lived together for two years. She too works at the University, teaching American studies.'

Hetty has already understood all this in her own mind but

hearing it put into words makes her fearful, angry and miserable so that she wants to lash out, to court her own destruction and yet to weep childishly. Instead she keeps her voice steady and doesn't pull her hand away. 'You say: "Not now"?'

'Not since I have met you.'

'Have you told her about me?'

'Yes. She knows everything.'

'Everything?'

'She knows I love you and that we are lovers.' The words stab her with a shaft of pleasure and desire.

'Is she angry?'

'Yes.'

'Angry with me?'

'No darling, with me.'

Whatever dies was not mixed equally; Hetty comforts herself with the half-remembered words that she had thought quite forgotten.

'There have been other people for both of us. It was not exclusive, you understand?'

'Yes.'

'You are sad?'

Hetty can't answer this and Helge after a moment goes on, 'You are sad, yes, because you are not like this.'

'It's not that I've got anything against it, I mean not in principle. I'm just not good at it. I seem to be temperamentally unsuited.' She tries to laugh at herself.

Helge laughs too. 'I know. I have felt this at once.'

'It isn't very exciting I'm afraid, but I can't help it.'

Later when they are together in a strange bed and have made love and the arm she has under Helge is going numb so that soon she will have to move her a little to take it away, and turn her back to sleep, Hetty sees the thin pillar of grey starlight holding the curtains a little apart and hears below in the street a car spurting away into the night and wonders at herself as she drifts towards sleep thinking: 'I'm taller than Helge. Does that matter?'

In the morning when she wakes Helge is still asleep with the clothes thrown back so that Hetty can prop herself on an elbow and contemplate the perfection of one breast, the dark fruit of the nipple surrounded by a dusky aureole tipping the pale olive silken swell, a pleasure she has never known before but that seems to her so unquestionably natural that it no longer even surprises her. Nevertheless, she makes a resolution as she watches the sleeping Helge that she must know more, must ask more, not wait passively to be shown whatever it is Helge wishes her to see. Like Psyche with the lamp trembling in her hand above the naked Cupid she has to know whether she has bedded with a monster or with love itself.

Yet in the end she doesn't have to ask. As they're sitting eating fresh bread and honey while Hetty at every indulgent bite thinks that she will get fat on lust and sweetness and then Helge won't want her, Helge says: 'I have been thinking that it is wrong and childlike of me to want to show you things without first telling you about them. You have the right to know everything not just to play at games. I wanted you to trust me but that is selfish and like a child with its mother and I do not want to think of you in that way at all.'

'Are you sure? It would be very understandable if you did.'

'And I, am I therefore your child?'

'Only a little,' Hetty laughs, hoping Helge will laugh too. And then she says, 'We all drag our past about with us. There's bound to be a psychological substratum that goes back to other experiences and to childhood in any relationship.'

'I don't want to be tied down by the past.'

'But you are a historian. You know the past, history, can't be suppressed. It has to be understood and then the present can be built in a more rational way. Or at least we can try.'

'You believe that Hetty? You believe it is possible to change people, lives, institutions?'

'Yes. Sometimes I feel I believe it against all the evidence and because I want to. But it's like the old doctrine of free will. We have to live as though we have freedom and choice even though we know there are genetic and cultural and historical determinants. Unless you believe in the possibility of change, of affecting events in your own life and others', you can't act. When I've felt there was nothing I could do, then I found I didn't even want to get up in the morning. I became inert, lifeless.'

'You don't feel this now?'

'I feel, I feel completely content.'

'That is different?'

'That is very different. I feel alive, and yet I don't care somehow if I die today.' Hetty is aware of an easy fullness in herself that she has only seen in the painted women of High Renaissance, the ripe goddesses naked on their couches, the toe of a kicked-off shoe protruding from underneath the washstand, the coverlet slipping from rich flesh that makes Hetty think of rose petals seething in a still for their scent. I feel like those Venuses, she understands suddenly, but she couldn't put it into words.

'Please don't die. Don't go so soon when we are just at the beginning. "I have thee by the hands and I will not let thee go",' Helge laughs, catching hold of Hetty. 'That is Byron, yes? He was a freedom fighter.'

'And a philanderer and a poseur. It depends on your point of view. When does a freedom fighter become a terrorist?' A spasm of fear makes Hetty's words seem harsh even to herself.

'Perhaps I cannot tell you.'

'Don't you have to?' Her doubt is increasing. 'No, of course you don't. You are free, perfectly free to do or say anything. I can't have any claim on you.'

'But I want you to have a claim, to make the claim, please Hetty.'

'What do you want?'

'I want to be with you, to share some life with you.'

'Shouldn't you share a life with someone more your own age?' Hetty has to ask.

'We have already discussed this, darling, and I have told you what I feel, what I think. You are not so much the older and I am not a child. We are happy together yes?'

'I am happy with you.'

'Then that is alright and I will try again to tell you.'

Hetty isn't sure now that she wants to hear. She wants simply to bathe in the warm scented bath that has been drawn for her, even if it turns out to be asses' milk. She doesn't want a fierce shower of reason, of hot and cold fact falling on her sensitive skin. She braces herself.

'It is true as that *Bulle* said that I was born in the East but my mother got out to the West when I was still a child, after my father died, just before it was completely closed off. My father had been a communist before the war and was sent to a concentration camp by the Nazis. He survived and he was finally freed by the Russians. But his health was gone and he couldn't endure the hard winters, the cold and the little food to eat. My mother worked as a teacher, here in Hamburg. She was in the union of teachers. I grew up with the economic miracle but until she died five years ago, my mother always said there were other things than cars and clothes and food, and that the people behind the Curtain couldn't all of them be bad and that there must be good in communism because my father had given his life for it. So I was forced to think and then there came the protests in sixty-eight when I was a student. Then everything went black and cold and here we were only concerned to live and make money and not die in a nuclear war. Now they say the West has won and communism is dead and it all begins again with swastikas and nationalism. There is a group of us throughout Europe in all countries who try to fight this.'

Hetty wonders what 'fight' means. Aloud she says: 'Isn't that a job for politicians and the police?'

'You don't know these people, Hetty, these new fascists. Sometimes they are the politicians and the police. In Germany, France, Italy and now in Poland and Hungary and in time in Russia, all over you open the box and all these things fly out. Anti-Semitism, discrimination against *der Zigeuner* and anyone with a dark skin.'

'And you are Hope,' Hetty laughs.

'Only I will not tremble in a dark corner and be shut up,' Helge says fiercely. 'You make a joke of it, Hetty. The British always make a joke but it is serious. You laugh as if I am a child playing a game.'

'I'm sorry. It's true: we do try to turn everything into a joke. It's our way of managing. Alright then, I admit there are a lot of unpleasant and worrying things surfacing. But what can ordinary people do in a democracy except speak out, use their vote. . . ?'

'It isn't enough, darling. Hitler was democratically elected by using this nationalism. They must not gain power these people or they will deceive and frighten.'

'But what can they do in a democracy as long as people don't give them power?'

'They don't wait. They organise. They buy arms and train people to fight under the disguise of hunting clubs. They distribute their propaganda. They obtain lists of those to be contacted and those to be killed. They have contacts in every country.'

We are having our first quarrel, Hetty thinks sadly. 'You know, that's a classic statement of conspiracy theory. You would have to prove it to convince me, and you can't.'

'I will introduce you to some others. Then you will see that this is not my invention. We have a group that finds out where the fascists will march and then we go there so that people can see that theirs is not the only idea and then, as you saw, the *Polizei* beat us up and accuse us of making trouble.'

'But that's freedom of expression, legitimate protest. There's nothing wrong in that.'

'You see, we agree really darling. Oh I am so happy we agree.'

And Hetty, whose determination is undermined by that soft word 'darling' that makes her stomach turn over every time with its sheer banal novelty in her ears, can't find it in herself to fight any longer but accepts the truce eagerly and agrees on lunch at the café they didn't reach last night through their simple inability to leave each other alone for long enough to get dressed and go out into the world.

There are several people sitting at the table that Helge leads her towards. The café is quite dark, the small windows fitted with opaque amber glass and the room itself heavily timbered like a hunting lodge. At first she can't make out faces in this light but when her eyes are accustomed Hetty sees that with one exception the people sitting there of both sexes are younger than Helge, indeed perhaps still students. The exception is a thin tense man in his forties wearing a natural tonsure of tanned scalp ringed by wiry brown hair that's just too unkempt down the back of the neck for Hetty's taste. She feels she knows the type: in some ways an extension of Jack, academic iconoclast playing to the gallery of students, and realises instinctively that he'll despise her because she's older.

'This is Lutz,' Helge introduces him. 'Hetty.' He nods and says what Hetty takes to be a surname she can't catch as Helge continues round the table with first names Hetty feels flying away out of the door as she tries to catch them: 'Uwe, Horst, Inge. . . .'

She can see they're wondering why she's here and feels old and weary. The conversation goes forward in German as she tries to keep in place a mask of alert interest to cover her boredom and deepening irritation, only reduced by the excellent coffee when it comes. 'I'm sorry about all that we are saying. We are making plans for a trip tonight and you must come too, to see. I will explain everything later. We can go after lunch. The drive will be interesting for you to see the country.'

'Where are we going?' Hetty asks as they set off through the clean and prosperous suburbs and then are out on the autobahn with the green signs offering 'Hanover', and trees with flickering yellowed leaves flowing away on either side.

'We're going into what used to be the GDR.'

'Don't I need a visa or something?'

'No, no, of course not. There are no more borders and any way who will know.'

Hetty sees that Helge is caught up with the excitement of the speed and the adventure, and has forgotten the ubiquity of

—179—

Maidstone and his international counterparts. How could they know? Hetty tries to comfort herself, but the words don't convince.

'It's a pity we don't have the time for you to see it,' Helge says as the sign for Hanover peels away to the right. 'It is the most British city because of your royal family and very beautiful. There is a big lake in front of the Neue Rathaus which is in the style we call sugar-cake, with swans and gardens.'

Hetty has forgotten for the moment her own period of the Enlightenment when the Elector was King of England. From the signs she knows they're going south. The houses have steep, tiled terra cotta roofs like those in fairy tales and stand among orchards that are hung with coloured fruits like Christmas decorations. They stop for coffee and cake at a roadside café, and then on again with the signs now showing Kassel and the country beginning to be less ordered. 'Here we turn towards the old border and we shall go through the Harz Mountains.'

I am there, Hetty thinks, where Tetta was. I am in her country.

'There, ahead was the old border.'

On either side of the road is a row of iron stumps that might have been part of a fence and a kind of block-house, deserted, boarded up and padlocked where once guards lounged and smoked and waited. Beyond a line in the tarmac, the road worsens sharply, narrowing its pitted surface to a country lane and, backdrop to the flat fields, the hills move steadily closer. 'I'm not sure but I think we must be getting near to where the letters were written from.'

'The letters?'

'The letters Tetta sent home to England: the ones you keep finding for me.'

'Where we are going is Erfurt which is very old.'

'That's it: Erfurt! There was a big double monastery there. I'm sure that's the place she mentions.'

'You will find it very different from what you have imagined. Don't be disappointed. But over there is beautiful. That's the Thuringenwald.'

'Thuringia where Berthgyth and her mother were sent by Boniface.' Past and present are knitting up again around Hetty in glinting gossamer skeins. She stares out of the car window at dusty weary fields as if looking for human figures to come across the cropped grass through a thousand years.

'Bonifatius, yes. But that is not an English name.'

'His name was Wynfyrth really: *Joyful Peace* in Anglo-Saxon. The Pope called him Bonifatius when he sent him on his mission to do good.'

On the horizon a pall of pewter smoke hangs in the air above three tall chimneys, spewing funereal Prince of Wales plumes into the sky. They begin to pass cars and people and push-bikes all leaning hard against a slight gradient. Streets close in on them, blotting out the landscape. The people they overtake are shabbier than Hetty has seen before, the women's heads scarfed against a light grey drizzle that has darkened the road. Lamps are coming on and there are lights in the shop windows as they drive on towards the town centre.

'Where are we going?'

'We will meet the others in a pub. Then we will go to the square in front of the Rathaus where the meeting will be. It is best if I go then with the others and you stay back where it is safe.'

'Why can't I stay with you?'

'Because, darling, you are not experienced in these things. You won't know when to run away, and you mustn't get arrested,' Helge laughs.

'How shall we meet each other again?'

'I shall give you the second key to the car and you can come back to it whenever you wish. We can park here I think. Now you must notice the way we go.'

Fortunately the rain is stopping as they leave the car, but it's dark now, and Hetty has a job to make out and try to memorise the street names. Helge dives into a Bier Keller called simply 'George' and Hetty follows. The others are there already with glasses of beer in front of them, and Lutz is speaking to them earnestly. Hetty doesn't think he's pleased to see her, from his brief nod and the spate of German that follows to Helge who flushes a little.

'Will you have some beer?' she asks.

'Yes, please. But let me pay. Maybe the others would like some too.'

Several of them accept, including Lutz, and Hetty passes her purse to Helge. When the beer comes everyone says 'Prosit!' Hetty feels the atmosphere relax a little. For the first time Lutz addresses her directly.

'Do you live in London?'

'No, in the country.'

'Where do you meet Helge?'

'At a conference in, or rather near, Frankfurt. Are you a teacher?'

'I teach political theory.' He says something to the rest and the glasses are emptied.

'Are we going now?' Hetty asks.

'Yes,' Lutz answers her.

They set out into the night, Hetty and Helge at the back of the little group. 'Will you know to find the car?'

'I think so.'

'You will stay in the safe place whatever happens and if I can't join you come back to the car until I come to you.'

Hetty can see Helge is becoming anxious, perhaps regretting the whole idea. She doesn't want to be a burden so she puts out a hand to touch her arm and says: 'Don't worry. I'll be fine. Only don't you get arrested. Not today.'

They have reached a narrow square that is already half-full of people. 'It is best if you stay here. Then you have only to go back down that street.' Helge hands her the key.

'Be careful,' Hetty says as she takes it. Helge looks at her a moment before turning away to catch up with their group who have almost reached the fringe of the growing crowd.

What will she be able to see, Hetty wonders, and how much will she understand? There's a raised platform with a microphone and a banner for what looks to be a party calling themselves 'Republicans'. To a sound of military music a march begins to move into one side of the square from a side street. It presses towards the platform escorted by stewards in armbands and by police. Hetty looks around the square and sees that more uniformed police have quietly ringed it. The marchers aren't cheerful, singing or chanting the usual 'anti' slogans but stride unsmilingly with a mock-martial discipline. Then comes a group of skinheads in the local version of their international uniform of studded leather and work-boots, with shaven heads and tattoos like bruises on the pale young skin. They line up along the front of the platform in a black guard below the microphone.

Hetty feels the old, remembered excitement, the compound of fear and anger which can turn so easily, curdle into violence, and that she has seen once on the faces of fellow peace-marchers whipped up by a handful of activists for their own purposes. She had stood back that time as the main body surged on, feeling the tug, the drag of the tide into anonymity, seeing Sandy's overbright eyes as she is swept past, back into Whitehall and hearing her cry out, 'I'm going round again; I'm going round again', and knowing as the flume washed past her feet that it could only end by shattering itself against the rocks and breakwaters of authority.

But then, she thinks, this is different! That had been a sudden almost spontaneous surge; this is orchestrated from off-stage, planned from the beginning. The speeches are starting; there's applause, shouting, raised arms. The speaker seems popular. Cameras flash and whir. One man in the crowd carries a cardboard eagle like a Roman standard. The black, red and yellow of the national colours flutter in ribbons or are formed into armbands and rosettes. Because she can't understand the speeches, Hetty's attention wanders. Where are the others? Now she finds them. They've worked their way forward and are bunched up together, silent when the rest of the crowd applaud and shout. There are men and women in roughly equal numbers and equally vociferous. Here and there Hetty picks out people not shouting, merely standing alert, observing like herself. Who are these observers? Plain-clothes police she suddenly understands, remembering Maidstone.

The first speaker is replaced by another, a tall spare man in a dark suit. He's the one the crowd have been waiting for. They fall very quiet, not shuffling or shouting but listening with an almost measurable intensity as he begins without histrionics in a clear carrying voice. The faces become intent, absorbed. Hetty wishes she could understand what's being said. The voice from the platform grows louder and faster. People in the crowd begin to punctuate his words with cries that are more like the non-verbal vocalisings of other-than-human animals. It's as if they have put on grotesque masks obscuring their humanity and begun to howl and roar through wolfish mouthpieces.

Suddenly above the growing clamour she hears a sound of singing, chorale-like, not a tune she quite recognises. It rises thinly from the front where Helge and the rest are now. Almost she thinks she can hear Helge's voice. Hetty cranes on tiptoe trying to see what's happening up there. She goes a few steps back, almost into the mouth of an alleyway in order to get a better view over the intervening heads. The singing and the clamour are louder, each struggling to overcome the other. There's a scream. She catches her breath sharply. The skinhead line has closed around the group of singers, submerging it. There are shouts and more screams. The speaker continues, reaching his climax as the crowd roars, drowning out the noises from the scuffle in the front. Hetty sees the police pushing their way forward through the massed bodies. She can't see Helge any more or what's happening there. The speaker has turned and left the platform. A police wagon that's come into the square unnoticed begins its two-tone wail. Struggling forms are being hustled towards it. Hetty knows Helge must be among them. The crowd is dispersing quickly. Hetty flattens herself against a wall as the people surge away.

What should she do? The square is almost empty apart

from a few stewards dismantling the loudspeaker system and the banners and posters. She doesn't know where Helge and the others might have been taken and she's unwilling to ask the people around her even if she could. She must find her way back to the car and wait as they've arranged. As long as Helge wasn't hurt she might be let go; charged, perhaps cautioned but freed. Hetty has no real choice. She looks about at the dark square. It's beginning to rain again. Can she pick out the street they came in by? She turns into the one she thinks she remembers.

It's as if the town has been swept clean of people by a neutron blast, dissolving flesh and bone and leaving only inanimate bricks and mortar, concrete and steel and glass. The rain gleams tarrily from road and pavement. Irrelevantly, Hetty decides it's an effect of the high pollution levels in these parts as she almost stumbles along, dazed, unable to remember properly that route she had tried to memorise. If this is the right street, there was a turning here. No it's further along than she thought. Is that the place where they had sat drinking their beer? Its diamond windows let out the same yellowish light only it isn't called The George but Hetty peers anxiously through the small distorting panes, looking for reassurance. Three men are drinking in an alcove. One of them is Lutz.

Her first instinct is to push open the door in relief. Then she hesitates. Neither of the other men is from the group. One is in leathers and boots; the second is in the mufti of the young men she had thought plain-clothes police: jeans and a light grey anorak. Hetty shrinks back from the window, afraid now of being seen. She must have taken the wrong turning out of the square. She must go back and begin again and not think about what she's seen and its meaning until she's safe in the car.

Back in the square she looks again at the street names, finds one she thinks she remembers and sets off once more into the rainy dark. This time the turning is in the right place. The George appears; she looks through its windows into emptiness and hurries on. Will the car still be there and Helge in it? But her heart lurches down on more emptiness. Her hands are shaking as she fits the key and sinks exhausted into the driving seat. She's aware now of being cold and wet. Tears run down the outside of the windscreen and her breath begins to curtain the windows with mist. Sometimes she dozes there in the darkness to wake with a start and see the hands of the clock have scarcely moved. But time does pass and it's when she's fallen into another cramped doze that there are running footsteps, the door is wrenched open and it's Helge.

'Darling I'm so sorry. I ran all the way.'

'What happened?'

'You saw?'

'Some of it. The beginning.'

'The *Polizei* picked us up and took us off. All except Lutz. He was too quick for them. They took statements from us and I thought they were going to lock us up but they let us go.'

'Where are the others?'

'They're looking for Lutz. He wasn't at the mini-bus. They wanted me to stay but I said I had to get back to you, that you would be anxious. Lutz is so clever. He usually manages to give them the . . . what is it?'

'The slip . . . give them the slip,' Hetty supplies, unable to voice her fears or even say what she's seen, in the face of such adulation.

'Let's go, shall we? You must be hungry and cold. And your coat's wet.'

'I lost my way coming back. I wasn't in a nice dry police van.' Hetty tries to joke as she moves across into the passenger seat. She wants the reassurance of Helge's lips and touch, the warmth of her, the living contact but she can't ask for them and she feels that separateness seeping between them like a chill rain. 'Do we have to go all the way back to Hamburg? You must be tired. Can't we find somewhere to stay?' Hetty hears her own querulous voice. She looks at the clock. It's only half past eight but it feels like midnight.

'Do you mean to stay here?'

'No, not here. I mean somewhere by ourselves, not too far but away from here.' As Helge had predicted, Hetty can't find any resonance of Tetta here, drowned out as the echoes are by Lutz's voice and the morbid music of the rally.

Helge thinks for a moment. 'I know somewhere. It's one hour and a half drive further perhaps but we shall find somewhere to stay. I have a number I shall telephone.'

Later when she returns in triumph from the telephone box, she explains: 'It's a summer resort so they have many empty rooms now, not like a city where everything is always booked up.'

Hetty can't see much beyond the windows but other cars and shapes of trees lining the road. Perhaps they can drive forever and she need never speak of what she's seen, safe in the car's warm pod. 'Are you alright? Not sleepy?' she asks Helge.

'No I am perfectly awake. Why don't you sleep? Trust me.'

Against her will Hetty finds her head lolling back. She knows Helge will look across at her, and is afraid of what she will see but she can't keep her own eyes open. When she wakes it's because her senses tell her they've left the straight road and are turning off.

'Are we nearly there?'

'If it was daylight you would see the hills covered in vineyards.' The car passes through an arch in high walls and on to cobbles. They drive through narrow unpavemented streets between old houses, past a church, a fountain and soon they are pulling up outside a small hotel.

'They say we must hurry if we want to eat here.'

'Well it won't take us long to unpack.' Hetty laughs with relief.

'This is such a good idea,' Helge says as they sit with large glasses of the local silvaner and menus that Helge explains are heavily weighted with game. 'In Hamburg, they would have been telephoning me. What is it called when someone is dead, the examination?'

'A post mortem.'

'Yes. Lutz would want a post mortem.'

'What's his name?'

'Lutz?'

'His second name?'

'Brehme.'

'Have you known him long?'

'Two years; I think it's as much as that.'

'Those people at the rally tonight, who were they?'

'They are a mix. Some are radical right-wing party; that is the legal ones. But with them are associated, as you saw, the ones in the kinds of uniform who are, we say, neo-fascists.'

'Do they do anything apart from talk and march about in a rather childish way?'

'They attack any building and any group that they say is anti-German. These are the ones who desecrate (that is the word?) Jewish memorials and beat foreign workers and gays. It will be worse if the economy doesn't improve because thousands have believed the Western dream and if they are disappointed they will look for someone to blame and it is always the same people. The minority of any kind. So we make the peaceful demonstration but if they attack us we fight back.'

'You don't think they might be using you, manipulating you for propaganda purposes?'

'How could they do that?'

'I'm not sure.'

'Let's eat and drink, darling, for tomorrow we die. Let's forget it all now. Isn't this a good wine?' Helge holds up her glass and Hetty is forced to agree, to chink glasses and look into Helge's eyes for reassurance, where reason drowns.

Later when they're undressing, each beside her bed as if in a dormitory, Hetty finds herself relieved that the beds are fastened down and can't be pushed together. She lies awake listening to Helge breathe and wondering what she should say in the morning. She wakes to find Helge naked beside her, pulling back a corner of the bedclothes to insinuate herself into the narrow bed and take Hetty in her arms.

It's as they're driving north again that she begins her tentative probe. 'You know I told you I got lost last night trying to get back to the car . . . ?'

'*Ja?*' Helge is concentrating on the crowding traffic.

'I came to what I thought was the place where we had our drinks, The George wasn't it?'

'Yes.'

'But it wasn't The George. It was another very like it and Lutz was in there.'

'Lutz?'

'Yes. At first I thought I'd go in and ask him to show me the way and then I didn't like to interrupt him because he was talking to two other people.'

'Perhaps he was having a drink to pass the time while the police might be looking for him.'

'Perhaps. I thought one of the people was a plain-clothes policeman I saw in the square.' Hetty is aware of fleshing out the truth a little. 'The other was a skinhead.'

'Skinhead?'

'The ones in leather and big boots with shaved heads.'

'I expect he was trying to get information.'

It's an explanation so simple Hetty doesn't know how to counter it, even though she also knows instinctively it isn't true. Where can she go now, except retreat into her own apprehension and anxiety.

It's Helge who gives her the next cue. 'Lutz said you would be jealous and try to break us up. He didn't want me to bring you.'

'Maybe he's the one who's jealous.'

'Yes that also because I don't sleep with him.'

Hetty feels a rush of bile into her throat. 'Does he want you to?'

'Oh yes. He says it is bonding.'

'Does he sleep with the others?'

'Yes, but only the girls.' Helge laughs. 'Are you jealous?'

'Of course. Wildly.'

'I am jealous of Jack.'

'But that was a long time ago, before you, us. In another country.'

'Yes but you loved him. That I am jealous for.'

'Anyway even if I am jealous of Lutz now you've told me, it doesn't mean I didn't see him with those two.'

If only I'd gone in, Hetty thinks, spoken to him, watched his face. If only I could speak the language. 'What will you do? Will you ask him about it?'

'No, because then he will be more angry with you.'

'But if he wasn't just trying to get information; if he was giving it . . . ?'

'That isn't possible. You don't understand what you are saying. That would be the end of everything. Is that what you want? You want me to give up, not to care, just to cultivate the garden?'

'Of course I want you to care. It's just that I'm not sure Lutz cares, that his motives are the same as yours, I mean the rest of you.'

'Darling you can't understand what it's like living here, what we have experienced. And now to see it all happening again. How can you understand safe in your island? These are my people. I can't see them throw away their freedom they only just have back and to bullies; yes, that is the word?'

'I'm afraid for you.'

'I've said it before: I am not a child, Hetty and some things I understand better than you.' Her face above the wheel is set hard and the speedometer finger moves steadily up. Hetty swallows her words, fearful of their effect as they roar northwards.

Eventually she asks: 'Aren't we going rather fast?'

'There is no speed limit on the autobahn and we have a long way to go.'

And Hetty thinks that she has no fear for herself of dying now, only of possible pain, or of Helge's dying, leaving her bereft forever but the mask of anger beside her won't let her lips speak again and the hand that wants to reach out and to rest on Helge's thigh stays still in her own lap.

The rest of the journey is done in almost complete silence. Only once Hetty dares to ask if Helge isn't tired and perhaps they should stop for some coffee or she should take over the driving. 'You're not used to these drivers. They would force you off the road. We shall be there by one o'clock.'

As the outskirts of Hamburg thicken around them, Hetty's misery increases. They go upstairs to the borrowed flat. 'Perhaps I should see if I can get on a flight,' Hetty says.

'If that's what you want. You could telephone the airport.'

Yes, they have a seat for her on the afternoon plane, she hears despairingly. She isn't to be reprieved by the kind hands of fate and British Airways. Nothing holds her there. Certainly not Helge who is withdrawn and strained. At the last moment before they go downstairs Hetty says: 'Kiss me, here, now.'

Helge puts her arms round her, kissing her on the mouth, hard, holding her as if she would break her bones. 'I love you, I love you. But you must trust me.'

At the airport she says: 'Call me as soon as you get back.'

'Where will you be?'

'Home. I'll go back to Saarbrucken tomorrow.'

'Please don't get arrested again.'

'Not for a little time. I promise.'

As the plane lifts up Hetty feels a retch of fear. To die with Helge in a car crash is one thing. To die among strangers, never to see her again, is another. But once the seat-belt light is switched off and the terrifying miracle has been accomplished, she's left to her doubts. There's the worrying difference between Helge's biography and Maidstone's official life; the father who was either a critic of fascism and suffered for his beliefs, or the serving soldier who died on the Russian front. Perhaps the clue is the mother who might have made a hero for her child out of an ordinarily dead serviceman and can no longer be asked which story is true.

She wonders when Maidstone will call or send for her and whether Lutz will be content with having forced her to return home and how he will try to bind Helge closer. For, turning it all over during the short hop from Hamburg to Heathrow, she has, with a sense of shock, to acknowledge his cleverness in planting his device, to go off in Hetty's face as soon as she shook it, with her questions to Helge. He had anticipated that Hetty might see enough to query and attempt to sow doubt, and it's thinking this through that finally convinces her that she's right, and that what she saw through the Keller window wasn't Lutz trying to elicit information, but him consulting his true colleagues.

She longs to be home to telephone Helge and warn her. She makes up whole paragraphs that will overcome Helge's resistance and Lutz's influence but even as the captain announces that they have begun their descent she realises that what her physical presence couldn't counter, her disembodied voice will be even more powerless against.

She reaches home in a state of exhaustion and confusion, unwilling to telephone Hamburg. Helge won't know exactly what time she will arrive. She has a brief pause in which she can think what to say while she unpacks, opens a cardboard carton of Long Life milk and boils a kettle for tea, spreads Helge's latest finds on the table. She is about to pour the hot water on a couple of tea bags when the doorbell rings.

'Ah, Miss Dearden, what have you brought back for us this time?'

... my dearest father, that I have been able to see you once more and if we do not meet again on this earth then surely we shall be together in heaven. Yet you must take care and do everything as I have prescribed. And you must be sure to keep always a strong band of faithful men about you, of good life and faith in Our Lord for the heathen grow every day more bold through our sins and weak men sell themselves for gold and betray their lords as was never known in the time of our fathers. Beautiful was it to see our dear land again and to kiss my father and I thank God that He has brought me to you and safe back again to continue His Service.

Our house I thank Our Lord had been quiet while I was away and the Frankish nation too but no sooner was I returned than I was summoned to Tours, which is where I now am writing to you, for my lady the Queen is still sick. It was hoped that she would amend here if she and the King together prayed at the tomb of St Martin but after a short improvement she is worse again and I have made the long journey here to see what I can do or at least to see her again.

For the first summer the Saxons are quiet and the King is not encamped against them as he has done for the last years ever since I came here. Among them must be our kinsman, Gundrada's brother if he still lives and has not fallen to the sword or sickness. We pray for him constantly, that God will give him time for amendment of life and to turn to Him but we have had no word of him and believe that he must have retreated further to the North, for the King settles all these lands with faithful Franks and the Saxons he carries off to other parts where they are surrounded by Christian people to keep them from backsliding until gradually they grow meek and gentle and in faith in the true God.

All this means that the dignity and riches of our house are increased together with our work, for many people throng to us for help in sickness or the baptising of their children, or travellers wanting rest before going north through the high mountains, and we have been forced to cultivate more land to feed them all. Also the fame of our work has spread so that other houses send to us for books and the work of our needles and what was once a quiet retreat among the hills and forests is full of people and the noise of workshops so that sometimes I feel that peace is fled, the world has come in and I long for that quiet garden in the wilderness of our beginning.

Here at Tours I have at last met that greatest of Englishmen, Master Alcuin, for he is Abbot here although not a monk or priest, and friend to the King and the Queen whom he loves as a daughter, and he has given me a new name as is his custom in play. It is Lesbia and I hope to be counted his friend.

His dearest friend among women after the Queen is the Lady Gisela who is known to him as Lucia and the King's daughter Rotrud, who lives with her in the abbey at Chelles, is Columba. Even the King himself is known to him as David.

When he heard that I had been home to our country tears came to his eyes and he begged me to tell him everything new, but I found that much of what I would have said he had already heard for he keeps a constant correspondence with men and women in every part of the island both priests and secular. And he talked to me long about the sins of our people and how he had determined never to visit England again lest he might be tempted to stay, and how the King will not let him for this very reason, and yet if he was determined upon it I believe the King would relent because of the great love he has of him. He urged me in my turn never to leave here but to dedicate myself to the King and the conversion of the Saxons.

He said that in the past too much had been done by force and that was the reason it bore bitter fruit not the sweet fruits of peace and faith, and that love must conquer where the sword had failed. Then I was emboldened to tell him of Berthgyth and of Gundrada, and he said that God had been good to the child in striking her body for Berthgyth's sin, and turning her mind towards Himself so that she might be saved and given a perfect form in the life to come. But he warned me to watch her closely for she is young and the Evil One will try to reclaim her for his own. Yet if she lives she will be a light to her own people. . . . (Now I am sent for to the Queen's chamber and must continue with this later.)

When I came in to my Lady Liutgard I saw that she was sick

indeed and, as I judged it, near to death but I said nothing for the King was sitting by her bed in great sadness and I was afraid to be the mouthpiece of ill news. He graciously raised me up and asked me to do what I could. Then he left us and I asked if she could hear me. Then she opened her eyes and gave me a sweet look and I gave her a little to drink of what I had brought with me and bathed her face with rosewater. Now she was enabled to speak. 'I am glad that you have come for I do not think I can live much longer and, although I am sad to leave the King and you my friend, yet I shall be glad to leave this worldly life of the court. And you know that had I lived my greatest joy would have been to spend some time with you in your house as much as the King would allow.'

Then I said that she should try to live a little longer for the sake of her friends and at that she pressed my hand and asked me to read to her from the Psalms for then she thought she might sleep a little, and so she did, looking like a child as she slept. Then the King came back and said: 'You have given her ease and peace which I shall not forget while I live and if God takes her to Himself out of this sleep His will be done.'

However it was not yet to be for she woke later and was able to speak and swallow a little more of my medicament and said that she was perfectly composed in her mind and felt no pain only a weakness and weariness in her limbs. She asked for a priest and for Master Alcuin to come to her and this was done, and when she had received the last rites she said goodbye to us all and folding her hands upon her breast closed her eyes. Her breathing grew lighter and lighter until it ceased altogether and when a feather was applied to her nostrils it did not stir.

So died my Lady and I never saw a more peaceful death and surely she is with God. But we who are left in this valley of shadows wept all together that we should no longer have her to sweeten our days with the honey of her presence. She is to be buried in the cathedral here near the tomb of the saint. I must return to our house but the King has asked me to go part of the way with him for he seems to find some comfort in speaking to me of her. Yet our progress will be slow by Orléans and Paris where I shall have a chance to talk to the Lady Gisela again. Therefore my father I shall not close my letter to you but keep it a little longer until I am safe home and can send Aelfwyn with it who will tell you more than I can write.

Which I did and now take up my pen again but much later than I expected and there are many things to set down before you. We were all much comforted at the House of Chelles and truly the Lady Gisela is most holy and wise among women and I think if I might speak with her often I should never feel that despair that is the temptation of our life. After Paris we continued to Aachen where the King now has his Palace and masses were said for the Queen in the Cathedral of the Holy Mother which shines forth as the most splendid House of God, it is said, outside Italy or Constantinople. I was pressed to stay a few days before continuing my way north both by the King and also Master Alcuin, to attend a great dispute between himself and Felix, Bishop of Ungel in the Spanish Marches, who had been summoned by the King to a great council there and the Bishop of Lyons sent to bring him lest he should be unwilling to attend.

My father, he teaches a heresy as great as the British heresy of Pelagius or that of Arius: that is that blasphemy of Adoptionism which holds that Christ Jesus was neither true Son of God nor even true God but only the Son by adoption and name. Felix has already been condemned once by the King and the bishops and by Pope Hadrian and repented yet now he rises up again in all his error.

For six days they disputed before an audience of scholars amongst whom I sat like Abbess Hilda at the Great Synod of Whitby as the arguments swayed this way and that, with all the strength and weight of Scripture and the Fathers hurled from both sides, until at last Alcuin conquered in the name of Christ and the True Faith, yet with reason and love not in any violent way. And now Felix is put into the care of the Bishop of Tours, Laidrad, to spend his days in repentance, and Laidrad, Benedict, Abbot of Amiens, who is like a son to Alcuin, and Nefridius,

Bishop of Narbonne, are sent into the Spanish Marches to root out the heresy that has grown strong as a vicious weed among the people. God keep it from our land of the English and from the British too who are ever prone to error.

So when this great matter was all decided I set out again with commission from the King and Master Alcuin to hold up the light of Our Lord in these parts under the bishop of Cologne and to teach all who will come to me. And the King confirmed me in our house and added further gifts with his permission to found a daughter-house when I judge that it is necessary, and to take any land for that purpose that is not already belonging to any one else which he will confirm to us by deed. And I am to make him a copy of the Psalms with our finest work, which shall be known as the Queen's Psalter, and he will keep it always by him to read from, for he said these were the last words she heard and they brought her such comfort that they will have equal power with him. He says that he will not marry again and I believe he intends this but matters of state in time may demand otherwise.

Father when I returned home this time I found the house disordered although I had left Adela in charge, for there is a certain sister, a troublemaker, who will not obey her because of the gentleness of her nature which should command the love of all. This sister had spread the rumour that the King had sent for me to heal the Queen and that her death had brought me into disgrace and I had been accused of sorcery and heresy. Thus is news distorted by malice. And she had locked herself with some of the sisters in the novices' quarters. So as soon as I arrived I ordered her to come out and when she would not I had the men break open the door and stood before her. The others were merely silly girls led astray but in her eye I could see there was the defiance of Satan when he stood before Michael.

Then I enquired of her why she had broken her vow of obedience and led others to do the same. And she answered that I had lost the King's favour and that the house should be returned to the Franks and that I favoured those of my own race, even if they were new in the faith, and that she was the most senior of the sisters from the Frankish nation. I replied calmly that far from losing the King's favour it was strengthened and I showed all the sisters the presents I had received from him for our chapel and the letter giving me permission to seek out somewhere for a daughter-house. Then I said that before me, as before Christ there was neither Frank nor Saxon, and called on God to witness, and all them there, that this I had always held to, and that in Christ it was not long years that brought reward but holiness of life as He made plain in the parable of the labourers in the vineyard when the last were given equal reward with the first. And I saw then that the others drew away from her but that unlike the heretic Felix she was not inclined to turn from her error and repent. Then I said: 'Since I see you obdurate and not returned to your vow of obedience I give you the choice either to go back to your own home or to be sent to Cologne to the bishop for his chastising, for if you will not be obedient to your mother in God surely you will obey your father and accept whatever penance he sees fit. And if you will do this and perform it faithfully you may come back again and renew your vows and we will accept you back into our sisterhood.'

Then she disputed a while within herself and finally said that she would go to Cologne where she will try to blacken me to the bishop but I have written him a full account of it all which I have sent by the hand of the trusted servant who goes with her. Those others who had joined with her at first I gave penance too, hard enough that they might know the pinch of remembrance but not so harsh as to sour their minds against me, whilst reminding them that I might send them all back to their families in disgrace.

No sooner was calm restored again then news reached us that a band of pagans was coming our way from the North-East. This I did not understand for this year they are quiet and it is said by Master Alcuin and others at the court that the Saxon wars are at last over and that people utterly broken. So we waited in some anxiety and the following day about noon we heard a noise of people and carts and saw coming over the bridge, which I have had built across the river, a band of heathen by their clothes, with some wounded among the men and the rest very cast down in spirit as appeared by their faces and their heads sunk on their breasts like people who have travelled many days without rest or hope.

I went out to meet them in front of our walls with the sisters and brothers and as soon as they came close I saw that it was Gundrada's brother who led them but aged and weary and with a bloody rag about his arm.

I asked him whether he came in peace and said there were no swords among us. He halted his band and rode forward by himself although he was hardly able to sit in the saddle. 'Where is my sister?' he asked. I answered that she was in England with our kin but would return soon.

'I cannot fight the Christian King and the Christian God any longer,' he said. 'I have come to ask for baptism and that we may be left in peace in that country of our fathers and not removed to some other land we do not know.'

'That is not mine to grant. Baptism I can give you and if you will all agree to accept Jesus Christ, forswearing those old gods of the Saxons, I will intercede for you with the King and perhaps he will show you mercy but more I cannot promise. Stay here and be healed and baptised and then return to your place in quiet and build a house for God and perhaps the King will spare you and in time will forget.'

Then we took the sick and the children into the infirmary and the rest camped beside the river and the next day when all had eaten and rested we carried the sick on litters down to the river and began to baptise all the people by turns and a miraculous sight it was to see them all going down into the waters, old and young, families together almost a hundred persons all told, and to hear them renounce the Evil Ones. But Ecgbert, Gundrada's brother who bears the same name as his father, would have none but me to baptise himself and his family, so I did.

In a few days most of them were recovered enough to return

to their former dwelling and I have promised to visit them and have sent one of the brothers with them to begin the work of teaching. Ecgbert's daughter whom I saw when she was a baby still has your jewel around her neck and has grown stout and strong. They have another child, an older boy whom I hope may in time hear the call of God but as yet he has no learning and cannot read. Whether his father will allow him to learn I do not know. Just now he is mild and penitent but we shall see if any true love of God can grow in that heart. My father, I ask you to send Gundrada back to us with Aelfwyn when he returns, for young as she is, God has work for her here among her own people and ours. I know it will be hard for you to lose her, for I saw when I was with you how she has won you with her quickness and bright ways and made glad your old age, and truly I am sorry to take her from you, yet I know that this is right and believe that you and she will think so too.

Is it not strange that I should come in search of a sister and find a whole family? And here we see the miraculous design of God for surely He sent me here in order that these people should be saved, Berthgyth's broken vows recompensed and His Son glorified. If they should have another child and it should be a boy and live I shall ask that it be called Baltheard so that your name shall not be forgotten when we are gone to Christ.

Now my father a last piece of news before I seal my letter and send Aelfwyn on his journey to you. Just before I left the court there was talk that the King will go to Rome later this year. He asked Alcuin to accompany him but he pleaded old age and infirmity. You know that the King protected the Holy Father, Pope Leo, when his enemies tried to blind him and cut out his tongue, and that many things were alleged against him of corruption and wickedness of life. When he returned to Rome he was escorted by our own bishop Hildebold and when his accusers were brought before him they had nothing to say so that the council declared the Holy Father innocent and referred those accusers to King Charles for judgement. The Queen's sickness and his war with the Saxons has made it impossible for him to go there before.

While I was at the court and the King's journey was being discussed I was emboldened to ask Master Alcuin if I should make my pilgrimage to the Holy City when the King goes, for surely there would be the greatest safety in such a concourse as would go with him, for you know dearest father that lone pilgrims, especially if they are women, often miscarry. At first Master Alcuin urged many arguments against my going, saying that God can be as well worshipped here or under the open sky as in the Rome of the martyrs. But I said, though I spoke in all humility, that, especially among the English, all people desired to make a pilgrimage there if possible and that I believed that as well as an increase of faith that I should learn many things by such a visit which I could put to use on my return and in particular for the better writing and illuminating of books which I might study in the great libraries there.

Then he saw that I was set on it but not in any frivolous desire of running about the world to see novelties, and he agreed that I should be safest as part of the King's company, and should in that way get the greatest benefit from my visit to the Holy City but that first I must have permission from Hildebold my bishop. I did not see that he could refuse it since he is only recently returned himself. So I requested it of him at once which he granted and it was fortunate that I was able to get this before I returned home and found all disordered for otherwise he might have refused me now, saying that the house could not be left.

Therefore my father unless you deny me, which I do not think you will, I shall go in the autumn of this year to pray for us all and make pilgrimage too for you who are no longer able to go yourself.

And now my father I send you some cordials against the summer flux and fur boots against the cold which will follow in God's season. Did I tell you that that Hibernian who accompanied me here on the boat when I first came, and had set up to teach in this diocese of Cologne, has been found guilty of eating meat in Lent and other misdemeanours, and King Charles has asked the help of the English to send him home to his own country? Greet the sisters at Wimborne for me.

'Surely you know,' Hetty says, 'I thought you knew everything.'

'Ah, not everything,' Maidstone answers from the middle of her sitting room where the ceiling's central beam almost touches his head. 'Besides we like people to tell us things. It shows they're co-operating. Who did you meet over there?'

'Dr Ebbesen.'

'Of course. But others?'

'Some student friends. I didn't get their names.'

'I expect they're known.'

'No doubt.'

'Anyone else?'

'Someone called Brehme, Lutz Brehme.'

Maidstone and Colin both have their notebooks out and are taking notes. 'How would you spell that Miss Dearden?'

'Don't you know?'

'And who is this Lutz Brehme?'

'I was hoping you might tell me.'

'We're glad you've decided to co-operate with us Miss Dearden.'

Is that what she's doing, Hetty wonders. Is she somehow betraying Helge in the belief that she's trying to save her? 'But who is he?' she persists.

Maidstone turns back a few pages. 'He does appear to be on our list of persons we're interested in. He spends a lot of time in the company of people rather younger than himself. Was a lecturer in political theory.'

'I think he's a plant,' Hetty says.

'And what would you mean by that?'

'I think he's a police informer who mixes with the students, incites them to get themselves involved in things and then shops them.' She's surprised by her own use of thieves' cant but is unable to think of any more academic terms to embody her suspicions.

'Ah, the French have a word for it, I believe.'

'An *agent provocateur*.'

'Funny we don't seem to have an English equivalent. Why do you think this Lutz is one of those, Miss Dearden?'

'Because he was the only one not arrested.'

'Perhaps he was too smart for the German police; smarter than the students. Where might this have been taking place?'

'A town called Erfurt.'

'And where's that?'

'In what was the GDR. Beyond the old border anyway.'

'Where your girlfriend comes from?'

'Somewhere near where Dr Ebbesen was born, and left when she was a child.'

'But still feels an attachment to.'

'As one would.'

'As one might. . . .' He has skilfully led her away from her question, Hetty realises. 'It must come expensive, keep flying backwards and forwards like this. You must think it's pretty important.'

'I'm a free agent. I have no responsibilities. Anyway I thought that was what the Common Market was all about: being able to travel freely, when and where you like, within Europe of course.'

'It gives us a lot of headaches now there are no proper frontiers.'

'That's progress, Inspector. That was what we used to condemn the communist countries for: lack of freedom.'

'But where does freedom end and licence begin? That's the

question no-one's ever answered. It was easier for us in some ways when we all knew where we were.'

'Them and us.'

'Exactly. Now everything's mixed up. You can't tell sheep from goats.'

'What about wolves?'

'You can usually tell them, except when they're in sheep's clothing of course.'

'Lutz Brehme might be one of those.'

'Indeed. Or he might just be a sheep in wolf's clothing. Have you thought of that Miss Dearden? We'll welcome your next bit of translation when it's ready. Turning into quite a little saga, isn't it. Where does it all keep coming from?'

'A manuscript collection in the state library at Karlsruhe.'

'Have you seen it?'

'No but it isn't something anyone would lie about. It's too easy to check.'

'But you haven't Miss Dearden. People might be relying on that.'

'There's no code to it, I'm sure. What would be the point?'

'To tell you something in a way no-one else could fathom out. It's got our chaps puzzled. They've got all sorts of questions and theories. Like if it's very old as you say why isn't it handwritten? How come it's all printed?'

'Because scholars, usually in the nineteenth or very early twentieth century when the world still had time to be interested in such things, transcribed it, edited it, published it in collections, mostly in Germany.'

'What's it all about then?'

'I thought you'd read my translations.'

'That's another department. Full of sex and violence is it?'

'In a way. It's about an English nun in Germany looking for her aunt.'

'My wife reads historical novels.'

'Then perhaps you should let her have a go at it if your department is so bothered.'

'Perhaps I should. Anyway we'll be grateful for your next chapter. Staying home for a bit now, will you be? Spending Christmas here?'

'I really haven't decided.'

'Perhaps you'd let us know when you have. And if there's anything else you think of. No doubt we'd get round to it all in the end but it might save us a bit of time and the public some money.'

Hetty sees them out into a cold dark night, wondering what her village neighbours who will surely have remarked them must be making of their repeated visits – the anonymous car drawn up on the verge and their grey presences. She isn't deceived by Maidstone's impersonation of Policeman Plod, a rôle of incompetence garnished with an aggressive sarcasm, either learned from television or absorbed by osmosis in the first years of duty from older lags. She's almost sure he knows about Lutz and was protecting him.

Now she can't put off ringing Helge any longer but when she dials the instrument goes on giving out the single melodious note with no answering voice and in the end she's forced to give up. Tomorrow Helge will be back in Saarbrucken where it isn't easy to telephone. Hetty had felt the presence of a listener as she had waited on the end of the line and had wanted to shout into the receiver: 'You can stop the tape, she isn't there.' And then she had imagined anonymous figures laughing at her and felt a wave of despair. She looks round the cottage, which she no longer seems to know or find comforting. Her life has totally changed and she sees no way of going back. The fox-at-the-door that she thought she had buried has caught her in its snare and refuses to lie quiet under the leaf mould. Yet she can't regret that lost quiet, the innocence of the old Hetty that's now buried deeper than the fox.

She rings Sandy. 'Answer me truthfully; what are you doing for Christmas?'

'We have to go up to Yorkshire, to Bill's parents for a couple of days as usual. I'm dreading it. Why?'

'Could I borrow your house while you're away? I don't fancy a country Christmas here alone.'

'Of course. But are you sure? I'd have thought it was much nicer. Log fires and all that stuff.'

'We've got a rapist in the district. I don't care for the idea of sitting here, starting at every creaking branch while the rest of the village is gathered round the Christmas pudding.'

'What about our local rapists?'

'Somehow they seem less frightening. There'll be people about in the streets and things I could go to.'

'Could you look after the cats?'

'Of course. They'll be company.'

'Why aren't you going away? Is anything wrong?'

'It's all very complicated. I don't know that I can explain. At least not on the phone.'

'Oh alright, I'll wait. But I shall insist on being told everything, well something. Come up the day before we go and we can have a jolly evening; get pissed. Bill was complaining he never sees you.'

Hetty has barely put the receiver back when the phone gives its hectoring British two-tone ring. 'You said you would call me as soon as you get there!'

'I tried. There wasn't any answer.'

'But I am here all the time. Never mind. You are there safe.'

'I've had some visitors already. When do you go back to the university?'

'Tomorrow. I will call you.'

'I'll write to you tomorrow. Where are you spending Christmas?'

'Always I go to my mother's sister in Frankfurt because she is alone. This year it will be hard for me not to be with you.'

'And for me. I shall be in London.'

'Where I cannot imagine you in bed.'

'Hush. Someone might be listening.'

'I forget. Then I tell them I am so happy in you. Do you hear whoever you are? You can't stop us to love each other.'

Brave words Hetty thinks them but wonders if they're true and whether the world doesn't bear down on lovers with its *peine forte et dure* to press them to death or at least destroy that first ardour. Is it just because I'm older, she wonders, that I find faith hard or is it the once-bitten-twice-shy of Jack, or just that I've always found it hard to believe; British pragmatism steps in with a sheaf of statistics, divorce, loss, heartbreak. And yet those same hearts keep coming back for more and maybe that's the secret, the perpetual renewal in individuals and generations.

They will know now that she's going away. Maidstone had asked her to tell him but she questions whether she's obliged to. She's not guilty, has done nothing, hasn't been charged with anything, merely blackmailed into a kind of connivance with them in their fantasies of terrorists, skulduggery. Almost she can laugh at them. Nevertheless she has to supply a copy of Tetta's translated pages, of that story they don't read but ransack for clues. Surely they can't tap Sandy's phone? That must be illegal. Bill would be furious! They wouldn't dare.

She gets up early in the morning to finish the translation. It's still dark outside and the air when she opens the back door smells of frost and chill earth. So Tetta is going to Rome. She has become part of the gaudy cavalcade of recorded history in the entourage of a great potentate, winding its way over the Alps with shouts and the cracking of whips, the ring of horse gear and arms. The bright tents pitch down like huge birds, flamingo or swan, beside the river, the smoke goes up from the cooking fires mingling with the chant of prayers.

By the time Hetty has finished her scribbling on the kitchen table and is on her third cup of tea a grey light has filtered in announcing the day. She's revised her decision of the night before and scrawls a note to put in with Tetta's tale, to the effect that she's going to London but she feels no obligation to supply an address which, she decides, they'll probably know already. Then she drives into Sarnford.

For once the winter sky is the colour of a blackbird's egg above her head. No Christmas-card snow is forecast, just earth hard as iron and water like a stone as the waits are carolling when she has managed to park in the market square and is picking her way between cars to the copyshop. Should she wish the dark young men, who may be Muslim or Hindu, 'A Merry Christmas'? Perhaps not. She comes out with her sheaf of copies and heads for the Post Office where all the world seems to be queueing with parcels for home and ranks of cards. She expresses a quick note to Helge giving her Sandy's address and telephone number. How will Maidstone be spending Christmas? Is there a nuclear family he returns to that will clasp him to its bosom reinforcing his Father Christmas image of those values he's presumably protecting?

Hetty passes the big dark tree with its garlands of lights, descendant of Tetta's idols pressed into service of the Christian god so that the two rebirths exist side by side, the dying sun in his green jacket who must be made to return and the baby of regeneration bringing back innocence, the lost childhood that never was in all of us. The Salvation Army in its navy and damson uniform blows a wavering trumpet and rattles a collecting tin under the branches, ringed by the overstuffed shop windows crying their wares. The green man is having his revenge, threatening us with his dying forever as radioactive dust and acid rain fall on Santa Claus' reindeer, scorch the Scots pines and strip beech and poplar in a lingering drought.

Perhaps her parcel for Maidstone will be lost in the Christmas post. Well that won't be her fault. In the afternoon she'll drive up to London and spend an evening with Sandy and Bill. Then she'll be alone and free to hope for Helge's call.

'So what's going on?' Sandy says when Bill has gone to fill up the car with petrol for their journey north in the morning.

'I don't really know. I've had several visits from the police and I think my phone is being tapped.'

'You can find that out you know. You have the right to be told if it is.'

'But what good would it do me? It wouldn't make them stop.'

'Anyway that's not the point. Why are they doing it, that's what I want to know.'

'They think Helge is some sort of terrorist and that the research material she sends me contains some kind of coded information.' Saying the name requires a conscious effort of the throat muscles. It sticks like cold potato in her gullet.

'Does it? Is she?'

'If it's a coded message it stops at me so where would be the point? And no, I don't think so.'

'But you're not sure.'

'She's involved in a political pressure group that may be manipulated by someone.' It helps, Hetty finds, to try to explain her thoughts to Sandy.

'And the police?'

'I suppose they must be MI6 or perhaps a special anti-terrorist squad. We know so little about these things, they may just be fantasists who have to find something to do now they're not chasing the old enemy, real communists.'

'Then they could be even more dangerous if they're making it all up.'

'When I was at that conference there was an American, a pretty wily old academic, who suggested the whole of the Cold War had been a fiction.'

'Just as Orwell said, predicted, ten years before. It must be hard for people to give it up, to think that so many, even us in our way, suffered for a fantasy: the wars, the trials and imprisonments, the fear. But whose fantasy was it?'

'Everybody's, I suppose. Children in the dark terrorising each other with ghost stories, except that some people were frightened to death.'

'The concentration camps, the genocides, they weren't fiction.'

'No, but they were based on myths of race and so on, fairy stories about who had the monopoly of truth and purity, ogres and giant killers.'

'Are you sure you'll be alright here alone?'

'I'm rather looking forward to it.'

But when she waves them off, of course Hetty feels a moment's doubt and desolation. Fortunately she has shopping to do and cards still to write and post. Helge probably won't get her letter until tomorrow: Christmas Eve. She can go out today without missing a precious phone call that's not being eavesdropped on. Hetty says goodbye to the tortoiseshell and the black tom, who seem perfectly content to be fed and stroked and let in and out by her, and follows what's now a familiar route down Putney Hill to the tube station and under the river up into central London. She wants to go to the British Museum again and walk about among the things she saw with Helge, in what feels both a long and yet such a little time ago, but first she gets out at Embankment, where the public address system is warning against unattended parcels in the threatened seasonal bombing campaign, and heads off for the Christmas fair at St Martin's to look for presents among the scarves and pots and handcrafted bright trifles in painted wood, glass and leather as if such substances themselves were tangible antidotes to the complex electronic circuitry our lives have become.

She wanders from stall to stall matching a piece of coloured silk or a silver bracelet to Helge's dark hair or against her skin. Among the cards she picks out a British Museum reproduction from a Carolingian manuscript Tetta might have handled: St Mark with a pen poised over his inkwell about to add a line to his story, Palace School Aachen as the reverse says 'showing Northumbrian influences', and buys several copies. Then she goes down the steps into Trafalgar Square with her small parcels safely in their plastic bag, drawn by a remembrance of Veronese Venus and Titian Diana, the opulence of their lit flesh, towards the National Gallery.

The square seems more crowded even than usual. The Norwegian fir towers mast-high against the Gallery portico, with a charcoal scribble of figures at its base darkly drained of all colour in the winter light. The fountain jets are dumb, their basins empty and a long dais has been set up to the left of Nelson's Column. A troupe of gowned and ruffled choristers have just taken their places aloft and will soon pour music down on to the upturned faces and passing heads below. Hetty crosses into the main square and turns north to cross again. Then she stops and steps back behind a leafless tree trunk. Ahead of her in a corner of the square under the ribs of a stone balustrade, two men are talking. As she watches, one grinds out a cigarette underfoot and begins to move away. The other pauses a moment, looks around quickly and then strikes down across the square towards St James's Park. Hetty emerges from her tree trunk, her breath harsh and cold in her chest, a taste of bile in her mouth and sets out after the first man. She is following Lutz.

She has to keep closer in the crowds than she would like in order not to miss him but he shows no sign of nervousness, walking briskly, hands in his raincoat pockets, heading, she thinks, for the Underground. Fortunately she's got a season ticket for the day, not knowing where she might want to go, or she might have lost sight of him while fumbling at the ticket machine. As it is, she's able to follow him through the gates and see his head with the slightly shiny crown being carried down the escalator in front of her and turning into the mouth of a District Line tunnel.

Would he recognise her even if he saw her? They'd met so briefly in rather dim cellar bars. Anyway she has to risk it if she isn't to lose him. Fewer people seem to be on this platform which she sees is for trains heading east. When the next drags its long caterpillar body down the length of it, she waits to see Lutz step forward to a carriage before moving towards the door of the rear compartment and strap-hanging where she can watch him through a couple of glass partitions.

Hetty keeps nervous track of the stations as they pass under a part of London she hasn't been to for years: Tower Hill beyond the Monument, going first back in time from seventeenth to eleventh century to emerge in the nineteenth beyond Mile End and the long-vanished city walls. She hopes Lutz doesn't have to change; she doubts her ability to keep him in sight through another set of tunnels and on to another train. At Whitechapel he moves towards the door and Hetty prepares to leave too, squeezing out at the last moment to follow his tonsure going ahead towards an arch marked 'Way Out', and reaching the open air in time to see him step on to a pedestrian crossing fording the main road.

On the other side he turns right and then left up another thoroughfare, standing out from the passers-by and more easily followed because the crowd has suddenly changed. And so must I, Hetty thinks among the brown skins and cotton trousers of the women under their top coats and the men in round embroidered caps shopping for clothes, Halal meat and strangely shaped vegetables among the hardware importers and rag trade factories. I might be where? Calcutta, I suppose, a world within a world. A signpost on the corner of the wide street says 'Museum of Labour and the East End'. That was where Helge had been going, Hetty remembers. Lutz crosses the road again and plunges into a hatching of smaller streets with old names – St Jude's, Clare, Vyner, Russia Lane – as Hetty hurries after, until, as she peers round the last corner, she sees him in front of a door pressing an invisible bell and shrinks back. When she ventures to look again he's gone.

And now the foolishness of her pursuit sinks her. What is she doing here on this wild-goose chase? What did she think she could accomplish with her sleuthing? What can she do now but turn round and go home to Sandy's? The adrenalin is souring in her veins. Hetty looks at her watch. She'll wait another ten minutes just to see, aware that she's growing increasingly conspicuous as she dawdles there with no shop window to give her an alibi. She crosses the road to watch from the other side. At the far end of the street an old man in cap and muffler is strolling with an open newspaper and attendant mongrel away from her towards a corner betting shop. Otherwise the cold streets are deserted and for the first time Hetty is aware how numbed she's becoming herself and of her cloudy breath hanging above her. She looks at her watch again. Only five minutes have gone but she feels the futility of her vigil.

Suddenly the street she is watching from her transverse corner is filled with cars from both ends. As she steps back from sight they scream to a stop outside the house Lutz has gone into and men jump out and begin to hammer on the door. One puts his shoulder against it. It gives. Several of them follow each other into what must be a narrow passage. In a few moments people, men and women, are being dragged out and bundled into cars. She thinks she sees Lutz among them but she's afraid to show too much of herself in case attention should fall on her. Two of the cars drive off. Another pulls up and more men go inside. One stations himself at the door.

Hetty is shaking with excitement and fright. She must get away, lose herself among crowds and make her way home to think. Noting the name of the street in case fear should make her forget, she retraces her steps, back to the main road, the still shopping and gossiping many coloured crowd and down the nearest Underground steps, the barred red circle above the entrance a symbol of safety she hurries toward with a gasp of recognition and relief. The train isn't full and she can drop into a seat still shaking, hardly capable of remembering how she got there and quite unable to register the first passing stations to judge whether she's going the right way.

When she recovers a bit she sees that if the plan stuck above the first seat is right the train should take her all the way to Putney. She hasn't finished her shopping but she feels too disturbed to carry on with her plans. She still has tomorrow. The rest of the day she spends walking the spikily frozen grass of the heath, feeding the cats, switching from television channel to channel, chasing news bulletins in search of any mention of what she saw, and finding none. We know nothing, she thinks, are told only what someone else decides we should know, and it can't even be dubbed a conspiracy because the different parts of our censorships don't work together, are even jealous of each other and their own corner of truth but the result is the same: a patchy knowledge that makes it almost impossible to decide or act in our clouded and partial democracy. You can't cover everything the newspapers would say. People would get bored. You have to edit, to sift. But there ought to be *one* source that just told it all and then you could decide. The worst thing is not even knowing what we're missing, and she presses another button in pursuit of her Will-o'-the-wisp.

She wants to telephone Maidstone and ask: 'Did you arrest Lutz Brehme today?' But she's afraid of revealing her own presence and of the cool sardonic response.

'Where might that have been Miss Dearden? We arrest a lot of people every day. I don't think we have anyone of that name on our books. But if you'd like to tell us what you know we could see.'

She sleeps fitfully and wakes early, hoping that her letter will have reached Helge but the first call of the day is for Bill. When the phone rings again she's resigned to disappointment so that Helge's voice almost seems an illusion. 'Darling is it okay to speak do you think? My aunt has gone shopping.'

'Yes, at least I think so. How are you? Are you alright?'

'Yes, I am fine, except I have lost my job.'

'Lost your job! How? Tell me.'

'When I showed up at the university I was sent for by the, what do you call it, "head"?'

'The dean maybe. Go on.'

'He said my political involvement is my own affair until it brings the university into disrepute. And now it does because I am all the time being arrested and therefore absent from my classes. So I am suspended from yesterday until the end of next semester on full pay and then I am expelled altogether.'

'Can't you fight it?'

'No, there's no point. I don't have permanence, *Amtsdauer*; what is it?'

'Tenure, I think.'

'*Ja*.'

'What will you do?'

'I don't know. I will think.'

Hetty sees at once that being sacked for such a reason will make it hard, if not impossible, for Helge to find an academic job again.

'Also, there is something else. I can't find Lutz before I leave for Frankfurt. There is no answer and I must tell him what has happened.'

Hetty takes a deep breath. 'That's because he's here.'

'What is that? What do you say? *He is here.*'

'Yes. Or no. Not there in Germany. He's here in London. At least he was yesterday.'

'It must be the mistake. He would have told me if he was going to London, leaving Germany. We are supposed to inform each other of such things.'

'Darling it's true. I saw him.'

'No you can't.'

'Listen; I have to convince you. Was it Russia Lane where you visited friends when you went to the Museum of Labour?'

'*Ja.* I told you.'

'No you didn't. Maidstone told me. But he didn't tell me the name of the road. Then when I asked you you told me about them but you didn't tell me the road either. Yesterday I saw Lutz in Trafalgar Square when I'd gone into the centre of London to shop. I followed him to Whitechapel. He went to a house in Russia Lane. I didn't get the number. Anyway, after he'd been there about ten minutes the police, at least I assume it was the police, raided it and arrested several people.'

'I don't believe this.'

'You must. How could I make it up, invent it; know the name of the street?'

'I could call the people there and check.'

'Do that. If you think it's safe that is. I don't know.'

'You don't want me to call?'

'Yes, I do. If it will convince you. But I don't want it to make more trouble.'

'For whom? If they know already to go to Russia Lane where can be more trouble?'

'Yes, you're probably right. What will you do about work? Have you got enough money?'

'I don't know yet. I will think. Just for now I have the salary until the end of the Spring semester and I have something saved.'

'You could always come here. Now you don't have to be at the university.' Hetty tries to keep the longing out of her voice.

'Hetty, thank you so much that you say that. First I must find out some things and get over the terrible Christmas. What are you doing?'

'I'm looking after two cats. Perhaps I'll find a concert to go to, carols maybe. I wish you were here. Will you be able to ring me again?'

'I will try. I have to go back to Saarbrucken once more to remove my things. I have told Christine.'

'Was she angry?'

'Yes but I cannot help it. There is no reason to stay there if I do not have the job.'

One day, Hetty thinks, she may speak of me like that to someone else. What happened to Europa when the bull got bored and wanted to go back to the open pastures, breaking the silk rein she'd put around his horns? Today she will try for the National Gallery again as if some guidance is encoded there among the luscious imaginings of the artists.

'There's an answering machine here. If I'm not in when you ring leave me a message. If you do telephone Russia Lane let me know what happens.'

Lutz could be back in Germany by now if they'd let him go, and if Helge challenges him he'll probably deny he was ever in London but the others will know he was there and could tell, that's if they're allowed to speak to anyone. Hetty feels like a swimmer barely staying afloat and not knowing whether if she tries putting her feet down she'll find firm ground or the abyss.

After Helge's call she switches on the radio to drown the silence while she makes herself toast and coffee, washes up the cats' overnight encrusted dishes and puts them down fresh food for the day. 'Why do cats never lick their plates?' she asks them and they wind themselves about her legs, keeping the answer to themselves as she opens a tin of dark fishy pâté and sprinkles it with stars and minnow shapes from their boxes.

> The holly and the ivy
> When they are both full grown
> Of all the trees that are in the wood
> The holly bears the crown.

There's the green man again, not quite chopped down, competing still with the infant god in its manger, waving its fists like baby Hercules strangling serpents in his cradle. Once there must have been more verses about the ivy, male and female alternating. Now all that's left is the dialogue between old god and young, claim and counter-claim. Choose. But we shouldn't have to choose because then we lose half our symbols and the trees are cut, the forests ploughed up, the delicate biosphere riven in the name of progress.

This time nothing interrupts her shopping and her progress through the Gallery so that she can almost think yesterday's events are an illusion. For a long time she sits in front of the small copy of the Veronese 'Rape of Europa' attempting to resolve its ambiguities. Are the waiting women trying to dissuade Europa or helping her on to the bull's back? She looks alarmed, anguished, but the bull lies docile almost smug, and the little lusts climb the skies or hold the fillet around its head, conniving at her destruction, knowing how it will rise and thunder away as soon as she's got both feet off the ground.

The walls are full of warnings to lovers how time and the world corrode the silken moment and only art can sustain it. The Gallery closes early and Hetty makes her way back as the short day slants down and the lights begin to battle with the dusk.

> Thyme, thyme it is a precious, precious root
> It's a flower that the sun shines on
> And time it will bring everything unto an end
> And so our thyme runs on.

Inside Sandy's front door is a welter of envelopes stiff with cards and an express from Helge. Hetty's heart is in her mouth choking her as she recognises the writing. She puts the other post on the hall table and goes through to the answering machine which is showing two calls. The first is Sandy, with Bill punctuating, hoping she's all right and the cats are behaving. The other is Helge.

'Darling, I called my friends. At first there is no answer. Then a strange person, a woman says they are away. So I don't know what this means. But she doesn't sound right this woman, not to be in their house, and I feel I am listened to which I have not thought before. So I don't know and perhaps I come after Christmas to see. I'll try to speak to you later.'

Inside the envelope is a letter full of tender banalities and some photocopied sheets. 'Now I have searched all the indexes,' Helge has written, 'and I think this is all to be found in our collections. But there was a note about the British Museum Additional Manuscripts so perhaps we must also look there?'

But first my father I will tell you of our journey here and of Rome itself, that centre of the world which all Christian people yearn towards more than any other except perhaps the Holy City of God, Jerusalem, which I may never see with these eyes of the body but only as St Augustine's City of God hereafter. And if it were not a sin I would envy the Blessed Willibald for his pilgrimage to the Holy Places as we read in his life by Sister Hygeberc but that I know that it was granted to him to tread in our Lord's footsteps because of his great faith and goodness more than is seen in these latter days. Yet I believe that as the

Blessed Bede never left his monastery and was able to encompass in his little cell all of time from the beginning, and the whole earth and heavens through the power of his mind and spirit, so it is not necessary to run about the world to know it, and that much I have learnt from coming here.

We reached Ravenna in November where we stayed to rest for several days and I was able to admire the beauties of that ancient city and its churches and I could see that much of the King's new palace is built after the fashion there and in particular the richness of the paintings and mosaics on all the walls. Then we continued our journey to Rome. On the twenty-third of the month the Holy Father Leo came out to meet us twelve miles to Nomentum where he and the Lord Charles dined together in great state. The next day we entered the city itself and truly it is the finest you may imagine with public buildings and private all built in stone and brick in the days of the Emperors of the West, bridges and temples and the great city walls which could not save it from destruction, in order that God might rebuild it after His own fashion, and perfectly preserved because of the mildness of the climate so that even in winter the sun shines and the sky is clear but in summer it is not healthy as even St Willibald found when he and his brother were stricken with black plague here. Nevertheless do not be fearful for me for I shall have left long before the summer heat. The streets are filled with people of every nation and every nation has its own quarter for pilgrims and merchants. There are great markets too, for every kind of thing, including the market where Pope Gregory first saw our people waiting to be bought and sent the Blessed Augustine for our conversion, but truly anything may be bought and sold here including the hearts of men. It was because of the treachery of the Roman people towards the Pope that the Lord Charles was forced to come here and I could see as the King's entourage entered the city, for we had left a large part of the army camped outside, that some faces were sullen among the crowds perhaps fearing that we might have come to sack the city like the barbarians rather than save it. The Frankish dress, which all the court and army which is not in orders wears, appears almost savage here and that is perhaps why the Lord Charles has on two occasions been persuaded to put on Roman dress although he prefers his own Frankish style which is indeed more suited to his way of life, which is to be much on horseback, and to the northern climate.

That day was filled with our visit to St Peter's for a festival Mass and I prostrated myself at last before the shrine of the Apostle. Then my heart was filled with great sadness my father because you were not there to share that occasion with me but I offered up special prayers for your safety and my own, and our houses and all our people. Then there came a lavish entertainment and feast which I did not attend but went with Gundrada and Aelfwyn to visit the shrine of St Paul at the crossroads where he suffered his martyrdom and so returned to the Pilgrim's House in the English Quarter where I had decided to stay because I thought I would be better able to compose my thoughts there than in the enticements of the court.

During the next week while the King's entertainment continued I visited the churches and Holy places of the city until on the first day of the month of Our Lord's birth the great assembly was held in the basilica and I once again climbed the Santa Scala to see and hear all that was said against the Holy Father Leo. St Peter's was crowded with clergy of every degree and with the King and his court and advisers. He had wanted Master Alcuin to go with him but instead there were Theodulf, Bishop of Orléans, Alcuin's friend, who was to receive the pallium of Archbishop; Riculf, Archbishop of Mainz, and Witto whom Alcuin calls his son Candidus, who stays with him at St Martin's when he is not in the King's employ at Aachen. Then, when all were assembled, the Lord Charles asked the Pope's accusers to stand forth and make their charges known against the Holy Father but none would speak out, and all the archbishops, bishops and abbots present said together: 'We do not dare to judge the Apostolic See. We ourselves are judged by it and its Vicar. Itself it is judged by none as has always been the custom.'

After this the Pope said: 'I follow in the steps of the Popes my predecessors, and am ready to purge myself of these false charges which have burst into evil flame against me.' It seemed as if this might be the end of the matter since where there are no accusers there can be no charges but still the murmurings continued and the doubts of some were not yet laid to rest. So on the day before the Eve of Christmas, in front of a vast congregation, the Holy Father ascended into the pulpit with the Book of Gospels in his hand and declared before God and His Angels and Saint Peter that he was innocent of any part in those crimes which were alleged against him and that he swore this oath of his own free will, compelled to it by no-one, meaning the King.

That same day there arrived two monks from the Patriarch of Jerusalem bringing the King the keys of the Holy Sepulchre and of Calvary together with the standard of Jerusalem, and thus commending the Holy City to his care. This might have seemed the greatest honour that could be bestowed on him but I was fortunate to be witness to the greater which was to follow. We had gone to St Peter's for the Mass on Christmas morning. When the King entered he went straight to the shrine of the Apostle to pray and as he rose from his knees the Pope placed a crown of gold upon his head at which all the people shouted in acclaim. Then the Pope said: 'To Charles Augustus crowned by God great and peace-making Emperor of the Romans, life and victory!' The whole basilica was filled with the joy of the people present and the choir sang the Litany of Praises calling on God to aid the Lord of the Franks, Lombards and Romans.

The Emperor, for so I must now call him, seemed surprised by the Pope's action and almost as if he would refuse it, and it was said to me after by Witto that if he had known what the Pope intended he would never have gone into the church, even on so bright a feast day, and now that men are calm it is clear that it must be a cause of trouble with the Empress Irene who rules in Constantinople though I do not think that she would

—221—

try to send an army against the Lord Charles whose might in battle is known to all. Yet there is more than one way to capture a city and I fear the plottings and schemings of the world more than open warfare, for it is such things that have brought us to the shame of Christendom where the Holy Father can be falsely accused, imprisoned and his mutilation attempted, because in this city, which ought to be the pure heart of the world, men jostle and scheme for power and riches contrary to the words of Our Lord and Saviour. And indeed if it be harder for a rich man to enter the Kingdom of God than for a camel to pass through the eye of a needle here every day, many professing to be servants of Christ must pass from this life into darkness through indulgence in every kind of luxury and evil that may be imagined, and I believe the very Emperor himself will be glad to return to the simpler life of his own court and people.

My father, that part of my letter was written while those great matters were fresh in my mind, and I had thought to send it to you as it was but before I could do so other more private matters, yet still miraculous in their kind, have taken place which I set down now.

After I had been in the city some weeks and the celebration of Our Lord's birth was past I began to wish to return to our house, being unwilling to leave it too long to Adela's guidance fearing that some might again take advantage of the sweetness of her disposition even though that morning I had received a message from her that all was well. Also I was eager to return to the life of contemplation and the spirit for there is something here in the very stones of the great monuments built by the pagans before the birth of Our Lord that leads to corruption and licence even in the Holy places. But when I expressed some of this to the Mother Superior she reminded me that I could not leave without the King's permission and that to travel alone was dangerous. Thus I saw that I must be quiet and wait on his going. 'But,' she said, 'you must use your time well and every day you should take a new part of the city and offer prayers at all the shrines for thus you will be occupied in God's service and you will be given light in contemplating the life of each saint and gazing upon the works and gifts of the faithful.'

Then I remembered too that, in all the public events, I had neglected to make my study of certain books and libraries and this I determined to do and to seek out copies of the Scriptures and the fathers not only in the great library of the Vatican but also in smaller churches, of which the city is full with one on almost every street, which contain many venerated treasures in spite of their smaller size. As for example in one to which English pilgrims go I found a copy of the Blessed Bede's book on St Cuthbert. It was only the second day of my little pilgrimages as I called them that I was passing along a narrow street near St Clement's when I came to a little square with houses all round, and the people, mainly cobblers outside making sandals which are the chief wear here with in the midst a shrine to the saints they venerate, the martyrs Crispin and Crispinian, where I decided to stop and pray, for was not Our Lord Himself a poor workman? But as I approached with Gundrada I saw on the opposite side a little bench in front of an iron grille with a basket for offerings and sitting on it that Hibernian who had been banished back to his own land for breaking fast in Lent, and other matters. Written on a board above the grille was the single word 'Paenitentia'. I tried to turn away and leave the place but the Hibernian who had seen me stood up and came forward saying: 'Lady, do not go. I said that we should meet again and God has so ordered it. I have something to say to you and something to show you.'

Then I said: 'Why are you here when you were banished to your own country for causing scandal to the people of God?'

'You are right to censure me and I will answer you. When I was banished I thought in my pride that I would not return home to Hibernia where every year the Northmen ravage towns and monasteries but would come to Rome on pilgrimage, for I was unreformed in my disobedience and sought only my own will. So I came here and lived easily, declining further into my sins until one day I heard of an English recluse who has been

—223—

shut up for years and to whom the local people come for instruction and healing. I thought I would go and see this marvel of an English penitent. So I came and I have stayed ever since to serve her, for here for the first time my soul is at peace. She turns away no-one who comes to her and she can see into all hearts, but most of all she has a message for those of the English race and as you are of that people she will wish to see you.'

Now I too was curious to see this Paenitentia and so I allowed myself to be persuaded while telling Gundrada to wait by the shrine of St Crispin in case there should be some trick. The Hibernian opened the grille and I stepped into a small dark room in which at first I could barely see until my eyes were accustomed and then I saw a further iron lattice set above a low wall with a window in it which could let down, and I approached it and said in Latin: 'Whoever you are thanks be to God.'

Then a voice spoke to me from behind the lattice very low and halting as if through disuse. 'Thanks be to God. Are you indeed of the English race as by your speaking you seem?'

'Yes. I am.'

And now she spoke in English, and moreover she used the tongue of Wessex. 'Where do you come from and what is your name?'

'I come from the House of Clingen in the land of the Franks. My name is Tetta.'

'And before that?'

'From the House of Wimborne.'

'I have waited for you a long time. I knew that one day someone would come from there bringing my forgiveness. What is your father's name and your lineage?'

'My father is Baltheard.'

Then I heard a little sigh, and a rustling from behind the grille. 'Is that Baltheard yet living?'

'He is alive in the land of the English,' I said and I began to have an apprehension of what might follow.

'Did he have a sister and does he remember her?'

'He has never forgotten her.'

'What was her name?'

'She was called Berthgyth. She went with their mother Cynehilde to the land of the Franks to the Blessed Boniface but was lost to God and her family when the Saxons took her. Yet her brother never forgot her and when I came to be head of our house at Clingen my father charged me to look for his sister and this I did as far as God guided me.'

'And what did you find?'

'I found not her but her son living, and his children and grandchildren.'

There was a little cry from behind the lattice but I could not tell if it was from pain or joy. Then the voice said: 'I who am called Paenitentia was once that Berthgyth. I have waited so long for you, and now your coming brings me reassurance that God will forgive me.' Then she began in Latin the *Nunc dimittis* in which I joined, singing it with her after the practice of the sisters of Wimborne. When we had ended and given thanks to God in prayer she asked me to come near and open the window in the iron lattice which could only be unlatched from the outside, which I did but I could see only a veiled shape within and she kept her face turned from me.

'I cannot tell you all my story,' she said, 'but I have written it down knowing that one day someone would come and trusting in God's mercy which he has promised to all those who repent.' Then she thrust several leaves of parchment, closely written and bound with a thong, through the lattice saying: 'Take it and read and learn. Let my life be a lesson and if you will, convey it to my brother Baltheard that he too may know everything that has befallen me.'

So I took the writings from her. 'Now close the window again.'

'Will you not leave this place now that God has sought you out through me, and either return with me to our house of Clingen or to your parents' home where my father still lives?'

I heard her sigh again. 'I am not worthy. Although God has given me this sign of His mercy I still have much to expiate so that the little time left to me here on earth will hardly be long enough. I am not the first of our people to become a recluse in Rome for our kinswoman Wiethburga, sister of Abbess Edburga of Thanet, died in a cell here far from her family yet close to God. Come to me once again before you depart from Rome and now leave me for my heart is too full to speak anymore.'

So my father I have read the book which I send to you with this. I had thought to make a copy as I do with my letters but there was no time and I thought further that I would entrust it to the hand of God and that if He willed it would come safely to you. I will not write of it and my thoughts on reading it but wait until you speak of it to me.

When I reached the other grille on to the square I found Gundrada and the Hibernian waiting for me.

'Sister Paenitentia has asked me to visit her again before I leave Rome,' I said to him. 'Meanwhile if she should become ill or is in need of help here is where you can find me and if it should happen when I have returned to the land of the Franks then I will leave you money either to send word to me or to care for her yourself and to buy what is necessary.'

When I went again today she had the low fever and was unable to speak yet I touched her hand through the window and begged her to take the physic I had brought, saying that God would call her when He was ready and that we should not hurry Him. Then she said: 'Beware of the pride of learning and of healing for unless they are of God then they are of the Evil One and will bring you to the same unhappy state as you see in me. I was impatient, not submissive to the will of God. I begged for a sight of my brother and when it was denied me I sinned with disobedience in my heart so that when my trial came I was weak and fell. When you come again to Rome I shall be gone. Of your charity let Masses be said for my soul and my name be entered in the Books of Life at Clingen and Wimborne, and wherever you may cause it to be set down, that I may be remembered and my soul saved by the prayers of those who have kept faith.'

So I left her charging the Hibernian once more to take care

of her and to send me word. 'You need not fear,' he said, 'that I shall not keep her on earth as long as I can for my own selfish reasons. She understands a sinner and when my soul looks to sink down to hell in the great scales it is she who will drop a tear in the other pan and bounce me up to heaven.'

My father I can write no more for we leave tomorrow. If it is God's will I believe this shall come safely to your hands. I know that when I set out on this journey my reasons were worldly, and it is only Our Lord Who in His mercy has preserved me from error and sin and brought me to a greater understanding, so that I can say as Master Alcuin: *What is man? The bondsman of death, a passing wayfarer, a guest sojourning on earth. What is death? The tears of the living. The thief of man. What is life? The joy of the blessed. The sorrow of the sad. The looking for death.*

They are standing outside the house in Russia Lane forlorn under its crust of old snow. The sky is lowering, sulphurous, as if the dirty heaps had been blown up there again and are about to fall, to rejoin the smirched droppings left behind at the edges of the pavement. Her mother, Hetty remembers, would have been out with shovel and broom clearing the stretch in front of their house so that no-one should slip. Hetty had always been sad to see the immaculate icing scraped into the gutter where it puddled and hardened in dirty alps until the council cleaners took it away in a lorry. But it had had its moment and everyone went safely dry-shod past their house.

Helge has rung the bell and they stand like waifs on a Christmas card while the ring goes through the house.

'Try again, and then if nobody comes we'll have to go.'

'How can they keep them all this time?' Helge puts out a finger again and presses the black button. Hetty thinks she hears a movement from deep inside. They look at each other, questioning. Now unmistakable feet are moving towards them on the other side of the door. Hetty isn't surprised when it opens to reveal the sidekick Colin. She's never told Helge that it was he she'd seen talking to Lutz in the square, feeling that she wouldn't be believed.

'It's Miss Dearden and a friend sir,' he calls back over his shoulder and then nods them inside.

The house is very bare. A few sticks of furniture stand around in the rooms like stage props that haven't been given their cue. Maidstone is sitting in the back room at a kitchen table with a half-empty cup in front of him. Colin's sits waiting to be finished at the other side.

'Ah Miss Dearden do come in.' He stands up, less tall under the higher ceilings of these rooms. 'Colin, get another couple of chairs from somewhere. Won't you introduce your friend? We thought if we waited about a bit someone might drop by, but I only half expected you. Why aren't you at home getting over Christmas?'

'Dr Ebbesen was worried about some friends who live here. She hasn't been able to contact them by telephone so she wanted to see if they were alright.'

'Yes, they're perfectly alright. They've gone away. Moved. They didn't own this house so they just moved.'

'They didn't believe in possessions, in owning things or people,' Helge says.

'Tell me about them. Ah, here are some chairs. Sit down. I'd like to hear more about your friends. Would you like coffee? Colin is quite good with the kettle.'

They find themselves sitting, declining coffee because somehow to perch there drinking it would be a betrayal, an act of complicity. Even to sit down increases their vulnerability by its very ordinariness. Instinctively Hetty senses Helge's puzzlement at these tactics.

'Now what was their name, your friends?' Colin has taken out his notebook Hetty sees with the corner of her eye.

'You must know their name if you have arrested them.'

'First, who says we've arrested them? You don't know that. And second,' he's picking off the points on clean round tipped fingers with bitten nails, 'people may have different names for different people. We may not be speaking of the same persons and then we might get into all sorts of trouble. What were yours called?'

'Rawlings, Jane and Dick.'

'And what did they do?'

'They worked in local government administration. Jane was at the Museum.'

'How did you come to know them?'

'I met Jane at a course in England.'

'What sort of course?'

'It was in social history. The history of ordinary things.'

'Do ordinary things have a history?'

'*Ja*, of course.'

'What about ordinary people?'

At first Hetty has felt frightened but now she's becoming angry at this game. 'We all have a history, Inspector. We're all part of history.'

'Some people don't seem to have a past though, not one they're admitting to that is. So you met at a course in England. Then what?'

'We became friends. We shared many interests.'

'Political interests?'

'Some yes.'

'Like terrorism, politically motivated terrorism?'

'No, no. They are Quakers, *Pazifisten*.'

'We found some pretty unpacifist things when we searched the house.'

'You find things? What things?'

'Oh the usual anarchist's bomb-making kit.'

'They are not theirs. They are *still* people. Someone puts them there, *unterschieben*.'

'But you did form an international political group?'

'Not party political. We have all parties. Like Amnesty International or Greenpeace.'

'Anti right-wing. Not averse to violent action?'

'Only protests. That is permitted in democracy.'

'It depends.'

'If it is not permitted it is not democracy.'

Hetty feels a surge of tenderness for the defiant figure fighting her corner. 'Dr Ebbesen would like to know what has become of her friends, where she can contact them.'

'We've found them a safer place to stay and advised them not to make contact with former colleagues while we clear this up.'

'They are under arrest?'

'No, they're co-operating with us. They understand things a bit better now.'

'Did you arrest Lutz Brehme when you raided the house?'

'"Raided"? Miss Dearden, that's a very emotional word. You've asked me about this person before. No-one of that name was found by us to be present at the time. Why would we have arrested him here?'

Hetty doesn't want to reveal her presence on the corner. She feels it a slight advantage in this power game that there is something they don't know. But Helge is speaking and Hetty can only hope she won't give away too much.

'He has disappeared in Germany.'

'Gone off for the Christmas holidays I expect. Will Dr Ebbesen be staying long in this country?'

'We haven't decided.'

'I must ask you to keep us informed. By the way, our chaps have decided those documents aren't in code so you needn't send us any more.'

They are being dismissed, let go as harmless, as of no account. Anger and relief alternate in Hetty as Colin shows them into the cold, darkening street.

'Come on darling, let's get out of here,' Helge jokes taking her arm and, beginning as they slither on the freezing pavements, holding on to each other, holding each other up, they laugh their way round the corner to where Hetty has left her car. Inside they laugh again, kiss quickly, their joint breath immediately shrouding the windows until Hetty can get the heater blasting it away. She rubs a hole in the windscreen mist and begins to negotiate the traffic already fleeing the city, home to tea and television.

By the time they reach the cottage they're tired and deflated. The fire is out and Hetty lights the Calor Gas stove letting warmth and the old cat's-pee smell of propane fill the small space. In the night the snow which they had outdriven reaches back to them so that the morning light dazzles through the windows and Hetty knows what's happened as soon as her eyes open on it. 'We're in an igloo, a snow house.'

'What shall we do today?'

'If the roads are clear enough I want to go into Sarnford to get some money from the cashpoint and check my account.'

On the way to the car they laugh again, bunching up the powdery snow into snowballs and pelting each other. The branches that surround the cottage and its drive are perfectly layered in fleece so light the least brush brings it showering down. Why did Jove only fall on Danae as hard gold, Hetty suddenly wonders and then supplies her own answer: to show it wasn't love but lust.

'Is there a good place where I can get German newspapers perhaps?'

'I think I know where you could try.'

She leaves Helge to browse while she calls at her bank. By the time they reach home, after a sandwich and a drink in the pub, Hetty is drowsy from driving between downs humped under blinding sheets and the blaze of the pub fire.

'You sleep. I will look at my newspapers.'

She falls asleep on the sofa, face turned away from the light Helge has to switch on to combat the short day. When she wakes and turns to face the little room Helge is sitting in the armchair with her head in her hands, a magazine open at her feet where it's dropped.

'Are you alright? What is it?' She gets up and goes to put her arms around Helge. As she does so her eye rests on the double page below, densely printed with German text with a row of postage-stamp faces its only relief. Among them, fourth from the right, she recognises Lutz. 'Tell me. What is it?'

'Just that you are right all the time. I suppose I knew it yesterday, some, but I don't want to speak of it. Now it is all here.' She picks up the magazine and offers it to Hetty.

'I can't read it. What does it say?'

'It's an article on the *Stasi*, the old East German secret police. They keep finding these records or rather as they find, where they are not destroyed first, they begin to examine and they find more and more informers and collaborators and agents. Now they have found Lutz.'

'But can you believe them? It might be just a piece of hack journalism.'

'No, it is *Der Spiegel*. They are very accurate. Not over the top. That is right? Lutz is on a list of agents with salaries. That is why he has disappear. Not that he is arrested here. But why did he continue with us?'

'I think he was a double agent or anyone's. Or perhaps even no-one's.'

'What do you mean?'

'Someone without loyalties; just an "agent".'

Other thoughts are jostling into Hetty's head such as that Helge will be on record somewhere as his associate, investigations will be made, more precise, the finger pointed. No life is without blemishes that might be shown up in a harsh light. She's unlikely to get another job in education or in any large organisation.

Helge has her head in her hands again. I am watching the death of an ideal, Hetty thinks, the brotherhood of men: the world my country; to do good my religion. 'What do you want to do?' she asks, afraid of the answer.

'I want to be with you. But I don't see why you should want me when I am such a fool, so deceived like a child. But, also, I don't know . . . I don't want to live in a world where there is only money.'

'We don't have to decide now. We have plenty of time,' Hetty says, wondering if they will ever be left alone.

Two days later they are in London. Hetty wants Helge to get over the hurdle of meeting Sandy and Bill. 'And we have some unfinished business at the British Museum.'

She can find nothing in the index under Berthgyth. The others are there: Boniface, Lul, Lioba, Eadberga, Tetta even, but a namesake not hers. What else might there have been waiting here quietly all the time that she could have missed? But then if she'd found it she might not have met Helge so, at one and the same moment, fickle and yet patterned is chance. She will try Paenitentia.

Vita. Her heart begins to race as she hauls the right volume on to the stand, traces the main entry, fills in the slip, goes to her seat and opens the heavy mahogany bookstand ready to receive the maroon-bound manuscript when it's delivered. She lifts it on to the stand aware of the cathedral hush around her and opens it at the first page.

Codex membranaceus saec XIV pulchra exaratus the catalogue had said and it's true. Even from the title page she can see the fineness of the black script, clear on the vellum, it seems, as the day it was drafted. In the top right-hand corner are the scribblings of someone trying to improve a faulty pen.

Iste liber est de libraria Sanctae Mariae et Ethelfridae virginis de Romsey, Hampto in quo continentur i Breve cronice de Regem Saxoniconem ab Hengistu ad Egbertum ii Vitae Sanctorum Angliae quorum nomina, ex ordine literarum, hic recensentur:—

They were all there, the names Hetty recognised, a roll call in alphabetical order she runs through until, after *Milburga abbatissa*, she comes to 'Paenitentia'. Romsey had been another of the great houses she remembered. It must be about twenty miles from Wimborne. Could Berthgyth's original have been taken from there, perhaps when the Northmen sacked Tetta's old abbey, caught up out of the library by one of the sisters while the flames ran up the altar hangings fusing silver and gold thread into a fiery web that dripped in roundels on the stone altar, uncurrent coin the pirates could sweep into their wallets once it was cold, and carried north to safety; to be copied into this repository of English saints after the Norman Conquest, as an act of patriotism by a subject people who were beginning to reassert themselves, the word against the sword? It made a kind of sense, story, epic, saga. Chronicles of the English Kings and saints. How strange that the Kings should end with Ecgbert.

The lives are written in double columns on each page with illuminated capitals in blue and red linear patterns as finely drawn and convolute as computer designs for the delicate fractol geometry of chaos. *Explicit de Milburga abbatissa. Incipit de Paenitentia anacherata.* Hetty takes down the details and goes to order a photographed copy to be sent to the cottage.

To my dear brother Baltheard if he be still living, and to all those of my family and friends, and the sisters at Wimborne, to those who remember me and those who shall come after me, I, once Berthgyth now Paenitentia, an unworthy sister of Saxon origin, last and least in life and conduct, venture to write for the sake of posterity, in the hope that others may learn from my narrative, relying on the Grace of God, the Giver of all Good.

Know then that as a child some seven years of age when my father was dead and my mother had taken her vows to serve God, I was brought by her to the land of the Franks at the request of the Blessed Boniface to teach the people of Thuringia, for my mother was very learned in liberal knowledge and became at once the magistra of a house, and educated me also to take my place as a teacher in due course.

In time I received my own house, the land for which had been given to our kinsman, Bishop Lul, but shortly after I became its head my mother died and I was left alone in a strange land. Instead of casting myself upon God who is the Father of us all, I began to yearn for my own land and people and in particular for you, my brother, begging that you would come to me and that I might see you again. So strong did this longing become that it invaded all my thoughts and when they should have been fixed upon God, even before the altar, my heart was full of weeping although none about me suspected it.

There came the day when having gone to gather herbs for healing with one of the sisters we were surprised in a valley beside a stream by a band of heathen. To my fear and wonder they took only me and sent the other sister away but not before I had given her a message to return to that place and I would try to get word to her.

We rode for some time. I was too frightened to notice the way we went but finally we came to a heathen village where I was thrust into a hut with a guard at the doorway and left. Eventually I was brought a gruel of half-cooked grains and then I was the more afraid for I had heard that the heathen feed their victims on such a diet before they sacrifice them to their gods.

At last I was taken again before the chief who had captured me. He said that they had heard of my skill in healing, that there was much sickness in the place and he wished me to use my powers on his people. I said that I could not do anything without my book of recipes and the right ingredients and that I must be allowed to send a message to the monastery and have the book copied but it would take time. This he agreed to but said that if I tried any trickery our house would be burnt down and all in it murdered.

Then I saw that I was being punished for my weakness and that God allowed the Evil One to test my faith, for by trying to save my own life I could imperil all those in my charge, and therefore I determined that whatever happened it should befall me alone. And so I arranged through the faithful sister for a copy of the book to be made and all my servants to be forbidden to attempt to rescue me and I set about making remedies and driving the sickness from the heathen with God's help, in the hope that they would set me free.

However after I had been there two months and the sickness had abated a little, far from letting me return to my own people the chief began to say that I must stay with them in case it should return and that to keep me he would marry me, his own wife being dead. In vain I tried to explain to him that I had taken a vow of chastity and was given in marriage to Our Lord Jesus Christ. 'Where is this Christ?' he demanded. 'Let him come and take you from me if you are his.'

Still I held out against him and would not marry him until one night he came to my hut and lay with me by force with his knife at my throat. In the morning he said that since I was a virgin and he was the first to know me that I was his and my powers would pass from me through him to his people. My soul was in great distress and I wished to die but I did not have the courage either to turn a knife against myself as Lucretia the noble Roman matron did, or to let him kill me before I would submit to his will.

Then I lived in a daily hell of lust and concupiscence among pagans, far from God's light, until it became clear that I was with child, and after my term was over I gave birth to a boy who was called in our language and theirs 'Ecgbert' but I was not allowed to give him baptism and feared all the time that he would die an infant and his soul be lost. When the baby was nearly six months old the pagan chief came in to me again to lie with me but I pleaded weakness through feeding the child and he left me alone for that night but I knew that he would come again. I could not resign myself once more to a life as the bedfellow of a pagan forever and determined that I would escape. . . .

That next day I carried the baby secretly to a place where there was a little stream and baptised him, begging God not to look upon my sin but on the child's innocence for did not Our Lord say: Of such is the Kingdom of God? Then I took him back to the village and when night was come I wrapped him up warmly and wedged him with cushions and then I took a knife and began to cut away at the reed wall at the back of the hut behind a bearskin hanging. From time to time I was forced to stop when I thought I heard someone approach and I was terrified that the chief himself might come to seek me out but God was my help and at last I had cut a hole big enough to squeeze through. Commending my baby to God's mercy and casting myself upon Him to do with me as He wished, either to let me be eaten by wild animals or killed by brigands, but not I prayed to be caught and brought back to a life of subjection and the loss of my soul, I crept out of the hut and into the forest. That night I went as far south as I could by the stars until exhaustion overcame me and I hid myself in a thicket to sleep. As soon as I woke I ate and drank a little from the food I had brought with me and then I went on always southwards by the sun. For many days I wandered through the great forest of Thuringia, thinking that I must be killed or die, eating berries and drinking water from streams or licking rain or dew from the leaves when my food was finished until I came to a place where some followers of St Kilian had set up a cluster of small cells where I was fed and allowed to rest and bathe myself. But when I heard them sing the office my heart was sick within me. I should have confessed all and cast myself on their charity but I was still hardened and not yet ready for God's chastisement that would save me from damnation. When a caravan passed going south towards Bavaria I joined them and, ministering to some who were sick, I travelled in their company as far as Salzburg where they stayed in the city whose Bishop Virgil was appointed by the Blessed Boniface himself, and it may be if our Holy kinsman had lived and had not suffered his martyrdom in Frisia I would never have fallen into that despair which was the beginning of my downfall.

In Salzburg I fell upon truly evil times, again through my pride which would not allow me to seek out the comfort of Holy Mother Church by making my full confession and accepting whatever penance might be laid upon me. I was forced to beg for my bread and when men demanded my body in return for their money, I gave it to them like the prostitute Thais, sinking lower in the filth, and my heart becoming a stone I carried about with me. I met others of my kind and race, some of whom had set out on pilgrimage and fallen by the way, and together we laughed and lolled and lamented and drowned our grief with wine. Then God might have forsaken me utterly but that I continued to pray for my child and you my brother even in my darkest days.

One morning I awoke in such despair that I determined to leave that place and end my life. I found a company going south again to the Kingdom of the Lombards and begged a place among them in exchange for turning the spit and fetching water. They were anxious to go there to trade for the country had been in rebellion against the Holy Father Hadrian but was now at peace again under the hand of Charles, King of the Franks and the merchants thought that the people would be eager to purchase their goods.

After we had been travelling some days the Alps began to rise up before us and we were forced to follow the river valleys in order to cross them. I had never seen such high mountains before and the wildness and terror of them began to make a softening in the stone that was my heart, like sunlight striking upon ice. Among the company was an old priest on his way to Rome, from the part of Bavaria where he had been ministering to the people since the days of Boniface's first mission although he was himself a Frank. Because of his age he was travelling in our company for safety but he meant to leave us at Pavia and go on to Rome. He said the offices at the appointed hours as if he were in the strictest order, and one day God put it in my mind to approach where he knelt on the wayside and kneeling behind him to join in the responses.

When we had finished and I rose to take my turn with preparing the evening meal he said to me: 'Daughter, if I am not mistaken you have not always lived the life of the world. When you have finished your work return here and I will hear your confession and that burden that you carry shall be lifted from you.'

As soon as the food was ready I took him a plate to where he was resting against a tree. When he had taken it and thanked me he went on: 'I do not know if I shall live to reach the Holy City. It may be that like your compatriot the father of the Blessed Willibald I shall die on the journey but if that is to be then I am content. Therefore begin your story for who knows the hour at which our souls shall be required of us.'

And suddenly for the first time my heart and my lips were as if chains fell from them and I could speak. Then I told him everything and after I had finished my story I wept, and asked him if he could give me absolution, and said that I would perform whatever he should lay on me. 'It is not I who must absolve you or demand of you but Christ to Whom you were dedicated with vows that may be broken but can never be unbound except by you. Unless you have forsworn Him in your heart, which I do not believe, you are still His and He calls you which is why He caused you to speak to me. Come with me to Rome if I am spared, or go on alone if I am not, and there you will find your answer in climbing the Santa Scala and throwing yourself on God's mercy before the shrine of St Peter, the fisher of souls to whom Our Lord gave the charge of us all when he bade him: "Feed my sheep." Now for the present I absolve you, and make this journey your penance and pilgrimage and that you should serve the Lord in the world until such time as He makes His will known to you, and yet although you serve Him in the world, in your heart and deeds you should as far as you can, follow the observances of your order and train yourself by them to accept His perfect will and become once more His handmaiden.'

When he had finished speaking he blessed me and I fell at his feet and kissed his hand and wet it with my tears, and the next morning being Sunday he said the Mass for all the company and for the first time for many months I received the Body of the Lord and felt it suffuse all through my limbs with living fire. We continued our journey slowly through the mountains. Soon he fell sick and had to be carried in a litter which did not please the master of the caravan although he was paid for it. Eventually we descended into the plain of Friuli and began to make our way eastwards. At Padua we parted with the merchants and turned our faces towards the South and Rome. He was by now very weak and scarce able to sit on a horse yet I sustained him as best I could and eventually we reached nearly to our goal and camped outside the walls above the city. 'It is thanks to God and you that I have come this far,' he said as we looked down at the many churches and buildings before us.

I asked him where we should stay among all those streets. Then he told me that he was heir to a small cell where he intended to spend his last days in prayer. 'And after me it shall be yours for as long as you need it and then in turn you must pass it to one whose need is great for prayer and quietness, whom God will show you, for so it came into my care.'

We had not been there long when his weakness growing upon him he composed himself and was taken with a quiet mind to God. And as I prayed by his body I was granted a vision of a light that shone about it that came neither from a lamp nor a candle and a voice saying to me: 'I give you a new name. Henceforth you shall be called Paenitentia and you shall serve only the living God with body and spirit.'

Then I determined to shut myself away from the world and wait until God shall pardon me and send one to me who would heal my wounds. And so I have waited on the Lord.

This is the Life of St Paenitentia as she wrote it. Glory be to God. Amen.

CODA

When Hetty put the cottage up for sale people trampled through it every weekend with the estate agent's description clutched in their hands, inspecting the amenities and making it over in their heads. The whole process filled Hetty with anger and sadness.

'You could grub that hedge out and have a view over the fields,' one said.

'Is that tree dangerous?' they asked of the chestnut.

They slammed the door of the carefully black-leaded kitchen range so that it fell off its hinges.

'I'd have that chimney breast right out, open up the fireplace.'

'The lawn must be awkward to mow with that steep slope.'

She didn't want to see it through their eyes but it was hard to resist. 'It's very small.'

'They brought up families of ten in these,' she wanted to say, irrationally defensive.

The most serious bidder's survey found a crack. The last few years of summer and winter drought had dried out the soil. The cottage was sinking to its knees. It needed underpinning. That would have to be allowed for in the price.

After the agents had gone she walked through the house into the garden and looked down on it from the top of the slope. She felt as if the cottage was being abused and she was its betrayer. Under the leaf mould the fox and the cat twitched indignantly. The new owners would probably bring in a rotavator and mince their bones into the earth. The house would be surrounded with stiff scentless blooms, fleshy gladioli, harsh orange Siberian wallflowers, scratchy French marigolds. The walls would be replastered with royal icing; the beams painted black.

Helge was in Gascony looking for a cheap farmhouse with enough acres for vegetables and a few rows of vines.

'How shall we live Hetty?' she had asked.

They could stay on in the cottage of course but Hetty knows that would be a mistake. It belongs to her solitude, and in any case she would always now see Maidstone's head brushing against the beams. They have been left alone but how long would that last if they stayed.

'If I sell the cottage we can use the money to buy somewhere else.'

'I have no money, no job. I have to begin again and perhaps no-one will employ me.'

But Hetty refuses to despair. 'We can go anywhere, at least anywhere in Europe. I have my pension and a bit saved. We can teach if we're in another country. Everyone wants to learn English and German.'

'You can write your book. I will teach and earn money. I won't be a problem to you.'

'What about France? Half-way between Germany and Britain. Cheap farmhouses because everyone is leaving the land. I'm sure I could manage to buy something there. We could grow things.'

'I've not lived in the country, always in the city. *Il faut cultiver notre jardin*. Yes?'

'If we don't like it we can always move,' Hetty says carefully, afraid that the bull will tear apart the garland that tethers it and trample the flowers to bits. What happened to Pasiphae-Europa? They shut up her monstrous offspring in a labyrinth until the hero Theseus came to kill it, ran off with her daughter and then abandoned her to be rescued by Dionysus, god of life and the blood of the grape. No wonder Europa rode away on the bull's back, leaving the stern law-giver and judge of the gloomy underworld, her husband.

> They are not long the weeping and the laughter
> Love and desire and hate:
> I think they have no portion in us after
> We pass the gate.

Hetty had written in a schoolfriend's autograph book, self-consciously, when she was fourteen, understanding the words but not their meaning as she does forty years later. Perhaps it won't work. Perhaps Helge will get bored and go away, she thinks, but it doesn't matter. I have *now*. We have now.

'I was in the library in Sarnford today and while I was waiting for my books to come I looked up a few things just to pass the time. Did you know your name, Ebbesen, means "child of Ecgbert"?'

'I think my mother said so, yes. She was like you, interested in those things, names and *ableitung*. Where things come from.'

Hetty had looked further. 'Helge' she discovered meant 'holy'; 'Ecgbert', 'a shining blade'.

'We will not become the *eremit*, Hetty, like your nun. Will you write her story perhaps?'

'Female power structures of the early Middle Ages: a feminist analysis,' Hetty laughs. 'No we shan't, mustn't become recluses.'

Mr Powers had come up for the last time on his bicycle to say goodbye, peering first through the window as he always did and then coming round to the back door. There were intimations of spring already in the garden, green bulb shoots nosing through. 'I shan't come here no more, not for they new people. You and me we done something together here, made something. You always treated I like a friend. I wouldn't work for no-one else.'

Hetty had sugared his tea liberally, realising that in a strange way she would miss him more than most, more certainly than her former colleagues at St Julian's. 'I never thought you could live anywhere else but here,' Jack had said. 'I rather envy you.'

While I was here, she thinks already using the past tense, I lived off the land, not on it. Yet I have loved it too.

'They never caught that bloke nor they won't now. Though some of us had a good idea but we kept our thoughts to ourselves 'cos you couldn't prove nothing. Only make yourself look a fool. What did they keep coming after you for?'

Reticence, caution, secrecy had all been partners in Hetty's life. Could she slough them off now and come out in a new brave skin? 'Who do you mean?'

'They plain-clothes police as was always knocking on the door and trailing after you.'

'Oh it was nothing to do with that. It was something that happened abroad, something I saw.'

'You was a witness?'

'They thought I could help them but I couldn't.'

'They'm like a dog with a bone once they get their teeth into you. Was that where you'm going to live?'

'Not in the same place. I'm going to France.' Would they be close to Alcuin's Tours?

'I've never been abroad so 'tis all the same to I.'

'Not even during the war?'

'Yorkshire were as far as I got. Well you can always come back. Us shan't run away.'

Is it me that's running away, Hetty wondered, before it's too late and I'm caught here forever, if it isn't already. Could they really make a go of it? Think of Tetta, she admonishes herself. Perhaps our idea, our image of our individual selves, is really rather weak and can only be grasped in terms of not being 'them'; unless there's something else to give it definition, seeing ourselves in someone else's eyes for instance, even if we have to invent them. 'Thou God seest me,' as the samplers used to say.

'I have found it Hetty,' Helge tells her delightedly on the phone. 'You must come and see soon but I know it is right. You will love it.'

Can I begin afresh, take all my anxieties and dump them in someone else's lap? Do I have any choice?

She presumes Maidstone will tell the French police to keep an eye on them since it's almost impossible to disappear in these days of the databank and the credit card without dropping into an underworld, underclass. She wonders if she should be angered by the way he seemed to drop them as of no account once he'd achieved his obscure ends, but she's too relieved. Sometimes they talk about Lutz and the others, but especially Lutz. Once Helge tried to find out what had happened to him by telephoning Uwe but had met only evasion. 'They are afraid. They don't want to speak with me.'

One day, after she has been studying an article in a German magazine, she says: 'I think I could have claimed some land in Eastern Germany but now it's too late. The date is passed.'

'Do you mind?'

'Not if you don't. I think it is better like this to start again. Not in my country or yours, but something new. But I wasn't wrong to try to make things right, better?'

'No of course you weren't wrong, not in principle. But we can all be used, especially through our ideals.'

'If Lutz was *Stasi* why did the English police use him?'

'Maybe the duplicitous have more in common with each other than with the rest of us.'

'But they thought we were like them.'

'They always do,' Hetty says though she's not sure where such knowledge comes to her from.

'We can't only dig the garden,' Helge insists.

'No, but we can't play their games either.'

'What then do we do?'

'Perhaps it's more what we don't do, like just making a new tribe with its own rules and loyalties. But especially we try not to let others do the thinking for us, and that's hardest of all.'

They are sitting out after supper watching the light drain from the valley. Hetty is practising her French on the local paper. Soon it will be too dark to see. The roof has been mended and a couple of rooms made starkly habitable. They have dug and planted. Sandy is threatening to be their first visitor in the autumn 'to help with the *vendage*, something I've longed to do ever since we saw *Bless the Bride*. I don't care if it will only make half a dozen bottles. It's the idea that counts. The god of wine and all that.'

'Someone's seen a wolf in the forest. I thought they were all extinct.' Hetty has a sudden picture of it slipping down from the mountains, green eyes glinting in the headlights of a home-going car.

'Maybe someone saw a stray dog after too many glasses.'

There's always a wolf, Hetty thinks, somewhere. But aloud she says: 'The Nationalists have got a march at the weekend in Toulouse. Do you think we should take a look at it?'

Sometimes when they're working, Hetty glances across to where Helge is intent on a task, sinking a sharp blade into the earth or spreading out the arms of a vine. She no longer sees her as a stranger but she still wonders, catches herself wondering, if anyone so seemingly transparent can indeed be how she seems, if there wasn't a grain of truth in Maidstone's allegations, if the affair with Christine had really been over. And then she feels weighed down by history, hers and ours. Perfidious Albion, will we never learn to be free and open, not retreat behind the secrecy of our veiling mists? Can you ever really know what goes on in someone else's head and heart? Should you try? Or shouldn't you just make an act of faith each morning by waking, and bathing, and eating the ritual grains we gave to the Spring sacrifice for the return of light, the sun, new growth, and then stepping out to whatever comes – like Charles I going to execution with an extra shirt on so as not to shiver or Europa hoisting herself on to the bull's back.

'Maybe,' Helge says. 'We'll see. Come to bed.'

Author's Note

Berthgyth's three letters to her brother Baltheard are among the collection of Boniface's correspondence begun by Bishop Lul, of which there are three main manuscript copies in Germany and Austria. Alcuin's letters are also extant but have never, as far as I have discovered, been given a complete English translation. St Lioba's life, and that of Charlemagne by Einhard, were both written in the century following the events described here. St Willibald's travels were taken down by the English nun, Hygeburc, from his own account. The rest is fiction.

MAUREEN DUFFY
NOVEMBER, 1990